Mountain Retreat

Garry Smith

and

Danny Arnold

DEDICATION

This book is a work of fiction and all of the main characters are entirely fictional.

We want to thank those who gave us invaluable ideas and constructive feedback: our brides, Peggy Arnold and Charlotte Smith.

PREVIOUS BOOKS

The Freedom Town Series

Bad Cat Jones

Freedom Town

Freedom Town Winter

Freedom Town Summer

Freedom Town '68

Cannon Mines

Freedom Town West

Gabe's Quest

The Mountain Series

Murder by the Mountains

The Mountains are Calling

Home in the Mountains

Chapter One

Wyatt Cannon, VP of Security for the sprawling conglomerate known as the Cannon Trust, was sitting in his office strategizing about the immediate future of the security division. Everything had been going smoothly in recent weeks, but he had a foreboding feeling.

The Cannon Trust had been established in Denver by his ancestors in the 1870s. His five greats ago grandfather, Grant Cannon, and Grant's brother, Clark, were fortunate enough to strike a significant motherlode of gold. They parlayed their wealth into land, cattle, horses, more mines, and banks. They soon established the family's Cannon Trust. Every descendant of Grant and Clark receives a sizeable monthly check from the Trust, which had grown in size and diversity over the decades.

Wyatt's previous career was as an FBI Special Agent. After marrying Ashley, the FBI job's stress on both of them led Wyatt to accept his current Vice President position and he loved the job. Ashley had delivered a baby boy, TG, who was almost a year old.

Wyatt, Ashley, and his entire top level security team attended a special wedding the previous day. Carrie Cannon had married one of Wyatt's best friends, Joe 'Koko' Sheffield. Carrie was the daughter of the Trust's Chairman, Harrell Cannon, and his wife, Virginia. Harrell was a descendant of Clark.

Joe 'Koko' Sheffield was a DEA Agent and worked largely undercover. He and Wyatt had worked on several cases together and had been in too many life or death scrapes. Wyatt trusted Joe with his life and offered Joe a position in the security division, which he had not yet accepted.

Joe was descended from Lily Sheffield, who also established a Trust for her descendants. Lily's wealth came from her father, brother, and husband—each man was a wealthy plantation owner and was killed during the Civil War. The Sheffield Trust was managed by the Cannon Trust. Lily had lived in Freedom Town, a Colorado community established by former slaves from her brother's Louisiana plantation. She accompanied the slaves on their perilous journey from Louisiana to Colorado Territory. She was a highly respected member of the Freedom Town community.

Grant and Clark Cannon had spent time in Freedom Town and were very close to Miss Lily. But despite the two family's closeness over the decades, Carrie and Joe's marriage was the first to join the two family lines.

Joe had been forced by the DEA to take a much needed R&R the previous year. He called Wyatt and came out to Denver to explore his Sheffield roots. Carrie fell hard for Joe the first time she saw him. Joe initially resisted the obvious sparks between them due to his dangerous job.

Carrie, however, would not be put off. While Virginia and Carrie wanted a big wedding, Joe could not risk being recognized in the drug underworld. Thus, everyone had to settle for the small, private wedding.....for now. The 'event of the year' wedding would occur when Joe resigned or retired from the DEA.

The wedding ceremony was held on the top floor of the luxurious Cannon Hotel in downtown Denver and the only guests were the Trust's security team and spouses. The floor consisted of four luxurious suites and a well-appointed shared common area. A brief champagne reception followed the ceremony. All the guests departed quickly and Carrie and Joe retired to one of the suites.

Joe and Carrie boarded the Trust's jet the next morning, along with John and Margie, Wyatt's parents. John had recently retired from the CIA and was now working for Wyatt.

The jet headed for Barbados, where the Trust's Spirits Division was located. It consisted of a large sugar cane plantation and a top level rum distillery. The current manager, Mark Cannon, was the fourth generation Cannon to serve in that capacity. He had recently obtained funding from the Trust's Board to greatly expand and modernize the distillery, which was currently under construction.

The flight to Barbados was smooth with only minor turbulence. They refueled in Miami and landed seven hours after leaving Denver. Mark Cannon met them at general aviation with two jeeps. Everyone was first taken to the Plantation House. Mark explained why.

"I went to Denver a couple of years ago to beg for funds to rebuild our rum distillery and met Wyatt on that trip. He suggested I go out to the horse ranch, and I'm glad he did. I fell in love with the horses and the Comanche dogs. I brought six dogs back and we keep two of them at the Plantation House—the other four patrol the construction site. I want to introduce everyone to them because they don't much like strangers."

As soon as everyone was introduced to Pepper and Blackie, Joe and Carrie were taken to the plantation's seaside villa. Two servants were assigned to the villa—one to cook and one to clean.

John and Margie returned to the plantation house to stay with Mark and his wife, Sheila. The house was the epitome of plantation houses depicted in movies.

The Atlantic Ocean lies on Barbados' east side, while the Caribbean Sea is on the west. The plantation was on the northeast Atlantic coast. It was located in a low mountainous area running down to the Atlantic near Cambridge. The villa Carrie and Joe were staying was across the Ermy Bourne Highway from the plantation, almost a mile from the house.

The worst thing about the villa's location was it was on the windward side. The hurricanes could sometimes be ferocious and do serious damage along the east coast. But most of the land was over a hundred feet in elevation so storm surges did not reach the villa. The villa, however, did occasionally suffered significant water and wind damage. Fortunately, the storms had not yet had a chance to build over warm Caribbean waters.

The Atlantic coast was dramatically different from the Caribbean side of the island. The ocean was much rougher than the Caribbean, with large waves most of the year. Boulders abounded in the surf and only a few tiny beaches existed, not very attractive to most tourists. It was ruggedly beautiful and Carrie loved it. Joe was not concerned much by the condition of the surf.

John and Mark talked late into the night about the plantation and the distilling operation. The plantation grew sugar cane and used much of it to make marvelous rum. Mark shared that construction had been slowed down by numerous vandalism incidents. Mark thought it was a group of rebels who did not want Americans or American businesses in Barbados. He had talked to the police but they were not helpful. It did not seem to matter that Mark was a fourth generation Bajan whose ancestors had lived on the island for well over a century. Perhaps it was

4

because the plantation and distillery were owned by the Cannon Trust, an American organization.

Margie went to bed as soon as she could. It had been a long day and she needed to rest. Shelia said they would explore the island the next day. Barbados was a wonderful tourist destination with many interesting things to see and do, especially along the west coast and in Bridgetown. The tourist area abounded with many wonderful restaurants.

John and Mark inspected the recent vandalism early the next morning and concluded it was more of a nuisance than heavy damage. Still, it was holding up progress, and Mark told him the damages were getting worse.

The two men were riding fabulous Paso Fino horses. John commented, "I saw a few Paso Fino horses on Grant and Angelina's original Denver ranch."

"Yes, the root stock there descended from Paso Finos given to Angelina by her grandfathers in the 1800s. We love them and so did Angelina, according to her diary and the letters she wrote to her grandparents."

After their ride around the plantation, the two men went back to the plantation to have breakfast with Margie and Sheila. The meal was wonderful, with mostly fruits and strong coffee.

They chatted for a while and Sheila said, "Not many of the Cannons visit us down here. Everyone says they want to come but nobody seems to have time for it. Is there anything you particularly want to see while you are here?

"I suppose just the regular tourist sites."

"Good. I thought we should explore the northern part of the island today. It's sparsely populated and we won't see many tourists. It's wildly beautiful, and we will see a few old forts and churches. It will give you time to get your feet back under you. We will have a jeep accompany us, since there's a few rebels in the north, or whatever they are called."

John thought to himself, "*Hmm. If we need an escort, I will also have a weapon.*"

Margie asked, "What about Joe and Carrie?"

"I figured they would want to entertain themselves for at least a few days." Everyone chuckled knowingly.

Mark showed John his collection of weapons. They were a mixture of modern and older collectibles. John was drawn to a pristine Winchester Model 1894, which Mark had purchased on his last trip to Denver.

John remarked, "It was the last long gun Grant purchased. A real classic. I also have one."

"Yes, I had the man who finds Cannon weapons for the Trust get it for me. It's actually one of my favorite rifles and I shoot it occasionally. I love its balance and it's very accurate. I have modern, smokeless cartridges for it. My newest rifle is this Kimber 7mm short mag. I think Grant would have loved it. I do an African safari every other year and it will take down almost anything, but I use a .416 Weatherby Magnum for elephants."

––––––––––––––––––

The trip around the north end of the island was just as Sheila described. The Atlantic side was ruggedly beautiful. The waves were huge and signs on all the small beaches indicated the water was dangerous for swimmers because of the boulders and rip tides. However, it was a great place for surfers. The area between Walker's Beach and Cuckold Point was obviously popular.

They saw a large rum distillery and sugar cane fields near St. Nicholas Abbey. The St. Lucy Parish Church was also interesting, as was the nearby Mount Gay rum distillery. They drove all the way to North Point. The waves there were huge as they broke around the point. Margie thought she liked the Cuckhold Point area best because of its huge waterspouts caused by waves pounding cave-like openings and shooting water high into the air from holes above. She thought it was like ten Old Faithful's spouting huge columns of cold water at the same time.

They stopped at a small bar and grill at lunch time. Mark told John the driver would buy their food and they could eat in the car further down the road. The area was rough and many people did not like Americans. John noted the people hanging around the building looked surly and was happy to eat further down the road. John wondered why they stopped at such a place, and then he tasted the food. He was not sure what it contained, but it tasted great. Mark told him he was eating fried flying fish. A dish they initially thought was mashed potatoes was actually mashed elephant ear bulbs, a staple on the island. All of the food was tasty and the local beer was refreshing.

While eating they saw a troop of monkeys cross the road, which startled John and Margie. They had certainly seen many animals walk and run across roads, but never expected to see a troop of monkeys.

After their late lunch, they visited the Speightstown Mural and Pier, which was much more touristy. It was an interesting town on the Caribbean side of the island. The waves were much calmer and many people were enjoying walking in the gentle surf and even swimming.

Joe and Carrie also rode around in their jeep after a leisurely brunch. They drove on the beach and explored the restaurants along the highway. They particularly liked one small restaurant. The menu was limited but what they tried was delicious—flying fish served on a hard roll. It was almost like a po-boy in the U.S. but subtly different.

They decided to drive by the plantation before returning to

their villa. John and Margie were surprised to see them.

Sheila said, "We're planning to visit the southern end of the island on Wednesday to eat at the Pisces Restaurant. It's one of the best on the island. If you would like to join us, we can pick you up."

Carrie replied, "Sure, that sounds great. What time?"

"About six, the sunset is fabulous at that time and the restaurant gets very busy later. I think you will enjoy it."

Joe said, "It seems to me most places here have really good food. Of course, we have only tried a couple."

John said, "Yes, I'm sure you have been too busy to be going out to eat."

Margie shushed John and Carrie turned very red. Of course, he was right. They had really enjoyed each other's company.

The next day, Mark and Sheila took John and Margie to Bridgetown, the capital of Barbados. It was a fairly large city teeming with tourists. Three enormous cruise ships were tied up at the docks. All the shops catered to the ships with both small and large souvenirs. Margie picked up a stuffed flying fish for TG. They spent most of the morning visiting the shops and watching the tourists as they were besieged by street vendors with all kinds of offerings.

Sheila suggested they drive down the southern coast to find a place to eat away from the majority of tourists. Mark added, "The small outdoor restaurants generally have great food. Let's find one that offers locally caught rock lobster."

They found one with only a few people dining in its garden room. Everyone ordered the rock lobster cooked in various ways.

John said, "This lobster is as good as I've eaten anywhere. But since they are half the size of a Maine lobster, I think I'll have another one."

Margie said, "If we stay here very long, you will have to go on a diet as soon as we get home."

They drove around the southern end of the island and found where most of the Bajan natives lived. The contrast between the northern end of the island and the southern part was striking. They drove by the government buildings, most of which were British Colonial style and several hundred years old. Barbados had been a British colony before it was granted its full independence in 1966.

They decided to walk the narrow streets a few blocks off the beach, most of which did not have sidewalks. An intense rain shower made them jump under a convenient portico, which turned out to be an old Bajan German restaurant. It was almost dinner time so they decided to see what a German eatery would be like on an island with no obvious German background.

When they went in, they were surprised to see pictures and memorabilia from the Third Reich on shelves and the walls. Many customers were speaking German and most of them were older.

Mark explained, "A number of Germans settled here after World War Two and remained close knit. I'm sure a few are still waiting for Germany to take on the world again. A few war criminals were caught here soon after the war, but they soon realized a small island was not a good place to hide. Most of them moved on to South America."

The food was close to authentic German food, at least according to John who had visited Germany many times. He said, "This is the best German food I've tasted outside of Germany. This restaurant would be successful in Frankfurt or Munich. But they would have to take the pictures off the wall because the Nazi stuff is no longer allowed in Germany."

The group drove back to the plantation, arriving at sunset. Tomorrow would be a rest day, except for Mark who had to get back to his job of running the plantation.

John got up early and was sitting on the wrap-around veranda. He was enjoying the peace and quiet when a pot of coffee and a mug showed up beside him. He sincerely thanked the maid who brought it. He was enjoying his third cup when Margie came out in her house coat. As if by magic, another mug and pot appeared.

They sat and mainly just enjoyed the wonderful morning. Margie said, "This is great, but I'm missing TG. I'm afraid he will be grown when I see him again."

John said, "I'm thinking we should go home in about a week and let someone else come down here to enjoy the serenity."

Sheila walked out in her housecoat to join them. This time two pots came out—one coffee and one tea. Sheila wanted the tea. Margie decided to join her while John stayed with coffee.

Sheila said, "There's a lot more to see on the island, but it's mainly more old forts and churches and new hotels built for tourists. If you would like, we can visit any of those."

John responded, "I think it's time we gave our favorite guide some rest. I'm going to look around to see if I can get any leads on the mischief going on around here. Maybe a worker can show me the edges of the property and where other vandalism has occurred."

"I will tell Mark to arrange it for you. I would feel safer if we could get the nonsense stopped. I will call him and get the ball rolling."

She was gone a few minutes and came back. "A jeep and driver will be here shortly."

John said, "Let me finish getting dressed." He did not add that he wanted his gun, but Margie knew.

Margie asked, "Can I ride around with you? I want to see the sugar cane fields and the distillery."

"Certainly. I'll even give you the Jeep's front seat."

If Margie was missing TG, she had no idea how much she was being missed in Denver. Ashley was ready to call and ask Margie to come home. Ashley and Ruth were waist deep in getting the Learning Centers put together for the large, remote ranches and farms.

The first time Ashley visited one of the Trust's enormous ranches, she was struck by the fact that she saw no children. She quickly found out the nearest elementary school was over an hour and a half away, and the high schools were even further. As a former schoolteacher, she was so appalled she gathered a group of interested women together and they proposed building one room Learning Centers on each large ranch and farm. Each would have a teacher and take advantage of the newest home schooling-type programs.

Ruth was Ashley's mother and had previously operated a construction company. She stayed busy getting the materials delivered to the right place at the right time. It was a constant job with the long delivery times and such. She had started using ranch and farm trucks to get the materials instead of waiting on deliveries.

Ashley was also consumed with finding teachers and getting them moved in. Housing for the male teachers was easy since they live in the bunkhouse the first year. But she realized housing for the teachers had to be added to the plan for some ranches and farms because some of the teachers had families and some were female.

Sara was also busy trying to make sure the technology was on site and set up correctly. Sara had just turned eighteen and was a master computer whiz. Joe Sheffield had rescued her from captivity—her father-in-law had her chained in a bedroom so she could help him stay a step ahead of the DEA.

Sara's biggest challenge was getting high speed internet to each site. It quickly became apparent they would have to depend on satellite connections to get the job done. She finally found a vendor who guaranteed high speed.

She reminded him the Trust would come after him if he did not live up to the guarantee. He responded, "I'm proposing we use near military grade devices and software for the system. It's the highest priced system available for a reason. But it's worth it if you want quality service day after day." She and the Trust's purchasing manager bought his story and his equipment.

Virginia was also helping with the Learning Center project, along with her civic work. She was on many committees focused on improving Denver's quality of life. The school project was important to everyone and Ashley knew Virginia would provide assistance whenever needed.

Caring for TG was largely left to Wyatt and Lenny. Lenny and Ruth recently married, which made him Wyatt's father-in-law. He was a retired Marine and had spent most of his career as an MP. He was also awarded a number of high level combat medals. Lenny was part of Wyatt's new security team.

Neither man claimed to be Mr. Mom and neither had a burning desire to become one, which meant TG had to be left with someone else. With hiring all the teachers, Ashley did not have time to look for a baby caretaker. Virginia came to her rescue with the woman who helped care for Carrie when she was a child. Ashley hired her to be TG's Nanny and she moved into their house. Her name was Cassandra, a Hispanic woman in her late fifties.

Cassandra was a marvelous addition. She prepared all meals for TG and herself, and occasionally for everyone else. TG accepted her very well and soon treated her like a mother or grandmother. This hurt both Ashley and Ruth, but they had to have to have the help, at least until Margie returned.

Lenny was helping Frenchy get a hunting and fishing proposal ready to present to the Board. Frenchy was another member of Wyatt's security team. He had served in the military and as a federal game warden in Idaho.

The proposal involved setting up outfitting services for hunts and fishing expeditions on existing Trust property. They decided to focus on the low hanging fruit in Louisiana and Texas. Both locations would be year-round operations with duck and goose hunting combined with fresh and saltwater fishing. A nearby motel would suffice until small private lodges were completed.

Two grain farms supported large pheasant populations. Nearby pheasant rearing farms replenished the birds after each hunting party finished their hunt. They simply needed to focus on improving pheasant habitat by not mowing fence rows and the areas between the large pivot irrigation circles. The waste grain from harvesting would provide plenty of pheasant food.

The entire security team had all the work they could handle. Wyatt hoped criminal activity against the Trust would remain low, but he knew it would not.

The bubble burst when Buster Moore, head of Internal Auditing, walked in one day and asked Wyatt for a few minutes. He said, "We think we've found embezzlement in the investment division. I don't have enough concrete evidence yet, but we think a big chunk of money is missing. It's been taken a little at a time and is difficult to detect. The accounts handled by Merrill Johnson seem to come up just a few thousand dollars short most quarters. The problem is his mentor, confidant, and champion in the division is the Vice President of Finance, Gale Mellot. The discrepancy has been noted regularly in our audit reports, but Gale seems to be blind where Johnson is concerned. I think we will have to make an airtight case before Gale will do anything. That will involve examining Johnson's accounts and his lifestyle to determine whether it jives with his income."

"Okay, talk me through what you have."

"Johnson has been with us ten years and was quickly identified as a rising star. Gale has talked him up at every chance and, to tell the truth, he's been good in investing the Trust's funds. The division has outperformed the market in most years, actually in all years, especially in the funds Johnson manages. But two years ago we first noticed the balances for several of his funds did not quite meet the expectations. Each was off only a few thousand dollars. It can happen because of timing and so forth and does not normally raise red flags. But the accounts were off similar additional amounts the next quarter, which raised the red flags."

"We dug deeper into past records and I think as much as a half a million is missing over the previous six years. We informed Gale and the next quarter had no variance, nor did the following quarter. Then it started happening again, for larger amounts and in different funds. Gale has taken no action, even though he knows about the discrepancy. His inaction could be because Johnson is a top performer."

"Okay, we will get right on it. It's hard to hide that much money where we can't find it."

Wyatt wanted Mitch to lead the investigation. He was a key member of Wyatt's security team. Mitch had a distinguished military career and Wyatt hired him away from a deputy sheriff job in Idaho after working with him on several cases.

Mitch asked Sara to check Johnson's bank and investments accounts to see if he or anyone close to him had a half million dollars more than would be expected. Surprisingly, she did not find the money. But she did find large amounts of money moving in and out of his accounts, which was not unusual for someone investing his own money.

Mitch decided to tail Johnson to get a handle on his lifestyle. His scrutiny was unproductive until the next Thursday afternoon. Sara called Mitch to tell him Johnson had purchased a plane ticket to Salt Lake City for the following day. Mitch managed to get on board the same flight and secured a seat behind Johnson. Fortunately, Mitch did not remember ever meeting Johnson.

When they deplaned in Salt Lake City, Johnson walked to a ticket counter and purchased a ticket to Las Vegas. Mitch was close enough to hear the destination. He bought a ticket and called Wyatt to tell him where they were headed. Sara began to search hotel and casinos and quickly found Johnson had a large line of credit at Caesar's Casino. She extended her search and found he also had a line of credit at the Golden Moon in Mississippi.

After examining Sara's results, Wyatt thought, *"He must be a better investor than gambler. He's always behind at both places and uses his entire credit line before he pays up."*

They had enough evidence to make an arrest. Johnson did have several large personal investment accounts and Wyatt made plans to seize those funds to pay back the Trust. He thought he should talk with Chairman Harrell before taking any action since Gale, a Vice President with long tenure, was implicated. Neither Buster nor Wyatt thought Gale was directly involved in the embezzlement—his mistake was not doing anything about it.

Harrell was not happy when Buster and Wyatt laid out the situation. In fact, he was absolutely livid, "Do you know when Johnson will be back here?"

"Sara found he has return tickets, through Salt Lake, and will be back late Sunday."

"Let's let him come to work as usual. I want him arrested in front of everyone. Maybe that will discourage anyone else trying to steal from us. Gale will have to go down with him since he did nothing to stop the thefts after being notified. He will be demoted and allowed to retire. I want his retirement check to be cut as much as we legally can. I will get HR on that. I will call a judge to authorize freezing all of Johnson's accounts so he can't get to them. Maybe we can get our half million back. We are going to make an example of these two."

Wyatt responded, "I will have Mitch follow him all the way back here and put him to bed. He will make sure Johnson comes to work tomorrow. Call the Sheriff or whomever you want to arrest him and tell them to come by here early Monday morning. They have an investment meeting early on Monday's."

"Great! Seeing Johnson arrested will be a great lesson for the other investment account managers. We will also have a meeting of the Board and Vice Presidents, in which I will deal with Gale. I think the message to everyone will be quite clear."

Monday morning was eventful at the Cannon Trust's offices. It went down just like Harrell planned. The investment account managers had an eight o'clock team meeting. Johnson sat at a large conference table with Gale and the fifteen other account managers. Harrell, Wyatt, and another man walked in at exactly eight o'clock.

Harrell said, "We are going to delay your meeting for a moment. As you know, I have told everyone we will not stand for anyone stealing from the Trust. Our security team and internal auditors came to me with the suspicion that over half a million dollars is missing from this division."

"We checked electronically and put a tail on one of you. Johnson, I hope you had a good time in Las Vegas because it will be your last one for a long time. Please stand up and come over here. You are fired, effective immediately. This is Deputy Sheriff Simmons. He will be taking you to jail."

Johnson began to protest but Harrell said, "Shut up! Don't even try to lie! We have every transaction logged and the evidence against you is overwhelming. I'm told you are an astute investment account manager. I also know you are a horrible blackjack player, based on the records at Caesar's Palace and the Golden Moon down in Mississippi."

Simmons said, "Please turn around and put your hands behind your back. You are under arrest for embezzlement." He then read Johnson his Miranda rights and led him from the room.

Gale, who was at the meeting, said, "There must be a mistake! He's one of my best account managers."

"Gale, I will deal with you later. In fact, the process has already started. You and I will have a meeting shortly. I can't have you arrested for being an incredibly bad manager—I tried. Be in my office in an hour. Don't be late!"

Harrell walked down the hall to a meeting of the Board and all the Vice Presidents, and he was still visibly upset despite having an hour to cool off, "Let's tackle the elephant in the room. Gale, you were told more than once about a shortage in one of your employee's accounts and you did absolutely nothing. You will either retire or be fired today. Our lawyers tell me I cannot reduce your retirement income, but I'm still looking for a legal way to do it. You may leave now and be sure you have the paperwork done by noon. Now, get out!" The meeting lasted about three minutes.

Chapter Two

John and Margie's driver/guide drove them over the plantation's property. Margie had never seen sugar cane. The long rows of nearly eight feet tall cane surprised and impressed her.

John, who had seen sugar cane in many countries, was concentrating on where attacks or mischief might originate. He found several stockpiles of material for starting fires. The driver said it was most likely the rebels. They stopped at each pile and emptied the cans of kerosene that could be used to accelerate the fires. Detonator wire and fuses lay by one of the piles. He could find no bomb making supplies other than those. He took those supplies with them in the Jeep.

John felt sure the rebels were planning to step up their attacks. A few blocks of C4 or some nitrogen fertilizer with a can or two of diesel could make a bomb strong enough to do a great deal of damage.

John said, "We're being watched. See how the monkeys and birds are reacting in the forest. Something deeper in the forest has them upset."

He checked his pistol to make sure it was ready. He knew it

was, but one should always check.

When they returned to the plantation house, he reported his findings to Mark, "We found several of stashes of material that could do a great deal of damage. We need to get the police out here and step up our patrols."

Mark answered, "We've called them often and they never come."

"Let's see if I can get their attention and get them out here."

John called his CIA contacts to see if they could shake up the police. He then called Harrell to see if he could call politicians to make sure they knew the police were not helping protect the Trust's assets. He also told him about the bomb making supplies he found.

Harrell said, "I'll get right on it. Why don't you and Mark hire extra people to patrol? I know we can't check them out as much as we like, but maybe Mark will know some people he can trust."

"I'll see if I can get them checked with my old employer. They have assets in the area. These rebels could cause problems for American interests, such as the hotels along the beaches."

"I'll see if I can get some of the hotel managers to pressure the police and government. They are heavily invested down there."

"Good idea."

"Have you seen or heard from Carrie and Joe?"

"Not much. They've dropped by a couple of times but did not stay long."

"I bet."

"We are having dinner at a restaurant on the Caribbean side in a few days. Margie and I plan to leave the next day and have someone replace us. She's really missing TG. I may decide to stay a little longer to help Mark with security. I think something big is cooking. No hard evidence but I have a gut feeling, and I trust my instincts about trouble brewing."

"Let's talk again when the police have had time to react. If they don't react strongly, we may need several men from our security team down there to help keep a lid on the situation. We're losing rum production with all these little attacks."

"Call you tomorrow or the next day."

The police came the next day to look around. They took the materials John found and said they would patrol the plantation on a regular basis, both day and night. They still did not seem to be highly motivated, but at least they made an appearance.

The six people in Barbados enjoyed a wonderful dinner in what was supposed to be John and Margie's last night. The plan was for the jet to leave Denver early the next day to bring Mitch and Theresa and take John and Margie back.

John told Joe about the bomb making supplies he found. He had decided to stay in Barbados so he and Mitch could investigate more. Margie wanted to get back to be with TG. She had many gifts for him. They dropped Joe and Carrie off at their villa.

Carrie said, "Let's sit on the porch and enjoy the sea breeze. It's such a wonderful evening."

She took Joe's hand and said, "I think I'm going to have enough of this beautiful island in another week or so. Besides, you are beginning to wear down."

"Me! I thought it was you!"

John, Margie, Mark, and Sheila were sitting on the front porch enjoying a glass of wine and pleasant conversation. John was smiling at one of Mark's stories when he suddenly became alert.

He said, "Everyone stay calm and casually but quickly walk into the house. I think we have unwelcome company."

When everyone was inside John said, "I just saw hundreds of birds fly away from the edge of the woods and heard the monkeys howling, probably at intruders. I then saw sunlight reflecting off metal, probably a gun or machete. Both dogs obviously heard something because they were staring at the woods and rumbling."

He continued, "We need to get armed quickly. Mark, I want the lever action rifle. You take the short mag and go upstairs—stay back from the windows, but where you can see the edge of the forest. Ladies, I want each of you to have a pistol close and a shotgun in your hands. Stay away from the windows. Sheila, call the dogs inside. They will be good protection if the house is breached."

As soon as everyone was armed, John slipped out the back door and swung around behind a row of thick bushes. He watched the woods intently. Four AK 47s suddenly roared with short bursts. John could hear the rounds hitting the house. He quickly slipped further down the line of bushes and found a place for a sniper nest. He put a box of shells on the ground to his right and waited for a target to appear.

John heard Mark take a shot and a man screamed. He saw movement, a man going to help the one who fell. John squeezed the trigger and the man also went down. He took a few more shots whenever he saw bushes rustling.

Joe and Carrie heard the unmistakable rattle of AK 47s coming from the direction of the plantation! He said, "Grab our pistols and I'll get the Jeep keys! I'm sure the plantation is under attack. We have to help them."

Joe drove as fast as he could. When they got in sight of the plantation house, Joe stopped and jumped out to join the fray. As soon as his feet hit the ground something hit him in the head. The culprit was about to strike Joe again with a baseball bat!

Carrie was holding both pistols and shot the rebel dead center of his chest with Joe's .40 caliber Glock. Another man was running toward her waving a huge machete. She shot again and the man fell across the first prone man.

She ran around to check on Joe, who was bleeding profusely from a head wound. She screamed and tried to hold him. He was unconscious and completely still—she thought he was dead.

John charged out of his nest and began running toward Joe and Carrie. He saw a man raise his rifle toward Carrie. He barely stopped and fired a quick round at him. The man toppled backward. The other attackers fled deeper into the forest.

Margie burst out of the house and began running toward John. He yelled, "Go back! Call the U.S. Ambassador and an ambulance. We'll call the police later. Tell Mark to stay upstairs and keep watch, and tell Sheila to turn the dogs out."

Plantation hands began to trickle toward the house. The Ambassador arrived at the same time as the ambulance.

Joe was alive but still unconscious. While Joe was being loaded into the ambulance, Carrie walked over and hugged John, "Thank you! You saved my life again. Hopefully, I helped save Joe's life."

"Carrie, his pulse is strong. All we can do is pray for him."

Carrie turned and climbed into the ambulance with Joe. John was slightly wounded and Margie was trying to the stop the bleeding.

The Ambassador asked, "What happened?"

John replied, "The rebels attacked in force, but the monkeys and the birds gave us a few minutes warning. We had time to arm ourselves. The police will find five or six dead rebels in the edge of the woods and three or four AK 47s. They attacked Joe and Carrie when they arrived from the villa. Joe was hit with a baseball bat. Carrie shot the man with the bat and another one rushing her with a machete. I shot another one who was about to shoot Carrie."

"Okay. The police, if they ever get here, will want to hear the story."

Sheila drove Margie to the hospital as soon as they could get away. The emergency room at the hospital was not what Carrie and Margie were used to. Everything moved far too slow for them.

A doctor came by after about an hour and said Joe had a bad head wound, "We don't have a neurosurgeon available to work on him. He will certainly need one, and soon."

John came in and heard the news. He called his former boss, the CIA Director, to ask if he had a medivac plane in the Caribbean to take Joe to Washington. They had one in Puerto Rico. It landed in Barbados less than two hours later.

The plane would take Joe to the Walter Reed hospital where a neurosurgeon would be waiting. Carrie and Margie boarded the plane with him. The CIA medical personnel started working on Joe as soon as his gurney was secured.

Carrie called her dad, Chairman Harrell. She had been handling the situation admirably until she heard her dad's voice. When she broke down, Margie took the phone to finish the call. She told Harrell that Joe was in extremely grave condition and would require surgery as soon as he arrived in Washington.

She moved away from Carrie and said, "That is, if he survives the flight. It's really bad."

"What do we need to do?"

"John and I talked about that. We think Virginia should go to Washington to be with Carrie and Joe. The police may try to arrest Carrie and everyone else here for killing five or six rebels, so you probably need to come to Barbados. Bring Wyatt and the others with you. John is wounded but still walking. I think they were the only ones hurt. The police are close to useless and they will be worried more about the dead Bajans. By the way, Carrie shot two of the rebels, including the one who hit Joe. She showed her Cannon backbone."

"Good for her! What time do you arrive in Washington?"

"Eight tomorrow morning is what I think I heard. The plane is carrying pretty good CIA medical staff. We will land at Andrews."

"Virginia will leave shortly for Washington. Wyatt and I and the rest of the security team will head to Barbados."

"We have men at the plantation standing guard. John called the CIA and DEA directors and they immediately sent agents to help out. I believe the plantation is safe. Those DEA Agents are rough looking characters and are very angry about Joe getting hurt. I think they are hoping the rebels will attack again. The only property damage was a fire in the cane field. Mark said the damage is minimal."

Harrell called Virginia to tell her what had happened. She was surprisingly calm and said she could be ready to leave in an hour. She would take one of the large twin engine prop planes and arrive before the medivac.

Harrell's secretary called everyone on the security team to an emergency meeting. Wyatt was hit hard by the news. Mitch, Wyatt, and Harrell quickly got ready to fly to Barbados. Lenny and Frenchy stayed behind to provide security for the compound. Ashley and Ruth stayed in Denver because they were head over heels in developing the school system.

When the medivac plane to Washington leveled off, Margie said, "Carrie, do you know how to reach Joe's parents?"

"They were killed in train wreck when Joe was in DEA training. He said it took him a long time to truly get over their deaths."

Virginia was waiting at the hospital when Joe, Carrie, and

Margie arrived in an ambulance. She ran toward Carrie ran toward as soon as she saw her. Carrie's clothes were covered with blood. The medical team on the plane gave her a jacket but it did not cover all the blood. Joe's head was bandaged but blood was still seeping through. Several bags of liquid were dripping through his IV.

A neurosurgeon met the ambulance and began giving orders for an MRI and other tests. He told Carrie they would be going straight to surgery as soon as he knew the extent of the injuries. He expected Joe would be in surgery all morning and part of the afternoon.

Virginia and Margie took Carrie to get her cleaned up. The hospital gave her scrubs to wear and she took a shower. She managed a short nap in the waiting room. None of them had slept much on the plane.

A little before eleven o'clock a nurse called from surgery and said they were about half through. She said, "It has been touch and go, but the patient obviously has a strong will to live."

The surgeon came down at two o'clock, "I think I have all the bone chips out of his brain cavity. I left the largest skull fragment out to allow for brain swelling. I will glue it back in a few days. He will move to ICU shortly. You can count on him being there several days or maybe weeks. We will keep him in a coma for several days to help prevent swelling. The crew on the medivac plane saved his life. I will be in the hospital the rest of day and tonight in case he needs me. By the way, my name is Chris Smith. You can have me paged if you have any questions. Since I know y'all won't leave to get a hotel room, I suggest you find a space in the ICU waiting room. I will keep you informed."

They went to the ICU waiting room and found three chairs together. They all made a nest of sorts and settled in for the long haul. All three were dozing when the nurse came to tell Carrie she could go back for a few minutes—only Carrie was allowed to go back.

She said to Virginia and Margie, "Visiting hours occur four times a day for the neurological ICU. I will try to slip all of you back during the next one, which is in three hours. Only two at a time can go back."

Carrie sat down beside Joe and took his hand. He was unaware of her presence and looked so pale and vulnerable it almost broke her heart. They let her stay only a few minutes and then escorted her back to the waiting room.

The nurse said, "There's usually food down here that everyone shares. When did you eat last? Don't get sick on us. It's going to be a long process."

Margie dug her phone out of her purse and ordered ten large pizzas. The least she could do was make sure all the people waiting on their patients had food. She would do better next time.

Dr. Chris came by at nine p.m. and said, "His vital signs are stabilizing and improving. That's a tough man in there and he's got a fighting chance. Is there anything I can do for you?"

Virginia asked, "Do you think we can find clean pillows and blankets. These appear to have been here a while."

"I'll see what I can do."

Clean blankets and pillows arrived a few minutes later for the entire waiting room. Carrie was sound asleep in a few minutes. Virginia and Margie talked a little about the bad things they hoped would not happen.

They too finally drifted off to sleep. They were very fatigued and there was nothing to do in light of the limited visiting hours. Chris came in just after daylight and drew up a chair.

He gave everyone a chance to wake up before he began, "He has a small bleeder that needs to be stopped before it becomes serious. We are going back to surgery to work on it. It should take less than two hours. I'll talk to you when we finish. His vital signs are much better this morning and he had a restful night. It's still too early for me to give you anything more. See you in a couple of hours."

"Thanks Doctor. We'll be here. You're the man!"

"Why don't you go get breakfast? I'm sorry, but you are going to miss the first visitation period because of the surgery. Tell you what, I'm going to take the three of you to see him. He's still in a deep coma but who knows about these things, maybe he can hear you. You can only stay a few minutes. He and I need to get ready for surgery."

They jumped at the chance to go back and at least see him. Carrie took his hand and talked to him as though he were awake. She talked about wanting a long life with him and a house full of children. Virginia and Margie cried. When they went back to waiting room, Virginia and Margie decided to go the cafeteria for breakfast.

As soon as they got to the cafeteria, they both called their husbands. Virginia asked Harrell, "When are you coming to Washington? It's not good here. He's back in surgery this morning to fix a little bleeder, if there can be such a thing. His surgeon, Chris, has been good about keeping us informed and I am confident in him. He was here all night monitoring Joe's condition."

"I hope to be there this afternoon or tomorrow. Several people in the hospitality industry have flown in and we will have a 'come to Jesus' meeting with the highest level government officials. Wyatt and his crew are out gathering evidence. The police are sitting on their hands. If my meeting goes well, I will leave right away. If not, you may hear me explode all the way to Washington. Have they given you any prognosis on Joe? How is

Carrie holding up?"

"Carrie is doing great considering the situation. Joe has not been awake since the attack. They have him in an induced coma to try to control swelling. It's still touch and go. He will have a long road to recovery if he survives. His odds improve each day, but Chris said he would be dead except for the excellent care he got on the medivac. We don't know if he will survive and, if he does, how he will be. There was a lot of damage."

"Let me get to my meeting so I can get there to help all I can."

"There's really nothing to do here, so get your job done there. That's more important than you being here."

Margie's call went much like Virginia's, except she was worried about John and his wound. "How are you doing? How's your arm? How are the rest of the men?"

"One question at a time. I am frustrated with the police here more than anything. My arm will be fine. Sheila is treating it with white lightning, which I must say burns but tastes great. There's no infection. Everyone is frustrated, but we're doing our own investigation. We're hoping the police stay in Bridgetown until we chase down the culprits. The one who hit Joe and Carrie shot was one of the leaders. We have the names of others. I will be talking to them soon, I hope. How are things there? Is Joe going to be okay?"

"Joe is day to day. They just don't know if he will survive or be okay. The damage is severe and he's back in surgery. You take care of yourself and y'all be careful. Those people have hurt us enough."

"Let me get back to helping run these suckers down. We think we're getting close to the primary suspects. It looks like a small violent group has been doing the damage. We think they are trying to get Americans and American businesses off the island. The group is likely financed by communists. That's why my friends were close when we needed the medivac plane for Joe."

"The doctor said the medivac crew saved Joe's life. They were better than most."

"I'm sure that's correct. Got to go."

With their calls finished they talked while they were away from Carrie. Margie said, "You know, they did not think Wyatt would live when he was ambushed. It was weeks before the doctor would say he had a good chance to live. Then it was months of recovery. I had to move to Salt Lake City to help him with the recovery. Joe has a head injury and I'm sure recovery will be even more difficult."

"I've been thinking about that. I have heard about people who have to learn to walk and talk again after a head injury. Some people never recover. I feel so sorry for Carrie. She may never have a 'normal' marriage or husband. They are so young."

"One good thing is I'm sure he will never have go back to work for the DEA. I don't think they can risk putting him in the field. I'm sure there will be some permanent damage or loss of function. We have to have something positive to think about. The waiting room is certainly depressing."

"Speaking of waiting room, we better get Carrie breakfast and go back to support her. She may hear from Dr. Chris before long."

"Yes, and don't let me forget to order food for the other poor people up there. It's the least we can do. Some of those people look like they are on their last leg financially."

Carrie had not heard from Chris when they returned. Virginia convinced Carrie to eat at least a little. She ate scrambled eggs and a few pieces fruit. They found better coffee and she devoured it along with two pieces of toast. Virginia was surprised at how much she ate.

Chris called thirty minutes later and said, "The surgery is over and the bleeder is repaired. Joe tolerated the surgery very well and the repairs we made yesterday seem to be holding. He is such a strong person with a huge will to live that I'm beginning to think he has a good chance. I will be there in about an hour to talk to you and maybe I can squeeze another visit in for you."

The news was really the first glimmer of hope for the women. Carrie was guardedly happy. Margie and Virginia tried to pump her up even higher.

Carrie said, "Let me go get my face on, I'm sure I look a fright and I don't want to see him looking this way." Margie and Virginia understood her point and both started to work on their hair and makeup.

Chris came in later and pulled up his chair, "I am encouraged. It's more him than us. He has a desire somewhere deep inside to live and it's burning strong. He may not know what's going on but he definitely wants to live. I'm betting on him, but he still has a long way to go. Don't be surprised if he needs additional surgeries. Carrie, starting tomorrow, I'm going to tell the nurse to let you stay with him for a couple of hours each day. I have a feeling you're part of the fire burning inside him. He may be in a coma, but he may know you are there with him. Now, let's go see him."

Carrie held Joe's hand tightly for the thirty minutes they were with him. She again talked to him about their future. Virginia and Margie laid a hand on him and prayed silently. As they were about to be ushered out Margie asked if she could say a prayer. Everyone agreed.

"Lord, reach Your healing hand down to one of Your good ones. He has protected others all his life and was running toward trouble to help his friends when he was struck down. You can make him well. We humbly ask You send him back to Carrie well and whole. She will help You care for him and so will all his other friends. We ask this in Your name. Amen."

Carrie gave him a little peck on his hand. She was afraid to even kiss the head bandages yet. They left the room.

Carrie unexpectedly said, "Let's go down to the Chapel."

They found it on the first floor and went in. Carrie knelt and prayed silently for several minutes. She was joined by the other two.

Everyone felt better after the prayers. Carrie asked if they could go outside to get some fresh air for a few minutes. She looked refreshed when they came back in. It really was the first time she looked like herself since the incident.

Chapter Three

The security team was making slow progress in Barbados. Harrell had assembled an impressive group of executives from the hospitality industry to talk to the government officials. The U.S. Ambassador agreed to accompany them to make it more official. Representatives from all the major hotels and resorts along with other business owners were also involved. In total, the group had investments of over five billion dollars and employed several thousand Bajan workers with some of the best paying jobs in the country.

The meeting started late, much to Harrell's annoyance. The Ambassador told him it was the 'Island Way,' which did not help Harrell's attitude. Everyone agreed Harrell should speak for the group. He was CEO of a firm that owned a large resort, a significant amount of land, and a large rum distillery. When the Prime Minister finally showed up, all the hospitality industry representatives were clearly irritated. Harrell was even more irritated when he saw no police were present.

Harrell began, "Sir, you have kept a group of people who run or own substantial assets in your country waiting for over an hour.

Besides being bad manners, it's really bad business. Why are police representatives not here? That's also bad business. If you can't get the proper people here in one hour, you and your country are going to lose significant investments."

"You can't talk to me like that! You know I am Prime Minister of this country!"

"And you can't tell us were to invest our money! Suppose we start shutting down our resorts? I'm willing to shut ours down first. I guarantee you the others will follow me. You may be Prime Minister, but if we stop your tourist trade, will you win the next election? How many Bajans will lose their livelihood? What would happen to the economy under your watch?"

The CEO of a major cruise line serving Barbados chimed in, "We have been asking for more security in the areas our passengers visit to buy souvenirs. Your police has ignored our requests. We will also pull out if our passenger's needs are not met."

Several others voiced similar positions. The Ambassador tried to calm things down, "Now let's don't make threats and keep the meeting moving ahead."

Harrell was still incensed, "These are not idle threats! My son-in-law is struggling to stay alive, thanks to your uncontrolled rebels, and all your police are interested in is why my daughter shot the man who bludgeoned him and why my people shot Bajan terrorists who attacked them in overpowering numbers. I want the police here now! You have fifty minutes!"

The head of the island's police force showed up thirty minutes later, along with a small contingent of officers. Harrell was still angry but the Ambassador had been working on him in a room near the Prime Minister's office.

He explained again that they were on 'Bajan time' which was not related to punctuality. He added, "We often laugh about it—

if you have an appointment in the morning and are able to see the individual any time in the afternoon, you have been very lucky. An appointment set for tomorrow is no guarantee of an appointment at all."

"Well, I don't like it, but I will try to be nicer the next round. I need to get to Washington to check on my daughter and son-in-law. I'm also wanting all the vandalism and attacks stopped immediately. My men will have the attackers caught before these so called police have even started to investigate."

They were called back into the Prime Minister's office two hours after the meeting was scheduled. The Ambassador took the lead, "As you gentlemen know, the plantation owned by the Cannon Trust was attacked. Two defenders were wounded, one seriously. He may not live. Six attackers were killed. The rebel who hit Mr. Cannon's son-in-law with a bat and was going to hit him again died in the attack."

Harrell said, "So far as I can tell, the island's police force has done nothing to catch the group responsible for the attack. You have refused to investigate the many instances of vandalism that led up to this armed attack. When bomb making supplies were found, you took them but, as far as I can determine, you did nothing to try to find out who was making bombs. All these American-based businesses have experienced similar problems. It's very difficult to consider making new investments in Barbados when serious problems like these exist. The distillery expansion, which will provide over a hundred well-paying new jobs for your people, is running almost three months behind because of the continuous vandalism. Now it seems the attacks are stepping up.

The ambassador spoke up, "The U.S. government demands you protect the interests of U.S. owned businesses or we will lower the ranking of Barbados as an investment site. I think these other men would like to add a few tidbits to my statements."

The owner of the cruise company was the first to speak, "We have asked for increased police protection for our guests many times and our concerns have been ignored. Guests keep returning to the ship with stories of being robbed or hassled as they shop and spend money here. Many other destinations will welcome our ships and we are now strongly considering eliminating Barbados from our routes. We need to see concrete action to protect the tourists we bring here to spend their money."

The manager of largest resort spoke next, "We have asked for better protection for our guests, to no avail. We have had to hire extra guards because the police will not even respond to a robbery that has already occurred, much less try to prevent it from occurring. I don't see any chance of us expanding in Barbados until the problems of petty and sometimes armed robberies of our guests stop."

Harrell stood up again, "Our Trust owned land here long before the island gained its independence. Yet we get no protection from the police. You often don't even answer our calls for help. We are making a multi-million dollar investment to expand our distilling operations. These rebels are disrupting construction. My son-in-law is fighting for his life and all the police want to talk about is why Bajan terrorists died while attacking my people. You seem to be doing nothing to catch the people who planned and executed the attack. We do not have to invest in Barbados. We own sugar cane farms in other locations, including the United States. If you can't protect our people and investments, we will have to move the operations to another location."

The police made a variety of excuses. The ambassador spoke up again, addressing the police chief, "These problems have been building for a long time. I suggest you take two weeks to come up with a concrete plan to protect U.S. interests and that you immediately begin looking for those who attacked the Cannon Plantation. Gentlemen, this is not going to blow over. If you don't develop a plan, the U.S. will take action and these businesspeople will also take action. Those actions will hurt the Bajan economy significantly. Oh, and do you really think it is necessary for Mr. Cannon's daughter to leave the bedside of her husband who is at death's door to talk to you about her part in repelling the attack? John and Mark Cannon have already told you what happened. I'd like an answer to that question immediately."

The police started looking back and forth at each other. Just as one started to say something about it being customary, the Prime Minister broke in with, "No! She is dealing with enough."

He turned to address the businesspeople, "We will develop the plan you ask for. I am aware of our reputation of not getting right on things. The chief and his men will begin working on the plan today. Their job security depends on the quality and timeliness of their report. In the meantime, we will increase the patrols at the dock and tourist areas. Patrol cars will be visible around the plantation and we will investigate who was behind the attack. If you gentlemen will excuse us, I have a few matters to discuss with my police force."

When the U.S. delegation walked out, the Ambassador said, "That's the most positive response we've ever received from the government. I will do my best to hold them to any plan they come up with. Maybe things are starting to take a turn for the better."

Harrell decided he could go to Washington to see if he could help with Joe. He called the pilots to tell them to be ready for takeoff in two hours. He found John and Wyatt at the plantation house.

John was getting his bandage changed after he and Wyatt spent the morning in the forested areas around the plantation. They found what appeared to be the main rebel hideout. No one was around, but it looked like five or six people lived their more or less permanently and several others came often. They found bomb making supplies in a small shed behind the main building. They planned to stake out the location with Mark and a couple of trusted employees.

Harrell said, "Let me call and get the police headed this way. They promised they would respond."

Wyatt said, "Tell them to not use the sirens or lights. Just drive out here. It would be better if they were in in camo. Someone will bring them to the site. We may be on the stakeout all night."

Harrell called the police chief who was still in the President's office. He relayed Wyatt's instructions, "Remember, no sirens and no flashing lights. We expect the whole group or a large part of it to be at the hideout tonight."

Two police cars arrived with four officers in head-to-toe camo. The group of nine men went to the rebel hideout, where they saw a car and four men. The Cannon group and the police settled down to wait for more rebels to show up.

Two hours later three cars with four men in each pulled up. John and Wyatt were close to the building so they could hear the conversations. One who appeared to be the new leader indicated everyone had now arrived and they should get the bombs made. The targets were the plantation house and the rum distillery construction site.

Wyatt eased back to the rest of the group to make sure they were ready. They needed to hurry because the men were already working on the bombs.

One policeman said, "Let me call headquarters so they can send a paddy wagon and backup." Wyatt thought that would be okay if they hurried to arrest the rebels.

They surrounded the shack and began moving in. A siren was barely audible but coming their way. Mark and the lead policeman stepped into the room and announced that everyone was under arrest. All but two complied by falling to the floor. One rebel tried to jump out a window John was guarding. John used his rifle like a baseball bat and knocked the man back into the building where he lay bleeding and unconscious.

The other rebel went out Wyatt's window. He decided to fight Wyatt, which was a bad mistake. His face and legs were quickly and awkwardly rearranged by two powerful kicks. The fight was over just as three police cars and a van with flashing lights and sirens blaring pulled up to the plantation house. John asked one of the policemen to lead the newcomers to the hideout. He wanted more men to make sure no one slipped off into the forest. None did.

———————

Just as Harrell landed in Washington, Wyatt called to give him the details. He responded, "Great! We should be able to get the expansion completed now. Tell Mitch to stay down there. I'll call and tell Theresa about Mitch staying. Maybe it will cool off and she can join him. It's better here, but still not good. They have done more surgeries and he's still in a coma. If he lives he may have serious issues with cognition and sight. He needs at least one more surgery to get his eye back where it should be. Chris, his doctor, says the surgery will be more complicated than the previous ones."

Wyatt responded, "John, Mark, and I had a long talk about

the Spirits Division Security. Even though we caught this group of rebels, we're not sure the mischief is over. Other groups may take up the gauntlet. John and I don't think we can deploy one or more of our security team down there permanently. So, what do you think about John and I calling our former colleagues to see if we can't find two or three recently retired agents to help Mark? Could be temp or permanent jobs, depending on what evolves."

"Yes, do it. We certainly need the entire security team in Denver."

Wyatt and John went straight to the hospital when they arrived in Washington. Joe was no better or worse. Chris came by to talk to the entire group that night.

He said, "We are going to gradually bring him out of the coma. Carrie will be allowed to sit with him. Even though I don't know if he can hear you, talk to him constantly. If you detect any signs like eyes fluttering or a twitch write it down. If he fights it too much, we will have to put him back under. I really do not know how it will go. Maybe we will get lucky."

Carrie was just grateful she could sit with him. Virginia asked if she could join Carrie. Chris answered, "Letting Carrie sit with him already has some nurses in a tizzy. Maybe you can work out shifts—she will need help. Does he have a close male friend, maybe from work?" Everyone looked at Wyatt.

Chris continued, "Good. Maybe you can give Carrie a break and sit with him tomorrow and talk about work. I just want him to get constant verbal stimulation as we reduce the drugs."

The plan came together quickly. Carrie would go in immediately and Wyatt early the next morning. Virginia and Harrell would take over later. John and Margie would head back to Denver to help care for TG. Ashley and Ruth were getting desperate for help as they got into the last phase of getting the school system ready for the grand openings. It was still a long way off, but they knew there was much work to do.

John called a former colleague and said, "Hey Wesley, John Cannon here."

"John, you old scalawag. How you hanging?"

"Great! Got a great job that has a little action from time to time. Wesley, I need help. I work in security in a very large organization that has property all over. I'm looking for a somewhat recently retired agent for a temp job that could turn into a permanent one. Would you believe it's on an island paradise in the Caribbean—Barbados."

"Hmm. You remember Alphonse Laborde?"

"Big Al. Sure, worked with him several times."

"He called me last month. He's been retired about a year. Told me he expected to fish and hunt in them Louisiana swamps every day for the rest of his life. But he's bored to tears already. Not enough action, if you know what I mean."

John pictured Big Al and thought, *"He's perfect. Mostly African American, with some Cajun and Indian blood mixed in. He would fit perfectly in Barbados."*

"You got his number?"

"Yep, give me just a sec."

John call Alphonse Laborde and Big Al caught a plane for Barbados the next morning.

Wyatt called Bennett and asked the same question. Bennett responded, "Maybe. I talked with Spider Jorgenson last week. He's reached that age, and he has to retire in a few months, at the latest. He and his wife were born and raised in Northern Michigan and do not want to move back to the cold weather"

"Give me his number and I will call him. I have a security job for him in Barbados. It's apparently seventy to seventy-two degrees there every day of the year."

"Hah! He might pay you to get that job!" Spider and his wife were on a plane two days later.

Mark called Wyatt three days to say Big Al and Spider were perfect. He also hoped he could keep them around permanently.

All the initial school planning had been focused only on elementary schooling, but it was now obvious high school classes were needed even more desperately. That would require more books, computers, learning tools and so forth. Ashley thought the high school students could help with the younger ones, as long as it did not interfere with their studies.

Ashley was also getting feedback that a surprising number of mothers also hoped to take advantage of the Learning Centers. Many of them did not have high school diplomas and wanted to pursue GEDs.

Tommy Cannon, the new Director of Ranches, spoke to Ashley about a similar issue, "You know, a lot of hands don't have a high school diploma. I think a number of them would be interested in getting one at night."

The GED issue threw Ashley into a tailspin for a few days. She mentioned it to Sara and got her answer, "All they need is a computer and the ability to hook up to the internet. I found many good looking GED programs, usually paid for by the state. I plan to get my GED as soon as the Learning Centers open. I'm already taking two courses and they are quite good." Another problem solved for Ashley.

Ashley worked on modifying and expanding the original proposal and planned to present it at the next Board meeting.

TG was ready to play with his grandmother and grandfather when they returned home. He had missed them a lot, probably about half as much as they missed him. He was beginning to talk a little. His vocabulary was limited to Mommy, dog, Roof for Ruth, and Len. Margie was determined to add new words, like her name. She worked hard but he did not want to say Margie in any form.

John walked into the room one day and TG said, 'Gamps!,' sort of, which almost crushed Margie. The next day, TG walked up to Margie and said something like, 'Memaw.' She was elated and played with him all day.

———————————

Wyatt called Margie and said there was slight improvement in Joe's condition. He had begun responding to Carrie and even more if Wyatt talked to him about work. His eyes were fluttering and he was squeezing Carrie's hand occasionally. Chris said they had removed all the medications used to keep him in the coma. He thought Joe would come around during the next week.

Chris warned everyone, "When he wakes up, he may not know any of you. I expect him to have at least a mild case of amnesia, which often comes with a severe head injury. His memory should begin returning more rapidly when he gets into a more comfortable environment. I wish I could give you better news. But just remember, a few weeks ago we weren't sure he would survive."

Carrie responded, "I'm so happy he has progressed to this point. If I can get him home, I think I can help get him well."

"I'm thinking we will get him home in two or three weeks. He still needs a major surgery on his eye, but that can wait. We will bandage it fully and hopefully he can see well enough from the other one."

Two days later Joe was sitting up when Chris came by. Sitting up was all he was doing. He had said nothing nor moved purposely. Chris used a large needle to stimulate his leg and foot and detected obvious involuntary movement.

Chris said, "This is great! He can move to a regular room and y'all can stay with him 24/7. He needs all the stimulation you can give him short of sex. We might try that before long," he laughed.

Carrie responded, "I'm game if you think it will help."

Joe's improvements were excruciatingly slow, almost undetectable from one day to the next. From week to week, however, his progress was very obvious. One day he picked up a spoon to try to eat, which was a major jump forward. Carrie and the others were elated. The progress was becoming more noticeable.

Chris asked, "What facilities do you have at your home?"

Harrell answered, "Doc, I am wealthy—really wealthy. I can have whatever he needs available in our house before our private plane can get us there. I can hire a doctor to stay with him if you say so. Just tell me what he needs."

"Okay. Tell you what, why don't you hire a physical therapist to stay at your house? He or she can tell you what to buy. I think PT will help him more than anything. Have the person you hire call me to set up a line of communication. When he's ready, he will need the surgery to fix his eye and all the related bones. I can do it or you can get someone there to do it. It's pretty complicated."

"Can you do it in Denver?"

"Hospitals don't like outsiders coming in and performing surgeries."

"They will allow it when the hospital's largest donor wants it done. If you are willing to do it, I guarantee they will accept you with open arms."

"We'll see when the time comes. You said you have a private plane to transport him?"

"Yes, and we will install a hospital bed. If you can give him something to keep him comfortable for five hours, I will have a doctor on the plane—and a nurse."

"Okay, I'm going to release him tomorrow morning and he will not remember the trip. Get the therapist hired and ready to start with his PT."

"Done!"

The Trust's jet was waiting at Andrews the next morning. John took care of getting the clearances to use Andrews. A medical team was on board and the seats had been reconfigured for Joe's hospital bed.

Joe was installed shortly after noon in the master bedroom in their apartment attached to Harrell and Virginia's house. Hilary, a certified Physical Therapist, was put in a bedroom next door. Two full-time nurses would share in caring for Joe. Chris had written his orders for the medical staff. Joe started waking up about dark and did not appear to be in any pain.

Ashley was very happy to have Wyatt back home and so was TG. He still knew his daddy and managed his version of 'dada' by the next day. Harrell and Virginia had to work to get him saying their name but they were ready to try. Harrell had to go to work, but Virginia had him saying something close to 'Gina' and 'Harl' when he came home.

Joe was a little groggy from the trip but had a restful night. Hilary ordered the equipment and had set up by the end of the second day. She wanted to start Joe walking as soon as possible. Speech would come second.

After a week, Joe was taking a few struggling steps. They were not pretty but he was moving. Hilary worked with him all day every day on some form of movement. Joe's rapid improvement was remarkable. She asked Carrie to help her to get him into a wheelchair so he could sit on the porch. Carrie talked to him until she could sometimes barely whisper. Different people read to him to try to get his brain cells reengaged with language. He had said nothing yet.

His first words came after two weeks at home. Wyatt walked over to his bed one morning and Joe said, "I let them get to us. Mistake."

Wyatt said, "Carrie shot the one who hit you and a second one waving a machete. John shot another one who was aiming an AK at Carrie. The rest of them ran off. They are in jail and hopefully will get long prison sentences." Joe did not seem to understand.

He asked, "Who Carrie?" Carrie's heart sank, but she recovered quickly.

"I'm Carrie and I am your wife. We got married a month ago. I was with you during the attack."

He closed his eyes and tried to remember, but nothing else came to him. Hilary delayed the physical exercises so Carrie could talk with him longer. She thought it was most important factor right then. Carrie poured out her heart to him all morning. She detected a few indications that his mind was flickering and spinning trying to digest the information. Carrie was encouraged.

The afternoon was spent working with his arms and legs. He was much stronger but still weak. Hilary let Carrie help her with light massages and movements. Joe looked at Carrie questioningly several times as though he was trying to remember her.

Late in afternoon, he looked at her and said, "Carrie wife."

She hugged him and gave him the biggest kiss his bandages would allow. His eye opened as wide as it could, "Carrie wife."

Two weeks later, Hilary and a doctor who came by every day

thought Joe was ready for the eye surgery. Hilary called Chris and told him.

He said, "Great! I can take some time off and come out there to do it. Ask Harrell to set it up."

It did not take much setting up. Harrell called the hospital and told them he would need the main surgical suite for a neurosurgeon to operate on his son-in-law. It was set up quickly. The only question he was asked was who would perform the surgery.

"Dr. Chris Smith of Walter Reed in Washington. He's been Joe's doctor through a half dozen or so surgeries. Do you want to contact Chris to see what he needs and set up a time? We will want the Angelina Suite for his recovery."

"Yes sir. I will get right on it."

Joe was remembering more and more, but in somewhat random snippets. He talked to Wyatt one day and said, "We have been in a few scrapes together. Some bad scrapes where people died. We were hard men, but not like John. I don't want to cross him if I'm thinking straight."

"You are thinking straight."

"I wish I could remember more about Carrie. I know I had....have....deep feelings for her, but I just can't unlock them yet. It's so frustrating."

Wyatt talked to the nurses and Hilary right after the conversation. He asked, "Would sex hurt Joe." They looked at each other and said they did not think it would.

Wyatt went in and told Carrie she and Joe should sleep in their apartment that night. He suggested she wear whatever she wore on their honeymoon. Carrie was taken aback, but ready to try it if they thought it might help unlock Joe's mind.

Wyatt said, "I don't know, but Hilary and the nurses said it might help and don't think it will cause a setback. I will bring him back to your apartment after our customary after-dinner drink. You just wait and come out after I leave. If you think it's causing him any stress, just call for me. Your dad and I may have an unusually long talk tonight. Just let things happen and don't push him."

Chapter Four

Wyatt was dying to know whether sleeping together had helped Joe and Carrie in getting to know each other again and could it have helped Joe's memories. He walked over to Harrell's to see if they were up. He, Harrell, and Virginia were sitting with their second cup of coffee when Carrie came into the kitchen.

"Mom, could you fix Joe and I scrambled eggs and toast this morning. Wyatt, if you and dad will help Joe to the veranda, we will eat there and enjoy the better world we're waking up to. He's feeling better this morning and seems to be thinking clearer."

With that, she turned and walked back to their apartment. The three in the kitchen looked at each other and wondered what caused him thinking clearer but no one wanted to ask. When Virginia finished making breakfast, the men helped Joe to the veranda. He could walk but was still wobbly and shaky. A couple of strong arms were more than he needed, but still comforting. Neither Joe nor Carrie gave any indication of how their night went. They both looked better than they had in a long while.

Carrie said, "Please send the nurses to help get him ready for PT in about an hour. I think I will go into town today to officially resign my job with the bank and maybe buy us a few clothes." She had more or less dismissed the two men as if they were servants.

Harrell said, "Humm." As they walked back toward the kitchen.

Wyatt added, "Indeed."

Virginia was waiting for a report. It consisted of two eloquent guys shrugging their shoulders. Something was different but they had no idea what or why, and Carrie and Joe were not talking.

Joe's eye surgery was coming up in a week so Carrie bought Joe two sets of really nice pajamas to lounge in. She also bought herself two sets. Joe had already mentioned going back to Freedom Town and to the ranch. She thought it might do both of them good when he recovered from the eye surgery.

When Chris arrived a few days before the surgery, he immediately visited the hospital to check on the surgical suite and equipment. The surgery would be delicate and consist of rebuilding the eye socket. He had begun the work back in Washington but now had to work on the orbital and get the eye aligned properly. A few hundredths of a milli-miter could make a big difference in sight and in appearance. He assembled the team to help him and felt good about them. The eye surgeon was the best in Denver and likely the best in the West.

He then visited Joe and Carrie and was pleased with Joe's progress. Hilary had him walking with only a little support. His arms seemed to work naturally and were strong. For a person who almost died a few months ago, he was in remarkable condition.

Chris asked, "How is your memory and mental condition."

Joe chuckled and responded, "Better than I could hope for. You may think I'm crazy, but I've had some really weird dreams that have helped me. An old codger with unkempt long hair and beard keeps coming into my dreams and telling me to hang on and that I will remember everything someday. He said Carrie and my friends will help get me back to normal. He gives me pep talks when I'm down and chastises me when I feel like giving up. He seems to have had a similar injury and somehow knows me."

"You just keep talking to him. I think he's doing you good and we need all the help we can get. Let's get everyone together to talk about this next surgery, which I hope is the last. Where do you want to meet?"

"The front porch has plenty of room and the weather is nice. I obviously want Carrie and her family there, and Wyatt. He and I have a special connection that goes far beyond working together. We have trusted each other in several nasty situations. I know he has my back and when I get better, I will have his."

Carrie went to tell her parents and to call Wyatt over. All were assembled when a nurse and Hilary brought Joe to the porch. Everybody but Chris sat down and he had their undivided attention.

"This next surgery is very delicate. We have to rebuild the orbital bones around the eye. We will try to do it through the nose, as weird as that may sound. I can't promise it will work but if it does, he will not have any scars. I will be assisted by an eye surgeon and another neurosurgeon from here. They are very good and have experience with this type of work. I have performed this kind of surgery on many war wounds at Walter Reed."

"The surgery will take several hours. He needs to go to the hospital this afternoon for an MRI. It will tell me if there is any residual work to do on the skull and exactly what we face in the reconstruction. I can tell you a little more after we see the results. He will be in ICU for at least a day or two and in the hospital for about a week. The recovery will take a week more if all goes well. He will have a plastic protector over the eye and nose area—essentially, something like a cast. He will be able to do whatever his limited movement allows in three weeks or so."

"Hilary, you can start PT again as soon as he comes home. You have done a wonderful job. His movement is excellent considering his injuries.

Hilary responded, "He has wonderful support around here. He's also a determined young man. His drive to get better is greater than most people."

Joe said in halting words because his language was still affected, "Can I travel after the three weeks? I have a couple of places I want to go. They're not far by car."

"The neurosurgeon here will need to check you, but it's certainly possible. Just don't be running after bad guys."

Carrie stated firmly, "He won't. Looks like I will have to do that for him!"

Joe added, "I don't think I could take TG down right now. I just want to reconnect with some people who many of you would not understand or believe. Wyatt can take me."

Carrie said, "I think I know where you want to go and you are not leaving me behind!"

"Yes, I think you should come with me. It might help both of us. Besides, I like sleeping with you next to me now that I am out of that blasted hospital bed." Carrie blushed a little and everyone else laughed.

Carrie, Virginia, and a driver took Joe to the hospital later in the afternoon. He had not been awake for the other cranial MRIs. The tube was tight and the mask they used to keep his head still was really confining and uncomfortable. The machine was loud, even with the ear plugs and music playing through earphones. He was ready for it to be over long before it ended.

His room in the Angelina Suite was ready when the MRI was

complete. Chris and the Denver doctors came in later to discuss the results of the test.

Chris said, "The MRI indicates we have nothing to work on besides the eye, which is very good news. All of us think this surgery can be done through the nose. We will see you bright and early tomorrow morning and get you fixed up. You will still have the plastic protector and a bandage for a few days."

He turned to Carrie and said, "You can go home and get a good night's sleep and be here about six in the morning if you wish."

"Doc, for such a smart man, that was a really dumb comment. I'll be right here for the duration. I'm planning to sleep in that bed tonight but we will just cuddle. He's starting to remember who I am and I don't want to give him a chance to start forgetting." Everyone laughed, even Chris.

"Yes, ma'am!"

Several people came by to wish him luck. Virginia and Harrell planned to stay in the apartment connected Joe's room. Wyatt assured Joe he would be there before the surgery began.

As she had said, Carrie eased on the hospital bed beside Joe. It was tight but neither of them complained.

She said, "If this is too uncomfortable for you, I'll get in the chair. You need to be rested for tomorrow."

"Why? I'm going to be asleep all day. One of the few things that feels natural for me is lying beside you. It's very comforting."

Carrie was thrilled with his comment. She was going to give Wyatt a big hug for getting them back in the same bed.

Wyatt arrived at the hospital at five the next morning. The nurses were already prepping Joe for surgery. When he arrived, the three who spent the night were already up and ready to get the show rolling. Carrie slipped over and gave Wyatt a hug.

She said, "I wasn't sure when you pushed me back into Joe's

bed. I wasn't even sure he knew me. Thank you for doing it—it helped us both tremendously. He knows me but the details are still fuzzy. He says he's in a place where it's murky and hard to see things clearly. I wish I understood how to clear the world up for him."

"If you have not read the section of Angelina's diary about Dale's injury, and losing and regaining his memories, you should. You're helping Joe just by being here and answering his questions, even when they hurt. We're going to get him back. It just may take more time than we want. The trip to Dale's cabin will help and the one to Freedom Town may help even more."

"There's something mystical about Miss Lily's room in the fort. I felt it, but not as intensely as Joe did."

"You may have some strange things happen at Dale's cabin. I have. So has Ashley. But you are a direct descendant of Dale and Martha. It could be quite interesting for you."

Dale and Martha Cannon were the parents of Grant and Clark Cannon, who established the Cannon Trust. Dale left east Texas for the Colorado gold mines. He was robbed and shot in the head. He fell into a ravine, but survived. Unfortunately, he had amnesia and wandered in the mountains alone for three years. Grant and Clark found him and the family helped him regain his memory. He also showed them were to find many gold nuggets, which turned into a very rich gold strike.

Joe was ready to go to surgery. He and Carrie shared a good hug and he shook hands with Wyatt, "Maybe I will be a new man when I come out. Let's hope so."

Carrie said, "I love you so much." Joe had not recovered to the point that he said he loved her and she ached to hear those words.

Chris said Joe would probably be moved to a recovery room around noon. Everyone but Carrie went down to the cafeteria for breakfast, which was typical hospital fare. Good enough to keep you from going out to eat, but just barely.

They took a tray up to Carrie. She ate a little but was not hungry. Her mother pushed her to eat to keep her strength up, and she finally ate the scrambled eggs and a little bacon.

An hour after they took him to surgery, Chris called to let them know he was starting. At the three hour mark, he called again to let them know they were almost through. He should be able to talk to them in a couple of hours while Joe was in ICU.

Chris called later and said, "The surgery went well. I think the rebuild of the orbital bones went particularly well. Those are a combination of his bones and artificial bone. All of us think we got everything straight. These heal pretty quickly because we were able to put a lot of something like glue to get them aligned and keep them that way. Two of you can go up to see him. He should be coming out of it in thirty minutes to an hour. We will move him to a regular room tomorrow if everything is going along at the normal pace. The team here will take over his treatment and make decisions about his release from the hospital and when he can take those trips he's so determined to take. His determination has got him to where he is, so I don't expect it to decrease. I will look in on him tonight and head back home tomorrow. He will be in good hands."

Joe had a peaceful night according to the staff. They expected to move him to the Angelina Suite shortly after lunch. The family was shooed away after getting that wonderful information. Carrie was ecstatic about Joe's condition and that he would be moved to a room where she could be with him all the time.

When Joe's move was completed and the family was allowed in to see him, Carrie was astounded to discover Joe resting the largest hospital bed she had ever seen—certainly big enough for two. Harrell was grinning from ear to ear and she knew who had arranged for the supersized bed.

Harrell said, "If you are going to sleep with him, it might as well be in a bed big enough for both of you." Carrie gave Harrell the biggest hug he remembered in a long time.

"Thank you, Dad! I did not even know they made such a huge hospital bed. Mom, I need a lounging set. Please have one sent up. Maybe you should send two."

Joe was in and out consciousness. He kept calling for Miss Lily and Dale. He also asked for Koko several times. Wyatt was sure he was being visited by ancestors and remembering the person he had been for so long. Wyatt hoped things were getting better aligned in Joe's fragile mind.

When he was more fully awake Joe said, "Carrie, where are you? I need you close to me. I love you."

Carrie was elated! She moved next to the bed and said, "I'm right here, Joe. I'm holding your hand. I will lay beside you as soon as they change you into fresh clothes."

He said groggily, "Don't need new clothes. I just need you near."

"Okay, I will lay beside you as soon as I can. You just had surgery so you must stay still. I can hold your hand until then."

He frowned and said, "Okay, that will have to do for now."

Talking in front of her mother and dad did not even make her blush anymore. She was also ready for something more than holding hands. When she lay on the bed next to him, he immediately calmed down and went back to sleep.

Virginia said, "I hope you don't mind us sitting here with you two in bed."

Carrie said, "Mother, I really don't care who is in here. He says he wants me here so I'm here to stay. He said he loves me and needs me beside him. That's the first time he's said it since he was injured. It would take wild horses to drag me out of this bed Daddy so thoughtfully arranged."

Everyone dozed most of the afternoon. Harrell went to his office at three o'clock for a Board meeting he had called. He had been neglecting his work for too long.

––––––––––––––

The first item on the Board's agenda was Ashley's proposal to expand the school program. With the cost of the buildings and computer infrastructure already funded, the cost of laptops for high school students and the parents was practically miniscule. She presented the modification and the housing issues and was astounded at its positive reception.

Jarrett Edens remarked, "I can't believe none of us thought about this earlier. The opportunity for the hands to further their education from their homes at no cost will help the manager's hiring efforts. I'll also bet many of the parents don't want their children looking down on them when they get their own high school diploma. All of us wants our kids proud of us. Geez, my mother got her GED when she was 71 years old!"

Every comment from the Board members was positive. Her proposal passed unanimously. Harrell closed the meeting by saying, "If you need more money than is in the proposal, come back and you'll get it. This is an important project."

Harrell asked Ashley stay after the Board meeting to chat about the Learning Centers. He began with, "We need someone here in the main offices to get these schools off on the right foot. Have you found anyone?"

She responded, "I've been so busy looking for and hiring teachers that I've not even considered someone to manage the whole operation. I can start looking for someone right away."

"I have a suggestion. You are the one who has the vision,

intimate knowledge about the schooling, and what is needed overall. I would like for you to take the position."

"I'm honored, but I'm not looking for a job. I have a family and I'm hoping to grow it soon. I don't want TG to be an only child and he's going to be two before I know it. I've just been too busy to even think much about it. I want to get reintroduced to Wyatt. We've had no time together lately."

"Would you consider it for the first year while we find someone to take the job permanently? We will pay you so you would not be volunteering your time."

"It's not the money. It's the time, but it should be more manageable after the grand opening. I feel like TG is growing up without me. I will consider it and talk to Wyatt. I do not want the job permanently."

"I understand. Find your replacement and you will be off the hook."

"If Wyatt has any qualms about it, I will not do it."

"Good enough."

She left the office feeling very torn. She wanted to see the program succeed, but she was also ready to return to being a wife and mother.

She and Wyatt had a long talk that night. He concluded by saying, "This program is your baby and you should stay involved to ensure it succeeds. I don't like you putting in the long hours, but I think you should do it. Once it's rolling, it shouldn't take as much of your time."

"I want to have another baby soon. TG is growing up so fast. I want him to have a little brother or sister."

"Well, do you want to get started on it tonight? I think I have the time if we can get TG asleep."

"Sounds good to me. You work on getting him asleep and I will take a nice long bath. Too bad we don't have a warm spring here."

TG was playing in his room. Wyatt got TG into his pajamas and read him a book about a horse. He loved horse books. He was sound asleep in less than an hour. Wyatt went to his shower and got a quick one. Ashley had wonderful candles going in the bedroom.

They had not had much alone time in over a month and both had been distracted for most of the summer. It was good getting acquainted again. Both woke up in a better mood.

She said, "I will tell Harrell I will take the position until we find someone."

"I think it's what you really want and need to do. You have put in too much work for the program to fail. Maybe we can still get together on special occasions."

"When we get together, it's always a special occasion. The occasions just need to come a little more often. I am serious about another baby. Hope I won't be bedridden for the next one."

"Me too."

"I need to see Harrell again. Can we ride in together."

"Surely."

They arrived at work early. TG spent the day with Margie. He loved staying there and played with Wolf for an hour or more. TG played while Wolf tolerated.

———————————

Wyatt called the hospital and learned Joe was doing great. He was still heavily sedated to keep him inactive. When he awoke a little, he began looking for Carrie. He did not have far to look. Virginia had bought her some lounge wear Carrie stayed right where she was even with visitors in the room. Staff made her get up occasionally so they could check Joe's vitals, but she went right back. She was also talking almost nonstop to him. She had repeated some stories many times. They revolved around getting home and raising a family. She discussed the merits of three and four children until Virginia knew it by heart.

Harrell called to see how they both were doing. Virginia responded, "We're good. Do you prefer eight or ten grandchildren? I think as soon as they get a green light, they are going to start on the first—maybe sooner. How is your day?"

"Ashley just accepted the position as School Superintendent for a year. I'm very happy about it. Now tell me about these eight or ten grandchildren."

"Every time Carrie talks about wanting a family, she has a different number. I think she is up to four on a consistent basis now, but I've heard up to ten! Looks like they will need a house of their own or we'll be overrun with them. I think she's planning one a year so they will have someone their age to play with. I'm not sure I can handle two or three in diapers at the same time."

"She might change her mind after chasing one around the house. Somehow, I don't see her as a stay-at-home mom for long. Do you think their house should be in the compound so you can help with them, or further away."

"I'm sure I will regret saying this but, having them in the compound would be better for me. I guess we should ask them what they want. We have a little time, but I am afraid we don't have much."

Joe's condition improved daily and he was getting anxious to return to their apartment. He thought he would get even better when he could see the mountains. The doctor was reluctant to send him home until he checked out the arrangements. Carrie explained he would have 24/7 nursing care and his own Physical Therapist to start him back on the road to mobility. The doctor finally agreed, but wanted him to travel in an ambulance, which was fine with Carrie—anything to get Joe home.

Joe's rate of progress began to improve as soon as he got home. He was talking better, if still a little haltingly. He was struggling to walk with Hilary working on him every day. He was getting around on a walker, but it was difficult. Carrie was thankful she could see improvement daily.

One day Carrie had time to walk over to John and Margie's house to tell him thank you for saving her life again. She had barely seen him since the attack in Barbados but knew he saved her and Joe's lives that night.

As usual, John said, "It was nothing. Just what I'm paid to do."

Carrie said, "You may say it was nothing, but I know you risked your life to save me and Joe. Margie, you were also running into the fray. So, thank both of you. Joe and I would both be dead if not for you."

John smiled and responded, "That's what we do. Cannon's and Sheffield's save each other's lives. Carrie, I've been meaning to ask you about shooting those two men. Have you had any feelings of remorse? It's usually tough on a person when they first kill someone."

Carrie blinked a few times before responding, "I've been so focused on Joe's survival and health, I have not had much time to think about those men. I probably would have reacted differently if Joe had not been almost killed. I suppose the fact they needed killing has blocked any remorse."

"Good for you! Just remember it could come to haunt you later, maybe much later. If it does, see a counsellor who specializes in treating PTSD. Until it happens, don't give it another thought."

Before Carrie departed, an alarm went off on Sara's computer. Sara ran to see what the problem was.

She yelled, "You devils! I knew you would attack again! I'm ready for you this time. I have a more powerful computer and a nasty little surprise for you. But let's play a little bit before I deliver the coup de gras."

John, Margie, and Carrie walked toward Sara's voice to see who she was talking to. She told them between keystrokes it was the Russian hackers.

John called Harrell because he knew he would want to see the battle. He also called Wyatt. Sara played with the Russian hackers for thirty minutes, just to show them they had met their match. There was much cheering behind Sara as she fought them off as much as if it were an armed invasion.

After toying with them, Sara launched her electronic missile attack on the hacker's system. She had installed animations in the program to show when her missiles were launched and when they hit their targets. All three bombs, as she called them, got through the Russian firewalls.

She finally turned with a big grin and said, "They will need new equipment and a lot of time to recover from those triple bombs." Cheers went up from what had grown to a large group of people.

Virginia said, "Harrell, we have to celebrate now. Order pizza for everyone and I will invite all the security families over. Sara just scored a great victory for the Cannon Trust!"

Chapter Five

Sara called Jake to come over for the celebration. John was not surprised when he showed up. Everyone was having a great time celebrating Sara's victory over the Russian hackers. She felt more special than ever before and looked absolutely radiant. When Jake came in, she ran over to him and gave him a hug and a kiss. John was not particularly happy, but he was also not upset. He sort of expected it.

During the celebration, Jake came to John and said, "Maybe we should have a chat. Can we take a short walk?"

"Yes, give me a minute."

When they were away from the house, Jake said, "I promised to let you know if Sara and I started getting serious. Well, I think it's happening. I know it is for me, and I think it is for her. I am not talking about marriage in the near future. I would never do anything to hurt Sara, but I do have romantic feelings toward her and I hope she has them for me. I'm just letting you know that if you plan to run me off, you better do it quickly."

"I think it may be a little too late for that. Jake, from what I can tell, you are a fine young man. You passed a thorough background check. I know I'm probably looking at my future son-in-law. I just ask that you take it slow and let her grow up grow up a little more."

"I can promise you that. I have grown to love her and will be good to her while we are dating and after we are married."

As they began walking back in, Jake added, "On a different but related topic, Sara is making lots of money each month. She has no idea what to do with it. Do you mind if I help her develop an investment portfolio? I will run everything by you, but she needs to get her money invested."

"Run it by Margie. She understands investments better than I do." They went back inside and Jake sat close to Sara the rest of the night.

When the party started to break up, the ones who did not live on the compound were the first to leave. Harrell said to those with houses in the compound, "Please stay a minute longer. We, Virginia and I, keep hearing talk about a bunch of grandchildren. We are probably going to need another house in the compound for Joe and Carrie. May I have the architect look at potential homesites for them?" Everyone welcomed the idea.

John stood and said, "You might as well look for two homesites. I have a feeling Sara is going to need one before long." Sara and Jake turned bright red and dropped their heads.

"Nothing is definite, but you know I'm a pretty good investigator."

The women gave Sara a hug. The men shook Jake's hand. Lenny leaned in and said under his breath, "Jake, you're a brave man!" All the men heard it and nodded their heads knowingly.

―――――――――――

The next couple of weeks were relatively quiet for everyone. No crimes against the Trust were reported. The Learning Centers were ready to open in three weeks. The landscape architect pinpointed two beautiful homesites on the Denver side of the compound. Both owned a good views of the mountains and would obstruct no one else's view. Both could easily be protected without adding any more major devices or structures. Joe would be a good addition to the protection when he healed, but Jake was unproven so far.

Wyatt, Joe, and Carrie made plans to go to the ranch, and then on to Dale's cabin. Ashley wanted to go, but would go only to Grant and Angelina's cabin. Lenny asked Wyatt if he thought he might need help at the cabin.

Wyatt said, "Yes, I need several people, including Hilary, to go as far as Grant and Angelina's big cabin. I can use your help getting us settled into Dale's cabin. I'm thinking it will just be Joe, Carrie, and me up there. If I thought they could manage, I would not even spend the night. I don't see any way for them to make it without help. If nothing else, the outhouse will be pretty far away for Joe and pretty scary for Carrie. It's warm enough for me to sleep on the porch with Quanah or Wolf. But what are we going to do with Choco? He's so protective of Carrie. I don't know if we should take him—he might chew mine or Joe's leg off."

Lenny responded, "I believe you should leave him with Virginia. I don't want to be the one trying to keep him from going up the mountain with you folks."

The plans were coming together. Wyatt was looking forward to the trip, perhaps even more than the others. He thought two nights there might make a great difference if the ancestors visited Joe and Carrie. With Carrie being a direct descendant of Dale and Martha, he felt confident they would show up. Joe was already being visited in the hospital.

They might even get visits from Grant and Angelina. In many ways, Carrie needed as much help as Joe. Not being remembered by her spouse of only a few weeks was hard to take, especially since she had shot two men to save his life.

They arrived at the ranch mid-afternoon and were met by Cole, the ranch's new manager. He helped them get Carrie and Joe settled in Grant and Angelina's bedroom. He had supper sent to them, a wonderful Mexican stew. Wyatt wanted everyone to get the meal over with and get to bed soon, but it was still too early. The women decided to go to the warm springs to relax.

Joe sat on the porch and wanted to talk about the attack in Barbados. John told him, "You and Carrie came toward the sounds of gunfire at the plantation. Unfortunately, you drove too close to where the rebels were hiding in the vegetation. One of them, the leader, was waiting behind some trees with a wooden baseball bat. He hit you hard as soon as your feet hit the ground. Before he could hit you again, Carrie shot him. Another one charged Carrie with a machete, and she also shot him. I came running out and shot another one who was aiming an AK at Carrie. Sometime in this I was hit in the shoulder by an AK47 round."

"I was careless. Koko would not have been so careless."

"Son, you were running into a full-fledged attack and did not know the enemy's location. Your appearance helped make them break off the attack and run. We killed six, I think. The plantation and distillery were not damaged."

"Koko would have known better."

"Koko does not exist anymore. You are Joe. You can't blame yourself."

"But Koko would have been ready."

"Joe may never be the fighting man Koko was, but Joe is a good man with a good wife. As soon as you are a little better, I would still go into a fight with you."

"I will need to return to my DEA job when I'm better."

"The surgeon doesn't think you will be able to do to that kind of job—even a light blow in the wrong place could damage you permanently. I'm sure when you are recovered sufficiently the DEA will talk to you about resuming your duties, but don't get your hopes up. If you can't go back with them, I'll wager the Trust job offer still stands."

It was finally time to go to bed. The bedrooms were a little cool so John and Lenny built small fires in the heaters in each room. Lenny and Ruth went to his cabin and the rest went to bed.

Almost as soon as they dozed off, visitors entered both Joe and Carrie's dreams. Grant talked to Joe, *"Keep being strong. You have the blood of Miss Lily and Manny flowing in your veins. They never backed down from a fight. Even when outnumbered by Indians or other bad men, they stood firm. When Miss Lily was taken prisoner by a bunch of slavers, she protected two girls she did not even know—Kate and Lizzie. She stood up to tyranny and prejudice many times."*

Angelina talked to Carrie, *"When we found Dale wandering in the mountains, he did not remember anything or anybody. Grant and Clark worked hard to help bring his memory back. They had some success but Martha, his wife, was the one who really brought him back. They lived a long and happy life together. Dale is the person who showed Grant and I where to find gold. This great life you live comes from that gold. Grant and I, along with Clark and Margo, went out and picked up sacks of gold nuggets and later started Cannon Mines. You keep working with Joe. He's worth it and you are worth it, and you deserve each other. I think Margo wants to talk to you now."*

Margo added, *"I was there when the men brought Dale in. He had been wandering around the mountains for three years. We worked so hard to bring him back to this world. I was a rich girl like you, but one of the best things I was ever involved with was helping Dale. Later in life, you will remember the strenuous effort with great fondness, even though it sometimes might be very frustrating. It will be worth it and the little girl growing in your belly will love her daddy so much. He will love her and never want to be Koko again. Stick with him and love him and you will have a happy life with many children."*

When the visitors left, Joe and Carrie slept like babes. The next morning Wyatt and Lenny were sitting on the porch with a pot of coffee. Others soon began filtering out to join them. Although it was still official late summer, there was a chill in the air. Most returned inside to fetch a blanket or jacket. The last two to come out were Carrie and Joe. She was helping him with his walker. Hilary noticed he was moving much better, which puzzled her a great deal.

Carrie appeared somewhat dazed, because she did not understand what had happened during the night. She was trying to remember everything mentioned by the visitors. She suddenly she jumped up and went to hug Joe and give him a kiss.

He asked, "Well, thanks, but what brought that on?"

She said, "Angelina and Margo came to me in a dream. Margo said I'm pregnant and going to have a baby girl. It must have happened the night when Wyatt made me sleep with you."

"Made you?"

She ignored the question and ran to give Wyatt a kiss on the cheek and said, "Thank you so much!"

Everyone was surprised at the news, but Carrie had no doubt it was true. Joe, Wyatt, and Ashley also believed.

"What do I need to do now? I've never been pregnant. Can I go up to Dale's cabin? Should I call a doctor? I'm so happy! Joe, I hope you're as happy as I am!"

Ashley said, "You might want to let your mom know soon since all of us know. I doubt if you need to change any plans at this point. Babies are born all the time."

"Not by me!"

Carrie ran to call her mother with the news. Virginia did not understand how Carrie knew and wanted to know which doctor said she was pregnant.

"Mom, I can't explain it on the phone and it's very early. I will try to explain when we are back in Denver. I am so happy! I will get a doctor's appointment soon so you will believe me. I'm quite sure you can start getting ready for a little girl. I have to go to kiss Joe again. I only got to once and I want more."

She went back out to sit by Joe. He was happy with the news, even in his clouded state. He returned her kiss rather emphatically.

She asked, "When do we go to the cabin? Maybe I will get more information."

Wyatt said, "Lenny and I are going up after breakfast to make sure the cabin is ready. We will take the two of you up as soon as we return. I will stay up there tonight—it's a primitive cabin. I'm sure Joe will need help getting to the outhouse. You will likely want an escort. I can help rustle up a meal or two. I will sleep on the porch so y'all will have some privacy, at least from regular humans. We will take Quanah to alert me if some marauding animals get too close."

"Outhouse? Marauding animals? What am I getting into!?!?"

"It's primitive, but I'm betting you will be happy when you get back."

"We will be ready when you and Lenny can take us."

As usual, the cabin was well stocked and reasonably clean. No bears had been inside and the rats ran when they opened the door and windows. They split wood for the stove and pumped water for the occupants. The cabin was ready after less than an hour of work.

Lenny obtained the ranch's most comfortable ATV. It had good springs and a long wheelbase, so the ride was not too bad.

Joe and Carrie had finished their lunch and Ashley and Ruth had packed Wyatt and Lenny lunch from the bunkhouse dining room. Everyone was on their way to Dale's cabin by two o'clock. They took two ATVs so Lenny would have a ride back down and leave the big one up in case they needed it. Wyatt took them by the best overlooks so they could see the area's true beauty. Carrie did not remember ever going up to the top.

They got the young couple settled in the cabin and Wyatt took blankets to the porch. He then cooked three steaks about the size of a platter. The menu was simply steak and bread. Carrie ate maybe half her steak and Joe ate only a little more. Wyatt ate all of his. Quanah enjoyed a great supper.

Wyatt made a pot of coffee to wash the meal down. Even Carrie enjoyed the strong coffee, although she added creamer and sugar. They all went to the porch to sit and watch the sun go down below the mountains.

Carrie was overwhelmed by the beauty. She said, "Wyatt, I have never been up here but some of those overlooks look familiar. In fact, a lot of them did. I wonder why?"

"Lizzie spent much time up here painting and drawing. Many of those paintings hang in the hotel and Trust offices. When you get back, you should look at those paintings again. They will look very different to you after seeing the real thing."

It began getting cooler as soon as the sun went down. Carrie said, "I better get acquainted with the outhouse, as much as I don't want too. After dark, it's bound to be scary. Can Quanah go with me?"

"Certainly. Quanah, guard!" Quanah followed Carrie to the outhouse door and sat outside until she came out. Carrie was definitely not impressed with the facility.

She said, "That thing is gross. Why doesn't someone spend a little Trust money and at least improve it. I am going to bring Mother out here and something will get done soon."

Wyatt and Joe laughed and agreed it would only take one visit to get her to demand something better be built. Wyatt thought he should ask Ruth about those fancy outhouses she sold to the government for campgrounds.

Everyone was tired and ready for bed as soon as darkness fell. Joe needed a little help going to the outhouse, but was able to get himself ready for bed with just a little help from Carrie. Wyatt got ready to bed down on the porch. Quanah was happy to have a bed partner.

The dreams started almost as soon as Joe and Carrie were asleep. The parade of guests started with Dale and Martha, who talked to both of them. Martha did most of the talking to Carrie.

She said, "*I know what you are going through. It's difficult for someone you love to not remember you. But you are helping him immensely and can continue to help him. Based on the little girl growing inside you, he knows you in the Biblical sense. He will get better but it will not come as quickly as you both want. Don't push a memory on him. He will ask as he starts getting bits of a memory back. Remember, you only knew him a short time before you were married and he was gone most of that time. You occupy an important part of his memories, but you are only a small part of his total memories. Just keep loving him and one day he will love you back like he did before.*"

Dale came to Joe, along with Miss Lily. They talked a long time and encouraged him to concentrate on getting those memories back. Dale said, "*Ask questions. Everyone around you will try to answer them or find the answer. You have a wealth of support, just like I did. Use it. The fog will gradually lift and you will see clearly. The woman beside you needs you, and you need* her."

The ancestors stayed until almost daylight and then faded out. It was eerily quiet after they left. Even Quanah realized something not quite normal was going on. Before she left Martha came out and gave Wyatt a kiss his forehead. She said, *"You are a good man. Help them. Joe is worth saving."*

Just as the sun peeked over the eastern horizon, Wyatt heard stirring in the cabin. He knocked on the door and Carrie said, "Come in."

He put a pot of coffee on and said, "Y'all may want to come out and enjoy this sunrise. It's going to be beautiful."

They came out a few minutes later and Wyatt got everyone a cup of the coffee. The sunrise was the most beautiful any of them could remember. The color lighting up the trees was spectacular. They just sat quietly and watched nature's beauty unfold. The coolness made Carrie snuggle next to Joe. He snuggled back.

Joe said, "I guess you probably know we had visitors last night. Dale is a real character, but he makes a lot of sense. Martha is also a strong woman. They both helped me. I hope they helped Carrie."

"They helped. 'Course I don't need as much help as you." She joked.

"I think I feel better this morning. The fog is not quite as thick. And I know you're my wife and that I love you. I'm truly sorry I did not recognize you when I first woke up. Your memory was hidden behind other memories that have been around much longer. My work and my relationship with Wyatt have been here a long time. You have not been in my life nearly as long, but you are most important." She almost knocked him off the bench with her hug which he returned.

She said, "I think we can go back down after breakfast. I have got to work up enough nerve to try the outhouse again. Quanah, come give me moral support. I am going to need it."

Wyatt built up the fire in the stove and started breakfast. They had cured bacon, eggs, and biscuits. Wyatt had become a more than decent cook somewhere along the way. Of course, anybody could make delicious food in a wilderness setting. He fixed what he thought was enough to feed six people. There was no leftovers—Quanah whined unhappily when he realized he would have to go catch a rabbit.

Wyatt and Carrie loaded up the ATV and they headed back down. Everyone below was waiting to hear what happened.

Carrie said, "If I told you, you would just laugh. It's something you have to experience, but I will tell you it makes a big impact. Joe and I both feel very different today. I think Joe jumped ahead a month in his recovery. I know I can now face his recuperation with a much better attitude. Martha especially helped me."

After a night in the big cabin, they went back to Denver. Wyatt, Joe and Carrie planned to leave for La Junta and Freedom Town in two days.

––––––––––––––

Wyatt went to his office the next morning to make sure everything was good with security. He had a message from Rosie asking him to call her.

When he called, she began with, "You remember the fellow who's has been staying with me, right?"

"Yes."

"We want to get married."

"Great! Congratulations!"

"I want the wedding to be at Freedom Town. That's where my people learned to be free of their shackles. I guess I want to get shackled there." She and Wyatt laughed.

"When do you want this to happen?"

"As soon as you can get someone up here to replace me for a couple of weeks. How soon can that happen?"

"Let me check around and see who I can send. I will let you know tomorrow."

Wyatt was happy Rosie was still planning to stay in Alaska after the wedding. He called Mitch and Frenchy in to see if either of them wanted to go to Alaska for around three weeks.

Frenchy said he really needed to be getting the hunting and fishing operations off the ground. Pheasant season would soon be open and the first weekend was usually the best weekend. Waterfowl season in the form of teal season would also be starting soon, plus fall fishing was usually big.

Mitch asked if he could take his family. They had never been to Alaska and might enjoy the trip before school started.

Wyatt said, "Mitch, it looks like you are the man. Your family can go with you. You will have opportunities to take side trips to the nearby towns and other points of interest. As you know, the mines are pretty isolated but in beautiful areas. Probably need to plan to depart next week—she's wanting to get married as soon as possible."

"I think it will work. Let me call Theresa."

Theresa loved the idea of a trip to Alaska in the late summer. It was still five weeks until school started.

Wyatt called Rosie back, "Mitch and his family will be up there next week—I will let the two of you decide on an exact date. He will come in on one of the planes and you and Lawrence can come back on the plane. Y'all work out when you will go back and he will come home. He needs to be home before school starts for his kids."

"Thank you for working this out on short notice. Will you be at the wedding?"

"I plan to attend, along with at least Lenny. I am sure others will want to attend. Let me know if there is anything we can do for the wedding. Kinda hard to plan one from Alaska. I'm going to La Junta tomorrow and will talk to them about your arrangements. They all know about Queenie and I'm sure we can get a fandango cranked up, which was a Freedom Town marriage tradition."

———————

With Rosie's situation taken care of, Wyatt was ready to head for Freedom Town. They would take a plane to La Junta and rent a car to drive to Freedom Town. They planned to spend at least one night in town and one or two out at Freedom Town's old fort. He was not sure how long Carrie would want to stay in such primitive conditions.

They boarded the plane early and were in La Junta well before noon. They got rooms at the best motel in town and went to the office of the Purgatoire Land and Cattle Company. Miss Jenny was glad to see Wyatt. He told her about the plans to visit the old fort and Rosie's wedding. The whole office came to hear about the wedding of one of Queenie's descendants. Wyatt knew Queenie was well known to the people of the company. Stories of her strength and courage were still taught in school and talked about around campfires. As often happens, her exploits had become larger than life as time passed.

An office worker said, "She's the one who killed ten white men with her bare fists when Freedom Town was being established." Wyatt knew the number was more likely two men, but Queenie was plenty tough so he did not try to correct.

He introduced Joe as a descendant of Miss Lily and a few of the office staff almost swooned. Few of them had ever met one of Lily's descendants and she was even more revered than Queenie.

Miss Jenny said, "Lily Sheffield is still viewed like royalty around here. She's the most famous woman in our Freedom Town history and she was white. Without her, the settlement probably would have failed. Her diary gives us much of what she did, but our oral history tells us about many things she didn't write in her diary. She was the source of the money which made Freedom Town more successful than other communities of former slaves. I have never read or heard a word about her looking down on our people. She treated them as equals and demanded others do the same."

Both Carrie and Joe were amazed at their reverence. Wyatt added, "This is Carrie, formerly Carrie Cannon—she's a direct descendant of Clark Cannon."

"My goodness, we are surrounded with royalty! Do you suppose we could get all of you to speak at one of our meetings? Direct descendants of Lily Sheffield, Clark Cannon, and Grant Cannon would be a really big draw!"

Wyatt responded, "What about arranging for us to speak when Rosie has her wedding? We want a fandango reception that will be remembered in La Junta for a long time. We can speak during the fandango. The Trust will be paying for everything, so don't skimp. A good band or two in the tradition of Freedom Town will be needed. Let's make it a celebration to fit the occasion—Queenie's four greats granddaughter is coming home to get married. She lives in Alaska now, but insists she wants to get married here."

"You got it! When is the wedding?"

"Here's her phone number. Call her for the details—I don't know them yet. I know she wants a regular wedding and to jump of the broom. Joe and Carrie jumped the broom at their wedding." A cheer went up in the office.

It was time to get Joe back to the hotel so he could rest.

Tomorrow would be difficult on him and Carrie. But it would be worth it if Joe could rip away more of the fuzzy curtain.

Chapter Six

Wyatt got up early to buy simple food for two nights. He picked up jerky, cheese, Indian fry bread, smoked ham, coffee, water, beer, and a few other items. They brought sleeping bags, a coffee pot, and a skillet for cooking.

Wyatt drove them around Freedom Town to explore a few of the deteriorating stone cabins. The walls were often still intact, but almost all the roofs were completely collapsed.

Carrie remarked, "How did they live here? The stone huts are so small and I see nothing indicating it might have been a comfortable life."

Wyatt responded, "If you read Miss Lily's diary carefully, and the early part of Angelina's, you will understand they experienced a hard life. Miss Lily had to have really missed her former life. She came from a family of wealthy plantation owners. She could have taken her gold and had a luxurious life in a big city, but she stayed out here with the former slaves. She was a great woman—strong and generous."

Joe said, "I hope I can live up to her standards."

Carrie said, "I hope our daughter can live up to them. Maybe we should name her Lily or something like that. I think she and Miss Lily would be appreciative."

"We will ask her tonight. I'm sure she will visit us."

As they were driving around on the rim, they came to a group of corrals and pens. Cowboys were loading cattle in a big trailer destined for the sales barn. The ranch did not carry many cattle over the winter. The snow sometimes got deep and the grass was sparse. They stopped to watch the operation. Before long, a cowboy rode over to greet them.

Wyatt explained that he and Carrie were descended from the Cannon boys who lived in Freedom Town in the early days. He introduced Joe, "This is Joseph Morales Sheffield. You probably recognize his name."

"Everybody out here knows the name Sheffield, especially if combined with Morales. I'm honored to meet you, sir. Your ancestor is revered out here. Why don't y'all come over to the chuckwagon and have lunch with us? Every cowboy here will want to shake your hands. The cooks will give the best and biggest plate they have."

Joe said, "Carrie may have descended from the Cannons, but she's a Sheffield now. We will be having a Sheffield baby girl in eight months or so. I want her to learn about this country and Miss Lily's story. Wyatt, let's go join them. Maybe it will rattle some of my ancient memories."

They drove to the chuckwagon and the foreman called the men to lunch. Carrie helped Joe get out and he apologized for not being at the top of his game.

He explained, "Some bad guys ambushed me in Barbados, and my beautiful wife shot the one who hit me with a baseball bat and another one who came at her with a machete. I think she's going to be a great Sheffield and produce a bunch of Sheffield children with sand, just like Miss Lily."

The cowboys loved those comments and Carrie became one of them instantly. They liked pretty women with grit.

The meal was delectable. It was a roast prepared with Mexican spices. It was not overly spicy, but it obviously was rubbed with a mixture containing scrumptious chilis. The meat was put on a piece of thick home baked bread and covered with another. The juices ran out when you ate and tried to get on their clothes. Carrie swore it was the best roast she ever tasted and Wyatt and Joe agreed. The cooks were elated and offered them more. Joe was temped but just too full to eat any more.

They talked to the men and a few women who were working the cattle. It was obvious that Mexican and African was the dominant ancestry and it showed in a variety of combinations. Several of the men had dark, almond eyes with green flecks.

Joe said, "Let's watch them work the cattle. I know they are just running them through the corrals and putting the correct ones in the trailers. I guess in the old days they herded them to market or to the railroad."

"Yes, they sold many cattle to the various Indian reservations, partially due to their contact with Bass Reeves, the first Black U.S. Deputy Marshall west of the Mississippi. It was sometimes a daunting challenge to get the cattle safely to their destination, and even harder getting the money back with all the rustlers and road agents in the Nations. Grant led at least one drive and said he did not get any sleep for most of the month it took."

"Let's go to Miss Lily's place and get it ready for tonight. We need to chase the rattlers out while we still have good light."

The mention of rattlers set Carrie off, "Are you telling me there's rattlesnakes out here!?!?"

"Sure, but we will leave them alone and they will leave us alone."

"Joe, I may smother you tonight. You better stay close to me and I mean really close. If you see Miss Lily before I do, tell her to shoo them away. I hate snakes!"

"Yes, ma'am! She can't let the mother of her descendant get bit by a rattlesnake in her old room."

Wyatt collected ancient weathered wood—it would burn easily and to give them decent light in the old Meeting Hall—Miss Lily had resided in a back corner of it. He thought, *"I'm sure the light will make Carrie feel better. Heck, it will make me feel better! A few sticks throughout the night should keep the snakes at bay, I hope."*

They sat on boulders worn from so many others using them over a century ago. They found them strangely comfortable. Wyatt got a good blaze going, but only after he checked the area for snakes. They sat and ate smoked ham and cheese washed down with beer, but water for Carrie. Once again, the meal was quite tasty and was something that might have been eaten all those years ago. The sunset was magnificent and the colors seemed to shift every few minutes. All three were contented and relaxed.

Darkness soon came slipping across the plains and into the Purgatoire Valley. Joe was the first to say he was ready for his sleeping bag—it had been a long, tiring day for him. He and Wyatt made a last snake inspection and rolled the sleeping bags out. Joe and Carrie slept in Miss Lily's living area. Wyatt's sleeping bag lay near the fire so he could easily keep it going through the night. The night was comfortable with the hint of a chill. Carrie slept as close to Joe as she could, just as she had said.

Joe dozed off first and quickly became restless. Carrie thought Miss Lily was probably visiting him, and she was right.

Miss Lily appeared in Joe's dream and said, *"You are a strong man descended from strong stock. You can beat this thing. You have to remain resolute and let the memories flow up from your* soul. *You are going to be a daddy and you need to be physically and mentally strong to help Carrie. The Sheffield's have always done what they had to do for the people around them. You will recover well.*"

Joe mumbled, "How will I become Koko again? Koko could protect those around him. Koko would not have walked into a baseball bat."

"*You will not need to be Koko again because you will never do such a job again. Koko is dead. He died in Barbados. You are now Joe Sheffield and you will work to protect the Sheffield and Cannon Trusts. I worked hard and took risks to keep the gold I brought to the Colorado Territory. You will now help ensure my descendants can continue to benefit from that wealth. That's your destiny, just like it's Wyatt's. Your life as a DEA agent is over and the character known as Koko will be buried. Love your wife and protect her and the kids you want. We need at least one son to carry on the Sheffield name and you are going to be the daddy of that son.*"

Miss Lily then turned her attention to Carrie, "*You are now a Sheffield woman and you must be strong. Joe's situation is testing your mettle and you are measuring up quite well. You will have Sheffield children and they will be healthy and sturdy. The blood of the Cannon's and the Sheffield's will combine to make strong, exemplary citizens. I am so happy you came here to see me. I had only one son and we were soon forgotten by most of our descendants. But the descendants of Freedom Towners remember me. You can learn more about me from Miss Jenny at the La Junta office. She knows more about me than Joe knows. Love Joe and keep him close. The child you carry will cause a great celebration in your world and mine. I will help you be strong, as will Angelina, Margo, and Martha. You and Joe will live the rest of your lives in Denver, or Freedom Town West as we called it. Bring your children to see me here when you can. The snakes will not be around when you are here."*

A few other people showed up briefly in their dreams. The last one was an older Black man who said a touching prayer that reached deep in their souls.

The threesome started to awaken when the eastern sky began to lighten. Wyatt made a pot of strong coffee and it was greatly appreciated by the others. Both Joe and Carrie wore strangely contented looks on their face.

Joe looked at Carrie and said, "I think I'm finished here. Maybe we should go back in and get a room so you won't be worried about snakes."

"Snakes will not be here while we are here. The children and I will be safe from them."

She said it so emphatically that Joe and Wyatt knew the message came from Miss Lily. They believed her.

She continued, "But I do want to go back to town—I need to talk with Miss Jenny. She can tell me a lot about Miss Lily and I want to know more. I want to uphold the Sheffield name."

They started back after a hearty but sparse breakfast. Miss Jenny was at the office.

When Carrie asked her to tell her all she knew about Miss Lily, she responded, "How long do you have?"

"As long as it takes!"

"You men can go on about your business—we will be here the rest of the day and maybe tomorrow morning."

Miss Jenny told Miss Lily's story as completely as she could. She intertwined Miss Lily's diary with the Freedom Towner's oral history. She began the story back on the Sheffield's Louisiana plantation and her first marriage and carried it forward. As she was talking, she asked an assistant find everything they had about Miss Lily, including textbooks the children studied as part of their history lessons. Carrie tried to absorb it all and it did take all afternoon and the next morning.

Carrie was truly impressed. Miss Lily was a woman she wanted learn more about and emulate as much as possible. She even wanted to visit the Louisiana and Mississippi plantations one day soon.

Wyatt called for the Trust's plane to come pick them up. He and Joe had a long conversation while waiting for Carrie to finish and the plane to arrive.

Joe said, "I realize I won't be working for the DEA much longer. I'm thinking I want to know their official position as soon as possible. What do you think about me working for the Trust, now that I'm not in top condition?"

"You will have a job when you are well enough to work. You can start coming into the office when Hilary and the doctor think it's okay. You are not ready to be in the field yet. You can work around the office until your mind and body say you are ready for field work, which will not be like the DEA. Maybe police-type work will help your memory. There's plenty to do. We have more data than you might expect coming in daily and I need help to stay on top of its analysis. I know you want to be back in the field chasing bad guys. You are not ready yet, but you will be."

"Yes, I can't hold up my end in a fight right now and I can't run fast enough to get out of the way. I think I'll know when I can trust myself."

Carrie joined them, "I have just found out a lot about a woman who should be more widely known. She was so strong and she did not have to financially support the community at Freedom Town—she wanted to support them. I want to find her grave and visit the plantations. She's the standard I want to live up to."

The plane landed and they headed back to Denver. Joe and Carrie were in deep thought all the way back. When they landed,

Joe called the DEA Director to inquire about his future with the agency.

The Director said, "I will come out there to talk to you. Can we keep my visit under wraps?"

"Yes. You can come to general aviation in one of the unmarked planes and put it in a hanger the Trust owns. A limo will be waiting to bring you to my house, which is part of a compound. No one will see you and we have plenty of protection here."

"I will be there day after tomorrow. I will leave Washington early so I should land before noon."

_____

Ashley wanted to talk to Wyatt about the schools after dinner. She said, "We have the Learning Centers ready to open. I'm sure we will experience a few glitches, but we have run several trials and all locations seem to be ready to go. I want to have a Grand Opening for each school. Even with the plane it will take the better part of a week and I really don't want to rush them. It might be better to have them at night, but that would take two weeks, which is far too long. What do you think?"

"Hmm, you do have a real dilemma. Let me take TG for a walk and think about it for a while. Maybe TG and I can come up with an idea."

He put TG in his stroller that looked like a horse and started pushing him around the compound. He walked all the way to the front gate and waved at Javier. On the way back, an idea started percolating. It seemed to be a very simple solution. He was sure Ashley was too close to the situation to see all the possibilities.

TG wanted his mother as soon as they got back home. Wyatt could not wait to tell Ashley his idea.

"I think I have a solution. Your Grand Opening should include some of the Trust's brass. Why not use the fine technology you've bought to broadcast the program simultaneously to all the Learning Centers? You, Harrell, Tommy, and whoever else you want to include can officially open the Learning Centers. It could be done the night before classes begin. You can order goodies for all the sites and have simultaneous parties. Ask Sara if it's doable."

Ashley ran to give him a fierce hug, and said, "Cowboy, I'm going to keep you around! I was stuck on a traditional grand opening. We are not a traditional school system, so why not show off our capabilities."

After a big kiss, she continued, "You're so smart. Maybe you will get a reward later tonight. I've got to go talk to Sara. Back soon."

Sara responded to Ashley's question, "It would be super easy with the equipment we have. When do you want to do it?

"The night before classes start, we will do one more test to be sure it's a go."

Ashley returned home and she, Wyatt, and TG cuddled on the couch. TG was not much of a cuddler—he was more of an action man. He was playing with his horses after a few minutes.

Wyatt said, "You know, it's time I talked to Tommy and Cole about a pony and horses."

"A Paso Fino for me. I'm sure you will want a buckskin quarter horse for yourself. If Tommy and Cole would let you, you would want a cutting horse. But the one named for you is far too valuable for us to keep. Didn't Tommy say he was offered five million dollars for Magic? I don't know if you are worth five million dollars for a breeding program."

"I think I certainly am! Maybe you should give me another chance."

"Cowboy, you are talking my language!"

The next morning Ashley ran the broadcasting idea by Harrell. He responded, "Sure, Tommy and I can say a few words, but you and some of the other women should also talk. Ruth did yeoman's work and so did Sara. Maybe even Virginia would like to say a few words. But you need to be the star of the show. Few people out there know it was you who generated the vision, solicited money for the program, and did most of the work to set it up. You should plan to be on stage for at least half the program. This is your beautiful baby."

Ashley and Virginia began planning the program. They wanted it to last no more than an hour. It did not take long for them to formulate the program's structure. Ashley worried about speaking for thirty minutes and how to keep it entertaining.

The DEA Director and two of his lieutenants flew to Denver to talk with Joe. The Director said, "Joe, I bring unfortunate news. We have to retire you. We can't afford to send you, especially as Koko, into the slime of drug organizations. Chris, your doctor, agrees with this decision. We could put you on a desk in D.C., but we both know a desk would be torture for you."

"We made some drug arrests after the raid in Barbados, so we can give you a work-related full disability, which helps you financially. We propose to perpetrate a scam that kills off Koko. We can say Koko was caught in a firefight and killed by DEA Agents. We will make a record of it and even have a mock funeral. I don't think anyone will show up for it, but we will erect a marker for Koko, a murky underworld drug guy who is now dead. Joe will survive and prosper, but Koko will die. What do you think?"

"Sounds like a story that happens all the time. Maybe they won't figure it out and come for me. I hope they don't. I can lay pretty low here and at a ranch in the mountains. I'm sure Carrie, my wife, will appreciate your effort to make our life safer. What do I need to do?"

"I have brought papers for you to sign. I suggest you have someone look them over before you sign. Your pay will continue until you are released by a doctor."

"Let me call Wyatt and Carrie and get them to look the papers over."

Wyatt brought the Trust's top lawyer to examine the contract. He thought it was straight forward and unambiguous. Joe signed and his career as a DEA agent officially ended. Carrie gave him a hug while a small tear trickled down his face—he loved his DEA work.

Carrie and Joe celebrated his retirement with a quiet candlelit diner. Carrie said, "I know you will miss the life you have lived for many years. I'm sorry it has been forced on you this way, but I can't help but feel relieved—you will no longer have to deal with drug cartels and those evil people. I hope we can get you in shape by the new year so you can work with Wyatt and his security group. I know it's still sometimes dangerous, but the quality of people you deal with each day will be infinitely better."

"That's a good way to put it. I'm going to miss the excitement of the work, but not the scum I had to associate with. You can't believe the depravity of some of the players. I'm sure I will feel better when I can go to work with the Trust. I really like those guys and I trust them. With the DEA, I could not trust many people."

Carrie said, "I'll do the dishes tomorrow. Let's go to bed and get up early enough to watch the sunrise. I will get the coffee pot ready to turn on when we wake up."

————————

Almost all of the residents of the compound had the same idea the next morning. Joe and Carrie walked outside and Virginia soon came out with her coffee mug. Wyatt and Ashley were the next ones outside, with John and Margie following by less than a minute. Lenny and Ruth came out and everyone started drifting toward Virginia and Harrell's large back porch.

The impromptu get-together had many varied conversations going on at the same time. The dogs were also having a great time playing with each other. Sara and Harrell were the last to join the meeting.

John said in a loud voice, "I know why Sara looks so sleepy. It's the young man 'helping her with investments.' What's your excuse Harrell?"

"I did not sleep well—I have a gut feeling that something negative is in the wind. I have no idea what it might be, but all you folks should watch your back. I don't have this feeling often, but it's usually correct."

The conversations continued for more than an hour and Virginia finally said, "I bought refrigerated rolls yesterday. I'll go warm them up. We have plenty for everyone."

She disappeared into the kitchen with Carrie and they returned in a few minutes with giant rolls that looked, smelled, and tasted divine. Everyone went into the house to get their choice of drinks. Most had coffee, with a few choosing milk. When the smell of the rolls wafted throughout Virginia's house, Hilary and the nurse still on duty came out to join the group.

Since they had started so early, they had plenty of time to enjoy the early conversation. But work called for almost everyone.

———————————

Sara rode in with John because her car was having its oil

changed. He noticed a car appeared to be following them. He evaded the tailing car but wondered what was up. The answer would come soon enough.

Harrell received a call from the Police Chief about a Rodney Merrit. Harrell said, "I think he works for us, but I can't be sure. Why?"

"We found his body this morning. It appears to have been dumped in the prairie near the airport. We found business cards indicating he worked the Cannon Trust's IT department. We're calling in a homicide."

"Can I send some of our security team out there? Several of them have worked for national security agencies and have experience in suspicious deaths."

"We've checked pretty closely, but sure, send them out. The body will be at the scene a little while longer. I will tell them to wait on your men before taking it to the morgue."

John and Lenny drove out to the site. The body was approximately twenty yards off the road and no car tracks led to the body. They were sure it took at least two people to dump the body—Rodney was a large man.

John took a close look at the body and said, "He was tortured by experts. Likely Russian—former KGB."

A policeman asked, "How do you know?"

John smiled at him and responded, "I spent over thirty years in the CIA. The evidence on the body fits the Russian MO. See his fingers? Something was forced under the nails. When you get him to the morgue, tell them to check his scrotum. I'll bet he will have electrical burns in the area. They were good and I'm sure they got whatever information they wanted."

The body was taken away and John and Lenny returned to the office. John sat and pondered, *"Now what could the Russian Mafia want from a Cannon Trust IT employee?"*

Suddenly he remembered the car following him and Sara to work. He grabbed his phone called Wyatt to bring the security team together, ASAP.

"I'm afraid the Russian Mafia is coming after Sara. Here's the dots I'm connecting. A Trust IT employee was kidnapped, tortured, and murdered. I think they wanted to know who thwarted the Russian hacking attempts. He most likely gave them Sara's name. Second dot, someone tried to tail Sara and me on the way to work this morning."

He continued, "She obviously irritated someone when she destroyed their hacking equipment. I'm betting they contacted Russian operatives over here. They obviously know where Sara lives. We have to get prepared, immediately."

Wyatt's phone rang. Javier said, "Wyatt, something's going on out here—I believe something's gonna' happen soon. A black SUV has driven up and down the road a couple of times today. They turn around and leave but it looks like they're casing the place. The dogs are also acting strange and some of sensors along the fence have gone off multiple times—more than normal for it to be bunnies."

"Thanks. We're heading home now to batten down the hatches. I expect an attack tonight or tomorrow night."

He shared the information from Javier with the team and Wyatt and John went to talk to Harrell. Wyatt began, "We confirmed that Rodney Merritt was one of our IT employees. He was tortured and dumped. Javier says there's been a lot of activity on the road leading to the compound and along the fence. Someone followed John and Sara this morning, but John lost the tail. John connected the dots and I agree with him. We think the Russian Mafia or some of their comrades intend to kill or kidnap Sara, either payback for foiling their hacking attack or forcing her to play on their team. We expect them to move tonight or tomorrow night, and they will kill anyone in the way. We need to prepare for a vicious attack. Everyone needs to get back in the compound early today. We are taking Sara there now."

Chapter Seven

John and Wyatt took Sara to the compound and called everyone else to be home by three o'clock. They began setting up the defense. The compound was as secure as any collection of houses could be and they had time to make sure all possible defensive measures were in place. Margie, Virginia, and Carrie began cooking a big meal, one that could carry them through a long wait. John and Wyatt checked all the weapons to be sure they were in working order. Lenny and Harrell came in soon. Jake also arrived.

John told him he should leave but he stood his ground and refused, "If Sara is in danger, I'm staying here to help protector her."

John said, "Son, I expect many people will lose their lives tonight. I don't want you to be one of them. Have you ever killed a man or had a man try to kill you?"

"No, but you were also inexperienced at some point in your life. I'm sure I can hold my own."

"Well, I'm not sure and I don't like fighting with someone I'm not sure about."

"I'm not leaving. Now, what do you want me to do?"

"Have you ever done any shooting?"

"I was the Colorado State Skeet Champion. I'm an excellent shot, especially with a shotgun."

John mumbled, "Bet none of those skeet birds ever shot back." He gave up on trying to get Jake to leave and started to find a place for him.

Wyatt talked to Joe, "Do you think you are recovered enough to help with the defense?"

"Try to keep me from it! I can still shoot. I don't have to move around."

"We don't know how many will come or which direction they will come from. I think they will try to come up the drive, likely between midnight and two o'clock. They won't know we have prepared a welcome for them."

"I agree. The terrain on the west side of the fence is almost impossible to get a vehicle through. Unless they come in almost one at a time, they will have to use a vehicle. I expect a force as large as twenty, but hope it's less. What do you want me to do?"

"We will go over all the plans at dinner tonight. My house is the most hardened of the group and has the best safe room in case we can't hold them off. I guess we will soon see if all our plans will work out. I'm betting they will, but you never know. I wish we knew their numbers and weapons. We have a few surprises for them. Being armed and prepared will be the biggest surprise."

Javier would stay at his house with four of the dogs inside. Both he and his wife were good shots and they were armed with shotguns and rifles. A shotgun loaded with buckshot is a formidable weapon—the effective distance is not far, but they are devastating at shorter distances. Few people will knowingly charge a man or woman holding a shotgun.

TG and Margie would go to the safe room, along with Hilary

and the nurse. Others were placed in strategic positions inside and outside Wyatt's house. Lenny and Jake were behind a rock berm across the road from the house. It was much like a fox hole with boulders on the sides. John was in a similar position by the barn, but he could move about more freely using the barn for cover. Lenny and John had automatic rifles and their handguns. John provided Jake with a Keltec shotgun loaded with fourteen rounds of buckshot. Wyatt, Harrell, Ashley, Ruth, Carrie, Virginia, Sara and Joe were in the house. Harrell was on top with an automatic rifle. The others were in shooting positions built into the house. Virginia was positioned at the safe room's entrance with a shotgun. If the attackers came up the road as expected, John had positioned two Claymore antipersonnel mines which shot balls in a sixty degree arc. The element of surprise was with the defenders.

Shortly after midnight, Javier called to say the cameras had just picked up two large vans easing down the road toward the front gate. Wyatt alerted everyone that the attack would begin soon.

Most of the defenders had dry mouths, until they heard something at the outside gate. The two vans burst through the gate or at least tried to. The first one got through but the second one got hung up in the wires.

Six men jumped out of the second immobile SUV. Two ran toward Javier's house and each was met with a load of buckshot at close range and were quickly out of the fight. The four others headed for the compound on foot. Two of them were taken down by the dogs.

The eight remaining attackers were still running toward the inner gate. John set off one of the Claymores just as the vehicle came to its effective range. The driver and the one on backseat driver's side were mortally wounded. Six attackers ran through the gate and advanced toward the house. The firefight was quick and brutal. The six attackers were outnumbered and in the open. Four went down in the first volley. The last two were running for the door when Jake used his best skeet shooting form to center each with a load of buckshot. The firefight was over long before the police arrived.

Harrell, John, and Wyatt were out checking the bodies when the police arrived with lights flashing and sirens screaming. Several of the women were throwing up due to them realizing they had just helped take people's lives.

Three police cars and a SWAT vehicle rolled in. They checked the two bodies near Javier's house and then the two bodies the dogs caught. All four bodies were mangled. When they got closer to Wyatt's house, they discovered eight more bodies on the ground, with two still alive. One might make it, but the other one was breathing his last.

It was impossible to determine who shot who. Most of the bodies were riddled with bullets. The two Jake took out were hit only by his shotgun blasts.

The police tried to ask questions but Harrell made sure no one talked until his lawyers arrived. He asked the Sergeant to call the Police Chief to the scene and found out the Chief was already on his way. The Chief and Harrell went to Harrell's house to talk. The other defenders went to Wyatt's porch and put their guns against the rail. It took the police the rest of the night to clear the bodies and the Chief to decide no arrests were in order.

Sara was the most visibly shaken. She knew the attack was all about her and knew her people risked their lives to save her life. She was sobbing and Jake did his best to comfort her.

Carrie was also sicker than the others. These deaths made her think of the two men she killed in Barbados. It was the first time she thought more than fleetingly about what she had done.

She threw up several times.

Only Mitch and Frenchy went to work the next day since no one else got any sleep. A police wrecker came and took the two vans away. Wyatt called the construction chief to come fix the damaged gate and they had it repaired by noon. Another crew came out to repair the bullet holes in Wyatt's house, but there was not many.

Everything was near normal by the next evening. Everyone, including Javier and Geraldine, had supper together. It consisted of pizza delivered from Harrell's favorite pizza joint. Considerable beer was consumed.

Jake came out for pizza and John took him for a walk. He began, "Jake, not everyone can handle it when the bullets start flying. I'm really proud of you. You held up your end of the deal. I'm thinking you may make a decent son-in-law after all. I won't complain if y'all start making plans. Just be sure you don't hurt her."

"I got it Mr. Cannon."

"Why don't you call me John?"

"Sorry Mr. Cannon, but I'm not quite ready for that." John grinned and slapped him on the back.

As they were sitting around eating pizza, Wyatt said, "I'm ready to call Tommy about getting a pony and a few riding horses. Ashley has ordered a Paso Fino. I will get a quarter horse."

Lenny and Jake also wanted quarter horses. The final decision was to get a pony, four Paso Finos, and three quarter horses.

Javier said. "I used to work with the mounted division. I would love to take care of the horses."

Jake added, "I grew up riding horses. We always had a couple around. I can also help with them."

John said, "Geez! Now you've given him another reason to be out here all the time—as if he needed another reason! Don't you have a real job to do?"

Wyatt said, "I will talk to Tommy about helping us find good horses. Lenny, are there any ponies on the ranch?"

"Should be at least one for sale. A lot of the kids have them when they are young, but they outgrow them. I will also try to locate appropriate tack at auctions. It's usually better than what the stores have in stock."

Ashley said, "It's my turn to talk now. We want to start preparing the video we will use for the Grand Openings of the Learning Centers. Harrell, you will have ten minutes, as will Tommy and Virginia. Do you want Virginia and me to write a script for you?"

"Yes, good idea. I want all of us to be singing from the same song book. I really want this to work and I think it's going to work beyond our dreams. It's something we should have done years ago."

"Okay, you got it. I think likely want a script. We do want to speak with one voice."

The rest of the evening was spent just visiting until Sara stood up, "I know I was the reason to last night's attack. I'm sorry all of you had to put your lives on the line for me. But I'm very thankful."

Harrell spoke up, "Yes, Sara, they were after you, but they were after you because you did your job magnificently. We were protecting a valuable Trust asset—and someone we all love dearly."

A cheer went up from all the crowd. Sara had never experienced people helping her just because they loved her. It was a warm and comforting feeling. She squeezed Jake's arm and wiped a tear away.

As everyone began preparing to depart, Carrie stood and said, "I want to verify that I'm definitely pregnant and we are so happy! Wyatt, thank you for making us sleep together."

Joe said, "I agree—a lot!"

Ashley stood and said, "Well Carrie, looks like Wyatt got to two of us, in a way. Mine was more direct. We will be pregnant together!"

Sara stood and John said while looking straight at Jake, "You wouldn't dare!"

Sara quickly said, "No! No! It's not that! Jake and I are thinking about getting married next summer, so we may have a busy spring and summer around here."

John said, "Better get those houses started. We surely are growing. By the way, when are we having the big shindig wedding celebration for Carrie and Joe?"

Carrie spoke up, "Guess it should be soon so I won't be showing too much. Hilary, when can you have him well enough to dance with me at the reception?"

"We will start working on dancing tomorrow. I think he will be able to handle a slow dance soon—no real boogie woogie moves yet."

Joe said, "I did not have many boogie woogie moves to start with."

Virginia said, "Oh, my gosh! I have to start planning tomorrow. Harrell, do you want to give me a budget so I will know how much I go over it." Everyone but Harrell laughed—he just shook his head.

The celebration started to break up. Margie came to Sara and Jake and said, "I've been expecting this, but let's go in and talk. Sara and I have to plan something everyone will like. When will a ring appear?"

"It will likely be Christmas before we get a ring. But I'm not sure John will be happy with someone taking his recently found and worshipped daughter." Jake was just stating the obvious.

Margie returned, holding Jake's arm as they walked to their house, "Oh, I think he will be at least civil. You scared him a little tonight and I loved it! He likes you too much to want to hurt you, but if she were pregnant, all bets are off."

"He has made me well aware of that! We may wait a couple of years after the wedding to consummate the marriage, just so there's no doubt in his mind."

John's comment was an emphatic, "Good!"

Sara grabbed John's arm and said, "He's just a big ol' teddy bear who loves and protects me."

"From the other side of the table, he's a big ol' grizzly bear who loves and protects you. You weren't on any of our little walks."

John added very calmly, "If you keep the part in mind about 'loves and protects her,' we will all be happy." Sara hugged his arm tightly.

Sara thought, *"John is the first man who loved me and protected me. Where was he during those beatings from my stepdad? I wondered what ever happened to him."* Only John knew for sure.

When they went into the house, John poured himself a drink and Margie picked up her calendar. She said, "I know you are not ready to come up with firm dates, but do you have a general idea, like maybe what month you expect things to happen?"

Sara said, "We will likely get officially engaged around Christmas, probably just before. We are thinking a late summer wedding—probably August. We are not sure where we want to go for our honeymoon, but probably to the mountains or a secluded beach."

John said, "It would be easier to set up protection in the mountains. The Trust has several beautiful mountain ranches. Jake, I need to get you trained with other defensive weapons. In addition to being important to you, she's a key part of the Trust and some miscreants may mistake her for the weak link in our security. They may keep coming after her. I saw you have the heart and grit to protect her. I just need to give you and Sara additional relevant skills."

"Thank you. I would love that."

"You won't be thrilled with the hand-to-hand instruction. May have to show you what the old man can still do."

Margie said, "Oh, John, quit threatening the boy. Can't you see he is a little afraid of you."

"And well he should be!"

Since they were only talking generalities about the wedding, it did not take long. Margie actually had two calendars she was jotting notes on both of them.

Just before she and John went to bed, she asked, "Do you want to have a big wedding at the hotel? The Trust pays for those, but we will need to get on the calendar with them. They stay pretty busy. With a Cannon descendant marrying an adopted Cannon, I'm sure it will be something really big."

Something set the alarms and the dogs off just after midnight. John came running through the living room and threw Jake a shotgun.

"You stay near the door and protect the women. It's probably just a deer, but you have to stay ready."

Javier confirmed quickly a deer had triggered the alarm. For Jake, it was much more— John gave him a weapon and told him to protect the women! That would not have happened before the Russian raid. Jake was more honored than anyone would ever know. To be trusted by John was a really big deal for him.

_____

The Grand Opening of the Learning Centers was rapidly drawing near. Sara helped Ashley get the speakers videoed. They decided to record Harrell first. Ashley and Virginia provided him with notes the previous day and he had studied them intensely. He was ready.

Harrell's message was built around the fact that the Learning Centers were something the Trust should have done long before. The women associated with the Trust, led by Ashley, had made the Trust's Board members officers aware of the dire need for providing better educational opportunities for the ranch and farm worker's children. The vote had been unanimous to fund the school system.

He ended his remarks with, "We at the Trust want to provide the workers and their children with the best education possible. Since it was impossible to construct traditional schools, the Trust is providing a new type of Learning Center consisting of a building and computer equipment. Each grade in all the Learning Centers will receive the same material electronically and have a teacher to coach the students through the tough spots. We are confident you will get an excellent education and you won't have to leave home or ride a bus for hours to get it. We also hope to provide experiences outside the ranches and farms."

Tommy's message was similar, except he had experience trying to get an education while living on a ranch. He talked about his experience of catching the school bus before dawn and getting home after dark.

He concluded with, "We are trying to make it easier for you to get a high school education while living at home. For those who have ridden buses, your school day will be three or four hours shorter. You will have ample resources on each ranch and farm to help you learn. Today you can find almost anything you want to on the internet. The largest libraries in the world will be available through the internet and you will have a teacher to help you organize your studies. I wish I had this when I was growing up on a ranch. Parents, the system will be available to you at night so you can finish your degree or simply find out what your children are learning. Let me know if you think of anything that could make your experience better."

Virginia's message was how glad she was the Trust was finally looking out for the children's education. She spent a few minutes talking about how they planned to add a culture studying component with trips on the Trust's new luxury bus.

She concluded with, "The ranches are fine places to grow up, but you can miss so many interesting things that happen only in larger cities. We plan to take you on field trips to cultural events help round out your education. Every field trip will also include fun activities. Ladies, we are also planning excursions for you, such as to plays, movies, and concerts, and maybe make time for some shopping sashays. Now, you are going to hear from the woman who brought your needs to the Trust's attention and put the program together. You should give her a big Thank You. This was her idea and she has pushed hard for a quality experience for every student."

Ashley talked more about the technical aspects of the program and how it was tailored around the home schooling approach, but with more structure. She went into some depth about how they would not be left alone in their studies. Their teachers had been selected specifically because they had experience in distance education. They had been training on the equipment and computer programs all summer and were committed to make this a great learning experience.

She concluded her remarks with, "We are sure we will

encounter a few glitches along the way, but we have a team here to help minimize and rectify those. I will be working as sort of a superintendent until we find someone else. I'm intent on making this approach work and so are the Trust's Board and executives. Let's all focus on making this work. I and the Board are committed. I hope you are. Now, refreshments should be available at each Learning Center. I will stay online for you to ask questions. Good Luck this school year! Have fun!"

Sara and a person from IT edited the videos to get the program down to an hour and make them even more interesting. Most of the people on the ranches and farms had never seen Harrell or thought he cared about their lives. None had ever seen Virginia. Only a few knew Tommy or Ashley. The adults would be impressed with the videos. The children would likely be more impressed by the cookies and drinks.

Ashley was like a cat on a hot tin roof during the days leading up to the Grand Opening. Wyatt and TG gave her a wide berth. In fact, Wyatt decided he and Lenny needed go to the ranch to look over the horses and ponies. Margie took care of TG.

The first order of the day was to find the right pony for TG. Lenny explained, "All ponies are not necessarily good first horses. They have spent time being smarter than their young riders. Some are pretty mean. They will bite and kick. They try to run away with a young inexperienced rider and TG is about as young as they come. But no one on the ranch is likely to sell a bad pony to a Vice President of the Cannon Trust."

When they arrived at the ranch, they drove around and saw several small ponies. Lenny asked the cowboys at lunch if any of them had a pony for sale, "We're looking for a pony for a very young rider—Wyatt's son. You don't want to sell one with bad manners to a Trust V.P.. Now, how many of you have a totally safe pony for a young boy?"

Cole stood up and said, "Tommy has a great pony he might sell. It carries some Paso Fino blood, but it's pony sized. It's as rock solid as any pony I know of." Several agreed.

"Where is it? Are there any others that might work." There were.

He got the locations of all the ponies and they started driving around with Cole. The ponies came in a variety of sizes. One was small like the ones used for kids at fairs. It might work but it was a really plain looking pony. The one owned by Tommy was the prettiest of the group but also a little larger. It was a loud colored pinto with obvious Paso Fino heritage. Wyatt liked its looks.

Wyatt called Tommy to ask if it was for sale and if he thought it might work for TG. Tommy replied, "No pony is going to be rideable by a one year old. My youngest son started riding her when he was three. He's ten now and just went to a bigger horse. I'll have to talk to him tonight about selling because it's his horse. Realize you will have to lead any pony around while someone holds TG on for a least a year or two."

"I understand. What about horses for the adults? We want four Paso Finos and three quarter horses."

"I'll need to come out there to help Cole find you horses we are willing to sell now. I think I can come out in the morning and help you find what you want."

"Great! We will meet you tomorrow. We probably need to find a few you are willing to sell and then let the group decide which ones they like."

"Makes sense. We can hold them in a corral until everyone can come out on Saturday to make their choices. I assume you might want Buck."

"I'm sure he would be my first choice."

"Lenny likely knows what he wants, also."

Lenny chimed in, "Yep."

"I will meet y'all tomorrow morning for breakfast at the dining hall."

They looked at horses all the next morning. By noon, Tommy and Cole identified six Paso Fino mares and geldings that did not fit into the ranch's breeding program. He also identified four quarter horses the ranch could part with.

He also added, "Tab, my son, says he will sell his horse, Chief. He would like to ride it for a week or so to get it back on its best manners."

"Perfect! We need to get the schools open before we take the horses home. Can you trailer them to the compound? Ask Tab if he wants to come meet Chief's new owner. Maybe he can give TG his first ride on Chief."

"That's a great idea! He will love it. Bring everyone out to make their selections and we will deliver them whenever you want."

Saturday broke clear and cool. The group went to the ranch early enough to have breakfast in the bunkhouse. It was a good break for Ashley because the Grand Opening was the following week and she had done all she could to be prepared.

Since everyone was not getting a horse of their own, a lively discussion preceded their final choices. Wyatt and Tommy thought they made good choices. The horses they picked were another buckskin, three palominos, two bays and a chestnut. They took turns riding them all. TG was excited to see all the horses. He seemed to have an attraction to the small horse called Chief.

They discovered Jake was indeed a good rider. Jake also spent time watching the cutting horse training. He was amazed at the horse's athleticism and the rider's ability to stay in the saddle.

Wyatt said, "I've ridden a couple of them and just held on for dear life. Maybe we can come out one day and let you try one."

It was chow time when they finished their business, so they ate at the dining hall. The cowboys were happy to have them and there was plenty of food. Virginia was again amazed at the quantity of food consumed.

The ride home was rather rambunctious for everyone but Ashley. She was thinking about the Grand Opening.

Chapter Eight

Ashley woke up early Sunday morning and soon hit high gear. She went over all the Grand Opening plans again. She sent an email to each teacher instructing them to visit the nearest town and buy three big trays of cookies, bakery made if possible, and soft drinks for everyone on the property. If anything else caught their eye, they should buy it and send the bills her. If visiting the town was problematic, perhaps they could challenge the mothers to bake goodies as their first PTA activity.

She soon heard TG clamoring to get out of his bed. She picked him up and took him to Wyatt to play for a while. Cassandra had Sundays off and usually spent it with her daughter's family. She had been a Godsend and they were hoping Cassandra would stay with them after Ashley's crunch was over.

Wyatt took TG to the kitchen and started making pancakes. TG loved to help his dad cook and also loved pancakes. The bacon smelled great and the coffee was brewing in the fancy coffee maker. Ashley had already drank one cup made on the single-cup side.

He put the food and drinks on a tray and took it to the back veranda. Almost every household was doing the same thing. It was a beautiful, cool morning and everyone wore a robe or housecoat. John had been sitting alone on their back porch since before sunup. Sara was still in bed but Margie brought John's breakfast out. Carrie and Joe were the last couple to appear.

Ashley planned a big day at the office. She was so wound up she was hard to live with. Wyatt and even TG felt her angst. Nothing they tried, including silly faces, comforted her. Margie fetched TG to keep him out of the line of fire. Ruth went over to take on some of the nervous behavior and shield Wyatt.

Wyatt ambled to Lenny's back porch and asked if he had any ideas for a road trip to keep him from getting runover by a steamroller.....Ashley. Lenny responded, "I was reading about an auction down toward Colorado Springs. The list of items contains several good brands of tack. We're gonna' need tack soon."

They decided to go to the auction as soon as Ashley settled down. Wyatt went back to his house and gave Ashley a big hug and a kiss. She sort of returned them.

He said, "I know your big day is coming and I know you have done everything you can to make the Grand Opening a success. You are also prepared for the start of school. Remember that you have a lot of backing. Lenny and I are going to a tack auction soon. Mom says she will keep TG until Cassandra gets back tonight."

Him leaving did not thrill her but she understood. Harrell and Virginia walked over while they were talking.

Virginia came over, gave Ashley a big hug, and said, "I am sure you are a bundle of raw nerves. I've watched you and you are ready. We are ready. This is a rather foolish statement, but you should focus on relaxing today. A nap would help if you're anything like me. You have done everything possible to make the Grand Opening a smash hit. Those children are going to be so much better off."

Harrell followed with, "Being the head of something as big as the school system is hard. I have faith in you. The whole organization has faith in you. It's pretty lonely when you are in charge of something as big as this. Everyone, including me, knows you've done a great job. The Learning Centers are going to be one of the best things we've ever done as an employer. Why don't you take a walk with someone? It always helps me."

"Thank you both for the kind words. I know you are right, but I can't help but think I'm missing something. I know we are ready, but I don't feel ready. A walk may help. Think I will see if Carrie wants to walk. We can talk about raising kids, which might help settle my nerves."

Carrie did want to walk as soon as she got Joe settled. They walked on a faint walking trail around the external fence. The four dogs were happy to have some human company and provided a rotating honor guard for them.

They talked of pregnancy and the thrill of having a baby. She offered to take Carrie on a shopping trip as soon as the Learning Centers were open and running smoothly, hopefully, the next week. They vowed to take these walks at least three times a week. The distance around the perimeter was a mile and a half of reasonably flat ground, with just enough ups and downs to make it interesting. They enjoyed watching the wildlife, such as rabbits inside the perimeter and a few deer outside the fence.

Ashley was much more relaxed after the walk. She decided to catch the nap Virginia suggested. She felt refreshed when she woke up. TG woke up from his nap a few minutes after Ashley roused. She picked him up and they spent the rest of the day playing.

Wyatt and Lenny found all the tack they needed at the auction. Lenny was a fountain of knowledge about tack, particularly saddles. He liked the Wilson saddles and told Wyatt they were extremely well made in Mississippi by a relatively small leather shop.

Lenny shied away from the highly decorative saddles, "If you ride in parades, those saddles with the fancy silver trim are fine. The roping and cutting saddles are built stronger, but generally are not very comfortable for other kinds of riding."

"The simpler pleasure saddles are better for most riding. I like the Wilson saddles in particular because they are well built and comfortable. A few of the big outfits build good saddles, but some are not so good. Most of what I see here are the cheaper ones built by the big firms."

Wyatt bid on the saddles Lenny recommended and got them at a good price according to Lenny. They bought bridles and halters for about half what they would pay in Western stores. It was a good day and they came back with Lenny's truck full of tack. Wyatt was especially pleased with a kid's saddle he bought. They unloaded the tack in the barn and were ready for the horses.

Wyatt was surprised when he went in and found Ashley was playing with TG. He led them to the barn, put TG's saddle on the corral fence, and lifted him aboard. TG played like he was riding a horse. He had a glorious time just sitting in the saddle and holding the horn, with a big grin on his face. Wyatt gently rocked the saddle and TG giggled with glee. He was definitely not ready to leave the saddle for supper, so they let him ride a few more minutes..

Ashley was still calm and collected. She said, "Wyatt, I decided I've done everything possible to get ready for the Grand Opening. I'm ready. The Learning Centers are ready. Worrying about it and making everyone around me miserable is not what I need to do. I'm sorry for my edgy attitude this morning. I'll try to stay calm from now on, but I can't promise. I've never done anything like this and I want it to succeed so much I just can't help myself."

"I understand and will try to keep us out of your way. We bought enough saddles and tack for the horses. Yes, it was partially to get out of your way, but we needed the gear for the horses."

They had an enjoyable dinner that evening. TG was played out and went to bed early. Wyatt and Ashley sat before a small fire in the fireplace. Although the fire was mainly for ambiance, the evenings brought a little chill to the mountain air. They chatted about a variety of things, particularly the highly anticipated second child.

Ashley said, "I would like to have a girl this time. What do you think?"

He fibbed and said he also wanted a girl. He thought, "*I hope that little white lie doesn't come back to haunt me. I've heard little girls twist their daddy's around their little finger. Oh, well.*"

Wyatt and Ashley went to bed early, knowing they were both going to have a big week, especially Ashley. The alarm seemed unusually harsh the next morning. Ashley began to get uptight again and Wyatt took her out to the rear veranda. Wyatt flipped a switch to light a small gas firepit. He was relieved to see the flames calming Ashley down.

She asked, "How did you know the firepit was just what I needed this morning? You can read my mind.....but only sometimes. Can we have dinner at the hotel tonight? I think looking forward to a Chef's creation might help me keep my nerves in check today. The Grand Opening is the day after tomorrow and classes start the next day. You may want to find a place to hide during the next few days. You can face down bad men intent on harming you, but not an uptight woman on the warpath."

Wyatt laughed and responded, "You are absolutely correct! I know what to do with one and have no idea how to cope with the other. It's difficult when the woman you love acts like she might rip your ears off any minute. I know you don't really mean it, but, at the same time, I'm never completely sure."

Ashley leaned over to give him a warm kiss and responded, "I'll always love you—I just forget sometimes. Maybe we can visit the ranch for a few days after things are running smoothly, which I hope is by the end of the week. I'm sure I will need to decompress. I'm sure TG would like to visit Chief. I also want to indulge myself in the warm spring again. By the way, why didn't you find land with a warm spring on it?"

Wyatt blinked and realized he had just found a superb Idea for Ashley's Christmas present. He wanted to remember it, so he wrote himself a note—'warm springs for compound.'

It was soon time to head for the office. Wyatt hoped no nasty outside action would raise its head this week. For once, he got lucky.

Ashley rode with him to her office to review the plans one more time. She could not find anything that needed to be done, which thoroughly scared her.

Frenchy and Mitch were putting the last touches on the outfitting operation. They were working with Sara and two IT people to get the website and reservation system set up. He hired a person to do the artwork for the site and the efforts were progressing well.

The first day of pheasant season was a month away and, so far, they had no clients. They put an ad in the *Pheasants Forever* magazine for the pheasant hunting and one in *Ducks Unlimited* for the duck hunting.

Sara created separate websites for the two parallel efforts. The websites and the magazine ads stressed that the land had never been hunted heavily, only by employees. The ads and websites included links to their computerized reservation system. Telephone number to call with questions were also included. The team thought both websites and the ads were splashy and good.

The website rolled out at midnight on Monday. The magazines hit at nearly the same time. By Tuesday night, the first weekend of pheasant hunting was fully booked with twelve hunters on both ranches. Each hunter was paying fifteen hundred dollars for a three day hunt. By Wednesday night only a few pheasant hunting slots remained open during the first month.

The duck hunting slots filled up more slowly, but Frenchy was sure they would book every weekend slot. He was right—by the end of the week, every weekend slot was filled.

Fishing reservations dragged a little, but they had sold a few trips. Once people saw the places to fish, Frenchy was sure they would also fill up. The outfitting operation would be a new source of income for the Trust.

They talked to Harrell and the Board on Wednesday and everyone was pleased. Their primary question was, "What needs to be done for next season?"

"We need small lodges at these four locations and a couple more locations for deer and elk hunting. Those five-hundred-dollar-a-day pheasant hunts would approach a thousand dollars a day if we had lodges. The lodges for waterfowl and fishing will stay full most weeks during the year."

"We need to figure out what we need to do on the northern ranches. They have big game, including elk and mule deer. The Canadian properties could be especially profitable. They also have waterfowl, more geese than ducks. The ranches along the Missouri Breaks could also be excellent. We don't intend to stop evaluating and planning. These four locations were the low hanging fruit."

"We also need to think about what we can do with the lodges in the off season. I'm not concerned much about the first off season because we need thinking and planning time. Might get feedback from the hunters. Cross country skiing comes to mind for the more northern properties and those at higher elevations. Excursions on tracked snowcats might be attractive, and perhaps jeep rentals and horseback rides. We just need to brainstorm the possibilities after hunting season."

Harrell added, "I'm beginning to believe outfitting can become a nice source of income for the Trust. We have thousands of acres in some great hunting areas. We may have to further develop some of the properties to take full advantage of them. I had no idea people would pay so much to kill three roosters or six ducks."

Wednesday was Ashley's big night. She was unnaturally serene. Wyatt and Ruth wondered who slipped something into her coffee. The night went remarkably well with no glitches. Harrell, Tommy, Virginia, and Ashley delivered their speeches like polished veterans. Most of the questions were about the bus trips and how the program would work for adults.

Ashley responded, "We have been concentrating on getting the Learning Centers open for the children. Consequently, we have not been able to devote enough time to adult education or the field trips. But I promise you we will get it done within the next two weeks. I'm sorry I can't answer your specific questions tonight, but I will be able to soon. We will schedule another night to present a plan for adult education, how the field trips will work, and to answer additional questions. If you have any ideas, please share them with me in the next few days via email."

Everyone was delighted that the adults on the properties were so interested in continuing their education. The interest in the field trips was also noted, for both the students and the parents.

When the Grand Opening event closed, everyone took a giant breath. It was a huge milestone and the first day of classes would be an even greater milestone.

Ashley would be able to sit in Denver and watch what was happening in each class. She could communicate with the teachers openly or send them a message.

The first day of classes went well. The students appeared to also want the Learning Centers to succeed, probably so they would no longer have to take the long bus rides.

Ashley wanted to visit the ranch to relax for a few days—she would work on the adult education next week. Most of the planning was actually almost completed—she just was not ready to talk about it. Plus, she did not want to detract from the children during the first few weeks.

Wyatt, Ashley, TG, and Cassandra drove to the ranch early Friday morning, with the grandparents following later in the afternoon. As soon as Wyatt arrived, he went to the corral to look at the horses Tommy and Cole had collected for them to evaluate.

Ashley got TG down for a nap and walked down join him. Ashley looked over the horses carefully. A really loud colored pinto and a dark palomino interested her the most. She rode both of them and they were as advertised—calm and easy on the bottom. After much back and forth, she chose the pinto because it looked like TG's Chief.

When TG woke up, they took him for a ride but not yet on his horse. Wyatt let him ride in front of him and TG loved it. They rode around for nearly an hour and he jabbered the entire time. Wyatt wished he could understand it. He was sure TG was giving the horse directions but, thankfully, the horse was not listening.

They left their horses tied to the hitching rail on the side of the house and went to get lunch in the bunkhouse. It was the day for fish, because many of the cowboys were Catholic. The cooks had prepared fried, grilled, and blackened fish dishes, along with two different fish stews. The fish were excellent, as the food always was.

Ashley ate a small grilled fillet and a small salad because she was trying to watch her weight. She really did not want to have to stay in bed for months the way she did with TG. Wyatt was not under those limitations.

They took Cassandra and small basket of fish, slaw, and hushpuppies back to the house. They and TG then took a good nap before the grandparents arrived.

It was so relaxing on the ranch, even though ranch work was constant everywhere they looked. Wyatt rode down to the cutting horse training with TG when he woke up. TG seemed to still be giving the horse directions, which he still ignored.

The grandparents arrived, along with Jake and Sara. As soon as they stowed their gear, John and Jake came down to the cutting horse arena.

Tommy had finished his day as the Director of Ranches and was back on the ranch helping Cole. He asked Wyatt, "You want to give it a whirl? They will be training for about an hour longer."

"Absolutely! Jake, how about you?"

Jake took a deep breath and responded, "Well, yes, if it would be okay."

Tommy nodded his head. John spoke up, "Let me fetch the women to watch the rodeo. I'm sure they will be amused. Y'all get suited up and ready to ride. Do both of you have insurance? I don't want to pay medical bills for a pair of drugstore cowboys trying to look like the real thing."

As soon as Ashley arrived, she said, "It you break you neck, I'm going to shoot you between the eyes, just to put your out of your misery!"

When Sara saw the real cowboys ride and how fast the horses moved, she kept saying, "Oh no! Oh no! I can't watch. Are you sure you can stay on? Please don't fall off!"

Wyatt rode first and managed to stay on, even though his ride was not pretty. Ashley quit threatening him and started cheering, "Ride him cowboy!"

Jake had been watching the other riders intently and knew he had to hold on tightly and let the horse do the work. He went into the pen and put his horse on the number Tommy called out. He directed the horse to the selected steer and then held on as tightly as he could. The horse was good, and Jake made it to the end. He actually looked a little more comfortable than Wyatt.

The rodeo was over for the day. They all walked over to the corral to see the horses they would be evaluating.

Sara said, "Jake, what do you think?"

"Well, the palomino looks really good and it's a Paso Fino. I also like the other buckskin quarter horse."

Since Lenny knew he wanted the quarter horse he rode for several years, only two more Paso Fino horses needed to be selected. Wyatt and Jake rode all the Paso Finos and said they could tell no difference in the quality of the ride.

Tommy pointed to two horses and said, "Those two have been ridden more and should be more solid. I recommend them." One was a bay and the other was a chestnut.

The other horses were turned out and only their selections were left in the corral. Tommy said, "I will get them delivered next week. Why don't you bring TG by my house and my son, Little Tom, will give him a formal introduction to Chief. You need to pay him separately. Chief was his horse."

It was seafood night at the dining hall. The women split crab legs from a huge crab. Tiny had two, along with a few other fish dishes.

Tommy came over to talk to Wyatt about the wedding and fandango for Rosie the next weekend. Quite a few of the ranch's cowboys had ties to Freedom Town and were planning to attend, primarily because Queenie was such a celebrity in the community's history.

It would be quite a fandango. Three bands were scheduled to play and it would last most of the night. It would be held at the high school in La Junta. Rosie and Lawrence would jump the broom at Freedom Town in what had been the original Meeting Hall.

Ashley and the other women went to the warm springs after supper. Ashley and Sara did not take swimsuits. TG went with them.

Jake said, "If y'all need someone to provide security, I'm available."

John said, "That'll be the day! I may make you wear a blindfold just in case."

Ashley said, "You can go down and look for snakes before we go."

John said, "You make sure you get back up here where I can watch you before they get in." The back and forth between Jake and John had become more of a joke, but Jake knew the joking had a serious undertone.

The weekend spent at the ranch was just what Ashley needed. She attacked the adult education issues on Monday morning and came up with a couple of field trips for each child. She also planned a shopping trip for the mothers. They would visit the nearest large city for the day during the week when the children were in school.

Another video meeting was arranged for Thursday evening. The night went well and most of the questions were answered.

Rosie and Lawrence arrived in Denver Thursday morning. They obtained a marriage license and drove to La Junta. Since every hotel room in La Junta was booked, the people from Denver decided to take three planes and fly back late Saturday night. Rosie and Lawrence stayed in one of the Cannon Hotel suites until Saturday morning. They planned to return to Denver after spending one night at Freedom Town's old Meeting Hall. Miss Jenny made sure it was as comfortable as it could be and she would also stay in Freedom Town to ensure everything went great on Rosie's wedding night.

The wedding itself was much like other weddings, except it was short and included the jumping the broom element. The fandango was not like most other fandangoes. A pig and a yearling had been slow roasted and many other somewhat unusual dishes of what might be called Mexican soul food lined the long tables. Many dishes combined food like hominy and okra brought by the former slaves with stews and beans which were distinctly Mexican. Whatever else one wanted to call it, delicious was the best word to describe it.

With Joe and Carrie Sheffield attending, everyone was ready to celebrate. Many of the Cannon's from Denver also attended. The broad mixture of races and ethnicities was truly impressive. Miss Jenny talked about the importance of Queenie, Miss Lily, and the Cannon boys to the success of Freedom Town. She spun a good story that held most people's attention, although many knew the story by heart.

Miss Jenny had spread the word about two Cannon descendants and a Sheffield descendant speaking to kick off the fandango. Everyone was looking forward to their comments, especially following the marriage of a woman who had the bloodlines of both Queenie and Cat Jones.

They each spoke for about five minutes. Their comments revolved around their understanding of the role Freedom Towners had played in helping the Cannons and Sheffields, even to this day.

Jenny had decided to provide only beer at the fandango. If anyone was upset, they did not complain. The bands began really cranking up about dark and a large bonfire kept everyone warm. Most of the attendees did not need heat—the dance floor was keeping almost every quite warm. All the Denver women, including Ashley, Ruth, Margie, and Virginia, danced until they were exhausted. Sara and Carrie were stars of the show. The young men were lined up to give them a spin. It was a fun filled night.

Jake tried just about every food available. He discovered his palate could not handle some of the dishes. He also discovered the dishes brought over from Africa were sometimes as hot as the Mexican dishes. As he and Sara went through the line, her job was to keep a supply of tortillas and a bottle of beer close in case he was overcome with the spices.

The Denver group had planned to leave at midnight but it was after one o'clock before they could break away. Everyone wanted to shake the hand of a bonified descendent of Miss Lily—few had ever seen one. Joe and Carrie had the most trouble pulling away. He vowed to come out and spend more time out here.

The planes landed in Denver three in the morning. No one gave a thought to working on Sunday. Monday was also questionable. Drivers were waiting to make sure there were no problems with DUIs. They would get their cars and trucks from the garage tomorrow—late tomorrow.

Chapter Nine

Sunday was a slow starting day for everyone after their long night. John and Wyatt were the first up and joined each other for their first cup on Wyatt's back porch. John said, "You know the Russians are not likely to stop trying to get at Sara. She has made them mad and someone back in Russia is likely calling the shots."

"I've been thinking the same thing. I don't think they will try a frontal assault again. They now know we're a tough nut to crack. It's too bad none of them lived long enough for you to question. Unfortunately, we are still vulnerable to a sneak attack or possibly a bomb."

"I'm thinking a solo assassin. It could be on the street or anywhere else. I need to talk to Sara and Jake about not being predictable in their movements and get Jake trained with a pistol. In fact, I'll start the training today. He needs to get good quickly because the man who comes after her the next time will be an assassin. I will start talking to them about how the attack might happen. I have experience in that arena and with Russian tactics."

"Good idea. I can help if you need me."

"Hmmm. A little hand-to-hand training might show Jake what this old man can do and might enhance our understanding."

"Yes, I'm quite sure it will!"

Others started getting up and Cassandra brought TG to his dad and granddad so she could fix breakfast for everyone. People drifted over and brought a cup of coffee with them. Lenny was the first to arrive.

He commented, "I can't do many of those fandangos in a week anymore. My body hurts from top to bottom. Ruth just rolled over and told me to bring her a cup of coffee."

"I don't think Margie has rolled over, and I'm pretty sure Sara has not even cracked one eye open. Jake stayed out here on the couch and he looks dead to the world this morning."

"If he knew what you had in store for him today, he would pull the covers over his head and stay in bed all day."

Lenny looked at them with a frown. Wyatt grinned and said, "John's going to begin Jake's hand-to-hand training today."

"I'm sure that will make his day!"

John said, "Cassandra is cooking a big breakfast for everyone. We need to talk when everyone is up and wide awake. We believe we haven't heard the last from our Russian friends."

"I agree. Sara has embarrassed them and we have embarrassed them. My understanding is they don't much like getting beat or embarrassed."

"You got that right! We may have to help break up the U.S. based group they are using. I'm sure it's one of the Russian mobs the KGB or whoever has contracted with. I can probably get help from the CIA."

"Didn't think they operated in the U.S."

"They don't.....officially."

Margie, Ruth, and Harrell were the next to join the crowd. All had a large cup or mug in their hand. Ruth said, "I am too old to dance 'til midnight and get home at three. Lenny, you make the best coffee I have ever tasted."

Margie said, "Have you noticed it's the older folks who are awake? If you can call the state we all look to be in being awake. What's that wonderful smell?"

"Cassandra will have a breakfast casserole ready soon. It will be Mexican and I don't know about eating it for breakfast after yesterday. I guess it's a version of 'the hair of the dog that bit you.'"

Cassandra brought the first casserole and plates out. The plates were paper, which suited everyone. The aroma when she put the dish on the table was out of this world. Ashley came out while everyone was serving themselves.

"Y'all having a party and didn't invite me!" She went for a big cup of coffee first.

Joe and Carrie came out with Hilary and the nurse. Cassandra brought out the second casserole and they dug in. Sara and Jake finally joined the group.

Sara said, "It took a while to wake him. I don't think he's used to partying like the rest of you. I know I'm not. But I did love the dancing."

Jake was hobbling a little and said, "She sure did. This girl loves to dance!"

"Don't think a little limp is going to get you out of what I have planned for you." Jake looked confused while Lenny and Wyatt snickered.

Everyone enjoyed Cassandra's casseroles and the strong coffee. John let everyone finish before he began the meeting.

"We don't think the Russian threat is over. We also don't think the next attack will be a frontal attack—the first effort was too costly for them. It's likely to be a solo assassin, or maybe a small team. Sara is their primary target but it could be any of us because of their failed raid. So we are going to talk about some of the Russian's favorite tricks."

Virginia innocently asked, "How do you know their tricks?"

"I used to be involved with them on a regular basis. I was a CIA operative for many years, so I have a depth of knowledge from going up against them. I'm still here, so I won those skirmishes. You can believe me. You can also believe me when I show ways to avoid getting hurt or dead."

Everyone got a chair and listened intently, "The next attack could be long distance, such as a sniper, which presents us with a problem. A good sniper could climb up in the mountains west of our perimeter fence and pick someone off. A good one can hit a human target at over a half mile, closer to a mile. Or, they could try an attack at close range—a few feet, maybe. An umbrella with a needle can infect you on a street, which is one of their favorites for protected dignitaries. A package with a poisonous agent is a good choice. Even a flower arrangement can be used. I could go on, but I will try to write this up for you. When you get the written material, study it. It might save your life. Remember, even if Sara is the target, they don't care how many get hurt."

Harrell asked, "What method of attack do you think they will use?"

"If it were my assignment, I would make a sniper nest on the mountain and shoot from there. We have a good setup to defend a frontal attack, as we and they saw."

He pointed to a rough area on the west mountain and continued, "One or two men somewhere in that area would be hard to stop. We will create a few surprises for them but if they are good, it will be hard to defend. I said hard, but it's not impossible. I will use every trick I know to swing the odds in our favor."

"In case they try the close attack, the people who will be

closest to Sara have to be prepared to take the attack to them. We're going to be practicing hand-to-hand fighting techniques and we need to brush everyone up on pistol use. Jake, much to my chagrin, you are likely to be the closest to Sara and right now, you are a weak link. You and I will work on your hand-to-hand technique while the rest watch. Have you ever had any hand-to-hand training?"

"I was in a dojo for a while. I was pretty good."

"Great! We are going to make you even better."

Joe spoke up, "John has sold himself short. He was one of the best assets our country had in the constant battles between our country and others. If you listen to him and follow his instructions all the time, everyone will get through this. He was the best at what he did and has defeated Russian opponents many times. The situation we are now in does not call for being nice or playing fair. We must win each encounter decisively. If you delay or hold back when someone tries to attack, someone is likely to die. If you act as John tells you, they will likely die."

"Thank you, Joe. What Joe said is true. The one who comes in second probably dies—only the winner will live. Let that rattle around in your head for a while. Under attack, you must win with extreme prejudice. In other words, if one of us is going to live, I want it to be me. Jake, do you have any old clothes with you?"

"No, sir. But I can get them quickly."

"Go ahead. We will find an area to spread hay so it won't hurt me too badly when you throw me."

Lenny said under his breath, "If the boy's smart, he'll just keep going." Wyatt and Joe laughed.

John added, "Before you leave, I have one more thing to talk about. You know the Russians kidnapped, tortured, and killed a Cannon IT geek to get information. Regardless of what they do next, they might do something like that again. That means everyone in our compound and in the security division is vulnerable. We've gotten a little slack on using bodyguards as we should—we have to tighten up until the threat is over. I'm comfortable about the compound at night, but only a few people are here during the day. And there's Mitch and Frenchy and their families. We should find about four bodyguards for, hopefully, short-term duty. Two of them should be assigned to Mitch and Frenchy's families. Two should be on duty here during the day. You ladies should never leave the compound alone. You need to be accompanied by your husband or a bodyguard, even for things like grocery shopping."

Virginia interrupted, "Oh, John, is it really necessary?"

"Absolutely. Anyone trying to kidnap you will be professional and there will be more than one. I'm assuming you do want to see your grandbaby grow up."

Harrell spoke up, "Virginia, we will do what he says."

John added, "Those of us who go to work should also drive in with at least one other person."

Wyatt said, "Does anyone know where we can find temporary bodyguards?"

Javier replied, "I have two friends who retired about a year before I did. Neither wants a full-time job, but they both pick up odd duty occasionally. I can call them."

"Do that. Anyone else?"

Lenny spoke up, "I keep up with a few of my retired MP buds. I probably can find two."

"Great! Please contact them."

Since most were still in their pajamas, gowns, and robes, everyone went to get dressed in old clothes. They started to reassemble thirty minutes later. A few stragglers took close to an hour. John scattered three bales of hay on an area close to the barn. The hay provided a little padding.

Jake got back and everyone was surprised when he showed back up in a loose white suit with a black belt. John said, "I see you have been holding back on me. If the outfit is yours, you know a lot more about self-defense than I thought. This may get interesting. Wyatt, you better get ready to save your old man."

Sara said, "Jake, don't hurt him. He's so much older than you." A chorus of snickers arose from those who had seen John work.

John said, "Let's begin with a few basic takedown moves. Remember this—if someone attacks you, the knees, nose, groin, and throat are the four most vulnerable areas. A blow in one of those spots may give you time to get away. Russians generally attack from the front. Jake, come toward me like we were walking down the sidewalk meeting each other. Act as though you have a knife. Here, let's assume this stick is a knife."

Jake came toward him and held the knife in a threatening manner. John grabbed the knife hand, gave it a hard twist, and moved the wrist backward. Jake dropped the stick as John went into his body and threw him over his hip. Jake hit with a thud.

John said, "Jake let me do that, but if he had resisted more, he would have been easier to throw. I used his forward motion to throw him. Now, in most self-defense classes, the action would stop here. But we are trying to stop someone who wants to kill us and we want to permanently dissuade the attacker of such a misguided notion. If I have no clear kick to his groin or knee, I would kick him as hard as possible in the arm I am holding. I want to disable his arm by dislocating the shoulder or elbow."

John showed them where he would kick, "Remember, kick as hard as you can. The attacker will be stunned and you will have time to draw a weapon. Do not delay before shooting!"

"One more thing, don't assume your attacker will be a man. Assassins come in both genders."

The training went on all afternoon with different people playing the attacker and the defender. Everyone was picking up the instruction very well. Ashley, who had some training at the FBI Academy, was already very good. Carrie and Sara were also good. Virginia and Margie needed work. John was giving more verbal instruction than he normally would.

"I'm going to set up a class for us with some people I know who can help you get better. We will work more on what the companion should be doing. I want all of us to travel in pairs or with a bodyguard for the next few months."

"We will also have sessions at the range with our sidearms. You can never practice too much. All of the security team should fire many rounds each week to stay sharp. You need to hit exactly where you aim and do it quickly. You can practice around the house and in the yard by pointing your finger at small objects. If you have read Angelina's diary, you know Bass Reeves himself taught Grant and Angelina to shoot this way. I learned this way. It works even though you may feel a little ridiculous."

"I want you to know this—I would try to get Sara with a sniper. I will be taking many walks outside the fence to pinpoint potential sniper nests. My greatest fear is them hiring a really good sniper."

Virginia asked, "Who is the best sniper you know?"

"Me."

John's reply in no way sounded like braggadocio. Everyone believed him and several knew he was right.

Everyone went to their house to rest and have a late lunch. John said to Jake, "You have much more skill than I expected. Now I have to make you into a killer, not just a fighter. You will most likely be with Sara and I want you to become a dangerous and lethal man. You've bought into this game because of Sara and you may have to kill to protect her. Don't hesitate!"

Jake said, "I'll do anything to protect her."

"That's really good because I expect you to be near her when the attempt is made. You always seem to be near her these days. I'm beginning to like the idea."

Jake realized John had just given him a great and sincere compliment. He was getting to be accepted by a man he respected immensely. Any of the security people would be happy to get such an endorsement.

That evening, Ashley said, "Wyatt, I think you should show Sara what you showed me about handling an assailant."

"You're right. Let's take the video of you destroying the carjacker and show it to her and Jake."

They left TG with Cassandra and walked over to see Sara. Wyatt said, "Sara, I want to show you a short video of Ashley taking down a carjacker."

"Really! Okay."

Wyatt played the video, and Sara and Jake were wide eyed when it ended. Sara said, "Oh My Gosh! Ashley, you absolutely destroyed that man!"

Wyatt said, "Let me play it back in slow motion and talk you through what she did."

He played it through three times, talking about each movement. They left the video with Sara, who later watched it a half dozen times. She then made Jake practice with her until she could perform every one of the movements correctly and quickly.

The next week involved much more self-defense training. Jake knew smooth movement and simply pointing was the name of the game in skeet shooting. But he quickly realized steadiness and accuracy were the keys to accurate pistol shooting. His targets soon looked like a big ragged hole in the chest or head of the silhouette targets.

John arranged to take Jake for a day of training on the police tactical course, where the focus was on making 'shoot or don't shoot' decisions as the targets appeared. It was much harder than simply shooting a target. It took Jake several hours to become proficient at shooting only the bad guys.

The four new bodyguards arrived early in the week. Javier's two friends stayed with them in the spare bedrooms. Lenny's buds were assigned to Mitch and Frenchy and stayed at their houses. All of them were comfortable with their assignments, including chauffeuring the women to various stores.

The horses were delivered mid-week. TG was excited, as was everyone else. Getting the horses settled in took all of an afternoon with Javier and Jake taking major roles. Sara and Jake rode around for a while, with him giving her pointers because she had only a little riding experience.

By the end of the first lesson, she was doing surprisingly well. Ashley and Carrie wanted to ride, but Ruth told them they should get permission from their obstetricians first. Riding horses was not normally recommended for pregnant women.

Sara and Jake rode around the perimeter on the trail Ashley and Carrie were walking on most afternoons after work. Ashley said, "Well, the horses should make the trail better, but we will have to be careful not to step in anything."

Javier and Wyatt saddled Chief and led him around with TG in the saddle. Javier, who was taller than Wyatt, held TG and Wyatt led the horse. The joy on TG's face was priceless and Ashley, Margie, Ruth, and Virginia marked every step with their cameras. TG was not happy when the ride was over, but had almost as much fun just sitting in his saddle watching the other horses. He would be easy to put to bed when he got over the thrill.

Javier remarked, "He's not afraid of the horses at all, which is both good and bad. We will have to make sure he does not come down here by himself. A horse could hurt him accidentally and that would scare him for a long time. He looks like a natural rider."

Wyatt thought, *"With Grant watching over him, he will learn quickly so he can ride some trails like Grant told me he would."* It was a warm thought.

The self-defense classes were going remarkably well. John thought everyone had reached much of their potential. Margie and Virginia were not very smooth but could handle an attacker with a little luck. They would have an advantage because most attackers would consider them easy marks.

John surveyed the mountains for good sniper positions and found three he would consider if he were the sniper. He and Javier checked the potential spots most days. They did not detect any sign during the first two weeks.

During the third week, they found signs another human had walked between two of the potential sniper nests. They could not find a different nest but were very suspicious.

Javier called John at the end of the week and said, "I think we might have activity up near the nests today. A small car I did not recognize passed here several times. I found it pulled off on a side road into the woods. I also saw a glint on the mountain. May have been the sniper or just a hiker."

John went straight home and they walked a faint trail. They found a spot where someone sat for at least a few minutes but no other signs of activity. A good sniper would leave little sign and John expected this sniper to be a very good one.

The next day was Saturday, and a day of horseback riding was planned. They saddled the horses normally ridden by Jake and Sara, as well as two for Wyatt and Ashley. Wyatt and Ashley were riding TG around the yard and Sara and Jake started up the trail they normally rode. Ashley tied her horse to a hitching rail beside the house and took TG inside. The OBGYN told her to limit her riding and to stop altogether at four months.

Sara challenged Jake to a race. She had quickly become an excellent rider. Just as they said 'go' and their horses lurched ahead, a shot rang out. The lurch of the horses made the sniper miss, but Jake heard the bullet whine past his head. Sara was unaware of the danger. Her horse hit a little dip just as another shot shattered the air. Jake caught up with her and jumped from his horse to take her to the ground. He got them behind a boulder and covered her body with his.

Wyatt jumped from his horse and retrieved a .45-70 from a closet just inside the front door. He spurred Buck and took off for the gate, with Javier close behind. Ashley gave TG to Cassandra and retrieved her favorite rifle—a .300 WSM and ran to the shooting position across the road. John jumped on Ashley's horse and followed Wyatt at full speed. Lenny came running with his .300 WSM and joined Ashley. The sniper took another shot and Sara screamed.

Ashley and Lenny saw the flash of the sniper's rifle and both opened up. They took turns shooting a full clip, while the other one was reloading. They had him pinned down. One of them hit the sniper and he was having trouble moving around. Wyatt and Javier were at the point the sniper used to start crossing the mountain's face. John was not far behind. The sniper was wounded in the leg but still able to fire. Wyatt got close enough for the .45-70 to be effective. He did not want to kill him because he wanted to question him.

Ashley and Lenny kept up the firing and the sniper could not keep Wyatt and Javier in sight. Wyatt crept within fifty yards while Javier covered him. He slipped behind a large tree trunk unnoticed by the sniper. He had a shot and wanted the sniper's gun. When a .45 slug driven by seventy grains of powder hits a gun's trigger mechanism, the gun suffers massive damage—so does the hand holding it. The man was wounded in his leg and the hand Wyatt shot.

Wyatt and Javier walked up to him, followed closely by John. He was so furious he wanted to make the man die a painful death but he had a much better plan.

He told Wyatt and Javier to get something to get the sniper off the mountain, or direct the authorities to his location. A person shot with a .300 WSM suffers massive damage. The sniper was bleeding profusely and the bone was shattered. John put a tourniquet on his leg and got the bleeding stopped.

He asked the man his name and got nothing. "Mister, I'm in a big a hurry and don't have time to be gentle. You will talk, now!"

John took the sniper's wounded right hand and saw it was so mangled he would likely lose it. He came down hard on it and the man screamed.

"My name Ulugbek Umarov."

"That's a good start. Who do you work for?"

"I am a contractor."

"Who hired you?"

No answer. John came down hard on the hand again and quickly received his answer. John could hear the ambulances and police sirens. He had the information he needed for now.

He stood and broke all the bones in the Russian's left hand. He growled, "You were trying to kill my daughter. You are lucky to be alive—so far. I think you will die an agonizing death after providing all the information you have. Regardless, you will never shoot again."

John dialed a number, and a phone rang in Washington. John gave his name and a number to positively identify him himself. He responded to a few more questions to make sure he was who he said he was. The operator put him through to the Deputy Assistant of Operations, whom John knew well.

John explained, "Our housing compound was attacked recently by Russians. We just captured a sniper after he shot at one of us. He's a contract killer used by the Russian mafia and the Russian government. The Denver police will be holding him after he has a little surgery. He has a lot of information and does not like pain. The CIA needs to put a hold on him until you can use enhanced interrogation on him—I didn't have much time and only wanted to know who hired him. I'm betting he has information that will lead to further action against his employers and likely reveal a few high-level spies."

The Assistant Director knew John was a man who could be believed and trusted, "He will be in our custody ASAP."

"Charlie, he tried to kill my adopted daughter—make it fun for him."

"Got it! We will treat him like he shot at our own daughters."

John heard and saw an ambulance at the compound. He had to resist taking the tourniquet off and let Ulugbek bleed out because his knowledge could be valuable to the CIA. He was convinced the man would not be alive much longer.

Another group of police and EMTs were headed toward John and Ulugbek. They bandaged both of his hands. The trip down was not pleasant for Ulugbek and John relished each moan and scream. John asked if the one at the compound was alive.

One of the officers said, "Yes, the wound was superficial from what I am hearing on the radio. They are on the way to the hospital."

John hurried ahead, thinking the six policemen could handle the seriously wounded sniper. His horse was waiting on him as he was trained to do. He rode to the compound as fast as he dared. Harrell grabbed his horse as he came to the houses.

He asked, "How's Sara?"

"Sara is fine except for the fall when Jake knocked her off the horse. Jake is wounded. He covered Sara with his body and has a nasty graze across his back. May spend the night in the hospital, but he will be fine."

The relief was easily seen on John's face, "Where's Sara?"

"She went with Jake. Wyatt and Margie are waiting to take you. Do you want to change? They are."

"Yes, all this blood is his. Ashley or Lenny hit him in the leg. He might lose it and one hand."

He changed quickly and they went to the hospital. Sara was an emotional mess.

"He got hurt saving me. A doctor is stitching the wound and making sure he's not otherwise hurt."

They all sat and waited for the doctor to come see them. He walked into the waiting room and said, "He's lucky. The bullet just cut a channel across his back. Should be back at work next week. He will be sore for a few days. I want to keep him overnight just to make sure. He took a pretty nasty fall from a horse, I understand. May have a concussion. You folks can go see him as soon as he's in a room, which will be about thirty minutes."

Sara asked, "Are you sure he is okay? He saved my life today."

"We can never be absolutely sure but I feel really good about him. We did an MRI while he was out to check the nasty bump on his head and detected no bleeding. We will watch him closely tonight. I assume you are staying tonight, young lady."

"Yes, can I stay in his room?"

"You certainly can. Try to get some sleep. He's going to sleep all night and will likely need a lot of care when you get him home. The placement of the wound will be painful for a while."

Margie and Sara spent the night. John and Wyatt went to the compound to let everyone know about Jake's condition. John planned to call the CIA again to make sure they kept him apprised of the situation with Mr. Umarov.

Chapter Ten

Jake rested well all night—Sara and Margie did not. John and Wyatt came to the hospital early to make sure Jake got a proper breakfast the next morning. He had a normal breakfast, not the broth and Jell-O they feared he would have.

John said, "Jake, welcome to the security crowd! You have killed men who needed killing and now you have a bullet wound. I think you are going to work out just fine. Seriously, you saved Sara's life without thinking of your own safety. I'm going to welcome you to the family, but all the threats are still in effect." John shook his hand and Jake was too busy grinning to grimace at the pain.

The doctor let Jake go home when he did rounds. He told him, "You need to stay quiet for a couple of days so you won't pull the stitches out. You will have a long scar, but it should heal fine. Do you have someone to take care of you for the next few days?"

Sara answered, "Yes, me. I'm even giving him my bed and I will sleep on the couch. I will also make sure he doesn't jump off any horses or get shot again."

"I think you will be well cared for, so I will release you this morning. You can get dressed and the nurses will be by with two prescriptions. Take the antibiotic for ten days—no cheating. The other one is a pain reliever. Take it only when you need it. I think this lady was worth the scar. Good luck!"

Sara said, "Jake, the clothes you wore here are a bloody mess. I'll see if I can find you something clean downstairs. Maybe they will at least have some decent looking pajamas. What size do you wear?"

"Large, I guess."

Sara returned with bright red pajamas and said, "Let me help you get these on. I don't think you can do it by yourself."

John spoke up, "You and Margie, please step outside. Wyatt and I will help him dress."

Jake's shoulders were stiff and his head hurt from the big bump. He tried to get the clothes on by himself, but could not manage.

John said, "I know Sara is going to take care of you, but call me if you need help getting dressed or undressed. I like you better than I did, but not enough to let her dress you." The men had a good laugh, including Jake.

As always, Jake had to leave the hospital in a wheelchair, pushed proudly by Sara. Wyatt waited in a large SUV at the front entrance. Jake had his own captain's chair, but Sara still managed to hold his hand. John just shook his head and said nothing. The die was cast for Sara and Jake, and, deep down, John was happy for them.

Sara quickly went to her room to prepare it for Jake. She arranged several pillows so he could sit up. She brought bottles of water and turned the TV on so he could watch the NFL games. She pulled a chair close to the bed on the side. She thought, "*I might sleep on the couch but I doubt it.*"

She sat in the chair and held his hand. His back started

hurting and she gave him a pain pill. She was determined to take care of him all by herself. He was a willing patient.

Sara got him ready for bed and put her gown on in the extra bath. She made a pallet on the floor and slept by his bed. Margie came in during the night and pulled the covers up on both of them. When John got up for his first cup of coffee, he looked in and was not surprised to see her in his room. He just smiled and walked to the back porch to enjoy his first cup. He saw Wyatt and TG on their porch and strolled over to chat.

"How's Jake this morning? You know he acted as fast as any of us getting her off the horse and behind cover. I'm very proud of him."

"You should be, and so am I. I'm certain he's going to be your sister's husband—your brother-in-law. She slept on the floor in his room. I'm thinking I may want to encourage a wedding rather than discourage it. My threats are having no apparent effect on either of them."

"I think he is gentleman enough that you don't have to worry."

"I am more worried about her right now."

Wyatt chuckled ,remembering his and Ashley's courtship. He just said, "Yep."

With all the other activities going on, Virginia found it difficult to find enough time to plan the celebration of Carrie and Joe's wedding. She and the hotel's staff had been working feverishly to get everything laid out and the invitations mailed. It was going to be a major celebration with a large crowd attending. Even more dignitaries would attend than were at Wyatt and Ashley's wedding. Many people knew Miss Lily Sheffield's story and everyone knew of the Cannons.

The Sheffield family was rather sparse but Virginia expected a nice delegation of Freedom Town descendants. The invitation stressed that it was a celebration of the earlier marriage of a Sheffield and a Cannon—the very first one ever, despite the historical closeness of the two families.

The ballroom decorating began in earnest a week before the event with the hanging of several paintings by Lizzie. One depicted Miss Lily in all her beauty and strength. Another was of Clark and Margo, Carrie's ancestors. Paintings of Dale and Martha and of Manuel Morales were also hung. A card was attached below each painting, which included names and relationship to the pair whose wedding was being celebrated.

The celebration was designed much like a wedding reception. Most men wore a tux and the women wore elegant ball gowns. Carrie was especially striking in her light blue gown trimmed in white lace.

The meal's entree featured succulent prime rib. A delectable crab dish was available for the few non-beef eaters. Eggplant lasagna was available for the even fewer vegetarians. The selection of vegetables, breads, and wine was vast. The desserts included bread pudding, pecan pie, and a heavenly chocolate concoction.

The speeches took a while with many governors and business leaders wanting to make the best short speech of the evening. When they finally finished, Joe and Carrie took the floor for the first dance. Hilary had worked to get Joe ready for the dancing and it showed. Few people detected the awkward movements on certain steps.

Harrell and Carrie danced next, along with Joe and Virginia. Most of the guests danced at least a few dances. Jake and Sara danced almost every dance.

It was the social event of the year, just as Virginia envisioned.

Both she and Harrell beamed all evening.

The security team was on the alert for any attempt at Sara. They and all the bodyguards were armed to the teeth. Fortunately, nothing happened to spoil the evening.

Harrell was besieged by people pushing investments in their state. Most had some type of incentive to offer for an investment. He talked to them more about education on the properties and all promised to help make sure the students got full academic credit for their classes. He also got several governors to agree in principle to the Trust determining the number of game tags for their properties.

The celebration began drawing to a close at midnight. The family and close friends retired to a private room for a nightcap. The toasts were eloquent and heartfelt.

Joe's may have been the best, "I want to toast those who helped me when I didn't even know my name. Without you I would most likely be laying in a mental ward with little memory. Carrie talked to me so much I had to start remembering stuff just to give both of us some peace. Hilary has got me almost fully recovered physically. I don't know if it was those voodoo needles she used or not. I do know I tried hard to get past that daily torture. To all of you, thanks! I love you all!" Joe's toast ended the festivities.

John called the CIA Assistant Director the next morning before anyone else was up at the compound. He asked, "Just checking in to see if we still need to be on high alert for the Russians, or have you brought them in?"

"We brought in everyone who Ulugbek ratted out. Colonel Atashikov was the leader of the group here. Watch the news tonight and you will likely see some arrests. I think you can reduce your alert level. We plan to trade these boys, or at least the leaders, to Russia for American and Ukrainian fighters. We will get word out that they talked and then give them to Russia. A short stay in Siberia and then they will disappear."

"Sounds like a good solution. Wonder if I might be allowed to help with the trade. I'd like to take care of them myself, but they have a fate coming worse than I could do. I'd just like to smile at them when they start across the exchange point."

"Since you gave them to us, I'll bet it can be arranged. The FBI handled the arrests. At least two of them will go on trial soon, so it will likely be a year before the exchanges can be made."

"Okay, I can wait. Just so Sara is safe. Arresting all of them should get their minds off her. Did you get any in Russia?"

"I think the Russian authorities will be arresting a group who does a lot of cybercrime in the next few days. They won't last long either—we have planted information about them working against Russian interests."

"Great work! I do miss it—but not enough to come back."

Lenny and Wyatt walked up just as John ended his call. John commented, "I think the Russian threat is history. Make sure you watch the news tonight. It should feature the roundup of several Russian operatives. Either we will take care of them or let the Russian government take care of them."

Both Lenny and Wyatt knew they had heard all they would get from John. He seemed happy with whatever had been worked out. They talked a while more about the weather and horses and other mundane topics.

The rest of the group walked over to join them and joined in the small talk. Harrell asked if the pheasant hunting season had opened. Wyatt told him pheasant season was set to open the next weekend and they had a full contingent of hunters.

Carrie and Ashley came out last. They both had little baby

bumps if you knew one was there. After they arrived, the talk turned to the double births in the Spring. Everyone was happy. Joe asked if Wyatt thought he was able to work yet.

Wyatt responded, "I think we can put you on limited duty.....if Hilary agrees."

Hilary said, "Limited duty is okay. I think he's ready mentally and the shooting around here didn't seem to bother him. He can't run very well, but we will start working harder on that today. It's just getting him to remember how to run and getting comfortable with it. Give me a week and maybe he can even go on assignments." Joe was happy beyond belief.

Carrie punched his arm and said, "So, you're getting tired of being around me all the time!"

"It's not that! I just have never laid around like this for so long. It has been months since we got married and I need action of some kind."

"Hah! Based on this little bump you've had some action."

Joe blushed and replied, "That's not the action I'm talking about. Chasing down bad guys is in my blood."

John spoke up, "Speaking of chasing down bad guys, everyone needs to watch the news tonight. I heard from D.C. about a few things that may interest you."

Even Virginia had learned it was futile to ask John questions. John was glad she was beginning to understand.

Everyone returned to their homes to have breakfast and get ready for work. Joe rode in with Wyatt.

A Trust plane was taking Rosie and Lawrence back to Alaska and they came by the security office before leaving for the airport. Rosie said, "Wyatt, although there's been no suspicious activity, I have a strange feeling that something's brewing back home—it started before we left and I still have it. We're bringing out a lot of gold and diamonds. The shipments at the end of each week are getting larger and larger. There's enough for someone to try to rob the courier."

"Okay, do you need backup?"

"Not yet. Lawrence has been helping guard the shipments. He has military experience."

"Hmm. We should get him on the payroll. He won't get the same salary as you, but it will be pretty good. No reason for someone to risk their life without getting paid. It will let you check on the gold mine a little more. If I were a criminal, I might pick the diamond mine since it's not ore, but the gold would be easier to sell because there's more gold mines in Alaska."

Rosie and Lawrence were happy. Their combined salaries would build up a nice nest egg since all their expenses were being paid. Lawrence signed paperwork in HR and payroll and they went to the airport.

Mitch, Theresa, and their kids were happy to be coming home. Alaska was beautiful but they were ready to sleep in their own beds. School would start for the kids the following Monday. That did not thrill them, but they had great stories about their summer vacation.

———————————

Harrell received a call from The Purgatoire Land and Cattle Company the following week. Cattle were missing and they needed help if possible. Since the Cannon Trust was invested in the PLCC, Harrell agreed to help and directed Wyatt to fly to La Junta. Wyatt asked Hilary about Joe going and she said it was okay.

Joe was ecstatic just to be working on a case! Since it involved the operation Miss Lily helped establish made the assignment even more meaningful to him. Wyatt decided they should take a helicopter to give them more maneuverability.

The ranch was large even by Trust standards. They touched down in La Junta to pick up Juan Salinas, the ranch manager.

Juan told them which area was missing cattle. He boarded the chopper and they flew to the herd. They soon found suspicious truck tracks.

Juan said, "We've not had any big rigs on this range in months. It looks they're heading to a set of pens on our eastern border—there's a gate and a paved road."

"Where's the nearest sales barn?"

"Almost every county has a small sales barn. But I read about a big sales event near Hays, Kansas this weekend, starting today."

"How far is it?"

"Almost three hundred miles."

Wyatt talked to the pilot, who replied, "We need to refuel. The closest place I know of is in La Junta."

Wyatt said, "Okay, let's go. I don't want to be involved in one of those autorotation things to get back on the ground. I believe you pilots, but I don't want to try it."

The pilot said, "Neither do I!"

They filled up and headed immediately for Hays, Kansas. The sale was beginning that afternoon. The Purgatoire Land and Cattle Company's brand was FT and had been since Freedom Town was established. Just as they had found when Cannon cattle were rustled, they discovered FT branded cattle in several holding pens.

Wyatt told Joe to call the Sheriff while he and Juan started asking questions about who brought the cattle to the sales barn. The man who delivered the cattle was quickly identified, along with the one who was to receive the check. They were sitting together and Wyatt and Juan took a seat several rows behind them. When Joe came in, Juan went outside to meet the Sheriff.

The two men apparently noticed the Sheriff's patrol cars roll up and began to converse with their heads close together. After a brief moment, one of them nodded and they both began to rise.

Wyatt used a deep 'command voice' and said, "Sit down!"

Both men whirled to glare at the speaker. Wyatt and Joe had opened their light jackets so they could see their Glock pistols—their hands rested close to the grips.

The men froze and Wyatt repeated, "Sit down! Now!" They sat.

Juan told the Sheriff about the rustling and that he wanted the cattle back. The Sheriff talked to him and the sales barn manager on how to best handle it. They decided to have the deputies immediately arrest the two men and the culprits surrendered quietly.

Wyatt took the auctioneer's microphone and gave a speech similar to the one he used when they caught the rustlers of the Trust's cattle, "The Sheriff has arrested two men who rustled cattle from the Purgatoire Land and Cattle Company. Their brand is FT. I am Vice President for Security at the Cannon Trust, which owns a share of the company—will be helping them with security from now on. We will prosecute everyone connected to rustling our stock to the fullest extent of the law. Do not buy cattle with the FT brand unless the sellers have papers signed by Juan Salinas, who is sitting here with me. We take this very seriously and will investigate until we catch any and all rustlers. Thank you for your time."

The cattle were loaded back up on the truck and taken home after the Sheriff got all the information he needed for prosecution. Cattle rustling was treated as a serious crime in Kansas. The two men would do a long stretch in prison. A Sheriff's deputy drove the truck, followed by another deputy in a cruiser. The helicopter with a full tank of gas took Juan back to the ranch, and Wyatt and Joe back to Denver.

Although the rustling and arrests involved no action, Joe still felt good. He was on the road to being back in the saddle with a solid security team. Carrie was happy to see him when they got back. She worried the entire time but handled it well.

———————————

Wyatt walked TG around on Chief during the afternoon. Jake and Sara took a long ride around the property and talked about the engagement ring and the wedding. They decided to go ahead and get the ring. She wanted a symbol of their love and did not want to wait until Christmas. She thought it would likely get pushed to a lower level of importance at Christmas and she was right. They decided to visit a jewelry store the next afternoon to pick out a ring.

They planned to surprise John and Margie that night. Jake was a little skittish about surprising John. Sara said, "John's just a big Teddy Bear."

"With you, yes. With me, he's closer to a big, bad Grizzly!"

"You know he likes and respects you. In his world, respect is very important. He even trusts you to back him with a gun. That's bigger than you probably realize."

"I believe you. I just don't like to surprise him when you are concerned. I think this will be fine and dandy with him. I surely hope it is."

They rode back to the stable and Jake unsaddled their horses. Margie walked over and asked him to stay for upper.

At supper, Margie said, "Jake, we still don't know anything about your parents. Can you tell us a little, including when we can meet them?"

"My parents live near Chicago. My dad owns a large investment firm there. My two brothers still live at home and are under Dad's thumb. I did not want to live that way, so I moved out here to try to build my own career. Dad has not forgiven me for moving out and probably never will. He controls everything my mom does. I doubt they will come out for the wedding. My only contact with them is a Christmas card, which he does not sign—just my mom and brothers. It's a pretty messed up family, which is why I don't talk much about them. You are now my family and I appreciate all of you. I love one of you, but I appreciate all of you and the others out here."

Margie said, "I'm so sorry. It must hurt not to see your mom and dad."

"I would love to see my mom and brothers. I try not to think much about my dad. As I said, he disowned me when I went out on my own."

John reached over and patted Jake's shoulder. Jake thought, *"Maybe he is a Teddy Bear. But I still need more evidence!"*

They had a nice time after supper and Jake left late. He and Sara talked more about the engagement, marriage, and looking for rings at lunch the next day.

Sara had never paid much attention to rings. She never had a ring and they had never meant much to her, until now. She was shocked at the price of diamonds. She looked only at the least expensive in the case.

Jake finally told her, "Sara, we are pretty wealthy. We both make good salaries and we both get large checks from the Trust every month. You can have any ring you want. Look at the expensive ones. They are what you deserve."

"But it's so much money! How can we afford it and still have enough for our house and children."

"Believe me when I tell you I am rich and you are rich. My Trust check has always gone into savings and investment accounts. That's about two hundred thousand every year for the last fifteen years. I'm actually a millionaire and you will be in a couple of years. Buy the ring you want, and don't worry about the price."

Sara eventually found the one she wanted. It was in the middle price range and she still cringed over selecting it. It was a beautiful three diamond cluster, with the primary one being well over a carat and the other two about half its size. The jeweler said he could have it sized in a few hours since it only needed a little stretching.

Jake said, "Now don't tell them around the office. We will surprise them tonight, not that anyone is going to be surprised very much."

Jake picked the ring up after work. He and Sara took a walk after supper. He proposed near where their house would sit, on the eastern ridge above the rest of the compound. The crew was already working on Joe and Carrie's house, which would be next door. Construction would start on Sara's house within the week.

It was getting dark when they walked back into the house. Margie immediately knew something was up just by looking at their faces. Then she saw the ring. John was in his room doing something to his gun collection. Jake thought about the song in which the dad tells the girl's date he will be cleaning his gun all night, which was not a pleasant thought.

Margie called him, "John, you need to come in here! Don't bring any of those guns with you. This young man is having enough trouble breathing as it is."

John walked in and saw how happy Sara was, which instantly melted his crustiness. He hugged Sara for a long time.

When he went to Jake, he said, "I gave my best effort to run you off, but you stood your ground. Lesser men would have withered and run for cover. I'm proud to have you in the family. Just remember—don't hurt her or break her heart. I will still put a hurting on you that you won't soon forget."

John then grinned and said, "I like her choice for a husband."

Margie went to the phone and called Wyatt, "You and Ashley need to come over here and see what your sister has done."

They grabbed TG and hustled to his parents' house. They were fairly sure what it was. Wyatt shook Jake's hand while Ashley admired the ring and hugged Sara.

Before long, everyone at the compound collected at the house, and a celebration erupted. Harrell said, "Jake, I don't want to put any pressure on you, but just remember I will give John all the time he needs to inflict whatever he has promised if you mistreat her." All the men volunteered to help John. Jake and Sara blushed and hugged.

Virginia and Margie were sitting in a corner, hatching up plans for a party to announce the engagement and throw another huge wedding.

With the Russian threat removed, Sara and Jake decided to go on a real date the next evening. They planned to go to dinner and take in a movie. The movie was a recent release about a girl being kidnapped and her father, a former Marine, taking on the gang rather than paying the ransom. There was a great deal of action and they both enjoyed it.

They were talking about the movie and when they neared the car, Sara said, "Jake, I see four men near our car and they are eyeing us. I don't like it."

The four men moved quickly toward them to block their path. Two stayed back while two others confronted the couple. The ones in the back held knives.

One of them said, "Stop and give us your money! Stay calm and no one will get hurt."

He then saw the large diamonds on Sara's hand and grabbed

her wrist. Sara instantly remembered Ashley's video. She did not resist. Instead, she lunged forward and headbutted the man in his nose! He grabbed his nose and she kicked him hard in his groin. When he grabbed his privates and leaned over, she drove a knee into his shattered nose and he dropped loose-limbed to the concrete. Three blows in three seconds!

Jake was also busy. The other man in front grabbed for Sara's purse, her concealed carry purse. Jake drove a short jab into the man's throat, kicked him in the groin, and drove a sidekick into the outside of his knee. He hit the concrete at the same time as Sara's assailant.

The other two stepped forward, flashing knives. Sara took a step back and a black Glock suddenly appeared in her hand.

One of them said, "Little lady, I don't think you can pull the trigger."

"Try me!"

He reached into his coat pocket and drew out a snub nosed revolver, but he never got it level. Sara shot him in the bicep, followed by a slug to his kneecap. She saw out of the corner of her eye the other man trying to cut Jake. She kept shooting— bicep and the outside of his knee. Four men writhed on the concrete.

Jake and Sara were breathing hard with the adrenaline flush. Jake said, "Holy Cow! How many times did you shoot?"

"Four."

"Wow. I heard only one roar!"

A crowd had gathered quickly and someone called the police, who arrived with weapons drawn. Sara put the gun on the ground and stood back. Jake explained what had happened.

Sara added, "I work for the Cannon Trust's Security Division and have a permit for the gun."

"The man who called 9-1-1 said he heard a shot, as in one

shot. I see four bullet wounds."

"Well, I was in a hurry."

"So you just shot wildly, right?"

Jake laughed and said, "Officer, she is the best pistol shot I've ever seen! I guarantee you that she hit within an eighth of an inch of where she aimed."

"Really! She should be shooting competitively if she is that accurate."

The policeman then laughed and said, "You two put down all four of these punks! They are a well-known group of petty thieves who have been menacing this part of town for months. Looks like they all need an ambulance. They will go from the hospital to jail. I need you to write an affidavit and sign it. Then, take your gun and you are free to go. I doubt you will have to testify, but it's possible."

When they arrived home, John asked, "How was the movie?"

Sara answered with a grin, "Movie was great but the fight after the movie was even better!"

Jake said, "John, if I ever make this girl mad, I will be sleeping on your couch so you can protect me! Let me tell you what happened....."

Chapter Eleven

The pheasant hunting was in full swing. Frenchy flew to the farms to make sure everything was running smoothly. He talked to many of the hunters during and after the hunts to see what kind of feedback he could get.

Most of the hunters were experienced and they liked to talk. The two things most often mentioned were a lodge and more dogs for the hunts. He assured them a small first-class lodge would be open the next season, and they would double the complement of dogs.

When he got back to Denver, he talked to the Board and told them what the hunters wanted. In some ways, the desires were different for the young strong hunters and those who were past their prime. The younger hunters wanted to walk long fields with the dogs, whereas the senior hunters preferred to block at the end of the fields.

He told them the best pheasant hunting was in South Dakota. If they really wanted to jump in, they would need a couple of pieces of land devoted to pheasant hunting, and build small lodges. The Board directed him to look for developed land or raw land they could develop. They were willing to invest in three more places, especially if they could grow crops and pheasants.

He said, "Okay, what's the budget for land and development cost? The lodges do not have to be really fancy, but they do have to be pleasant and comfortable, with good food. I think a lodge will cost around three hundred thousand dollars. I don't know about the cost of land."

They said, "You have up to seven hundred thousand to build the two lodges in Kansas. We will let our land people start looking for properties in South Dakota now. They know more about land and land values. What about the lodges in Texas and Louisiana?"

"Those likely need to be built better. They will need to withstand the occasional hurricane and they will be used year round. My best guess is they will be at least half a million each. I can get you some more exact costs if you approve of the idea. The farms are in the heart of great hunting and fishing, so I am not recommending adding to our holdings unless something comes along you want for farming."

"Okay, get us estimates so we can get started. What about big game?"

"We have great land for developing big game hunting. The two properties that contain part of the Missouri Breaks have wonderful habitat for mule deer and whitetail. We can develop it into trophy property without much effort. Smaller lodges may also work there. Those properties can be used for more than big game. They can have great goose hunting and good duck hunting by planting better feed and keeping the cattle away during certain times of the year."

"The mountainous ranches could have great elk hunting. A quality elk hunt can sell for ten thousand dollars or more for a week if we have good bulls, particularly if it comes with a good lodge. Some hunters, however, want to tent camp—they have dreamed of it all their lives. With quality bulls involved, the ranches will have more problems with poaching, which will require more riders all year. Once the season opens, our guides can be on the lookout and we can send people to discourage the poaching. A few arrests and prosecutions will help a lot."

Harrell said, "All I can say is 'go for it.' Your duties will change more toward game management than security. Your pay will be adjusted to match your increased duties. Remember, we have construction crews and land people to help get this done. I think outfitting at the level we are talking about will be a nice little gold mine. I will talk to Wyatt about your adjusted duties. But you will still be on call for any major security developments."

Frenchy was happy to get the promotion and the new duties. Theresa would be happy with the new salary. He was not happy to be leaving security because he liked the security team members—more than liked, he trusted them. He would be happy to go into a firefight with any of them on his six. They were a superb team. But he would still have one foot in security.

Wyatt was not happy to lose Frenchy. He was a solid performer who always kept up his end of the job. He and Ashley talked and decided to throw a party to celebrate his promotion. It would be a small party with only the people who lived in the compound, along with Mitch and Jana. Tommy and his family were invited since he would be working with Frenchy on the properties and because Wyatt liked him.

———————————

Wyatt cooked steaks on an outside grill and Margie and Ruth brought over vegetable dishes. Everyone had a great time. Mitch and Frenchy's children rode the horses and loved it. Javier and Jake spent time showing them how to do it right. Most were riding well before the party was over, partially because the horses were gentle. Little Tom, who had owned Chief previously, spent time with Chief and TG.

The group was like many others gathered across the country in the Fall, except most were millionaires many times over, and all had very well-paying jobs. Although a wealthy group, they did not really act like it. Virginia had her moments, as did Carrie, but for the most part, they were just a group of people who shared a common relative who had been smart enough to ensure their offspring were well taken care of. The party lasted until well after dark. They enjoyed each other's company, so no one felt the need to leave early.

Frenchy asked Harrell if he had thought of where he would be officed. Harrell responded, "Hmm, I had not even thought of it. Wyatt, you got enough space for him to stay on your floor?"

"Sure, we have several available offices. We can set him up and maybe the person who will be handling the reservations and dealing regularly with the hunters. I have a feeling he's going to need more people and more room by next year. I think we can handle that growth."

Tommy said, "We also have vacant offices and are going to have more soon. I have too many people between me and the properties. I'm clearing out some unnecessary barriers."

Harrell responded, "That's what I like to hear! I've got to find a new VP of Finance and I think we are going to have a couple of new Board members. I will the lawyers looking at what it will take to add a couple more. Five is not many for an organization our size."

Virginia overheard him and said, "You need at least one woman if you add any new slots. It's time the Trust entered the twenty-first century."

All the women gave a cheer. The men nodded their heads in agreement.

When the party broke up, everyone returned home. Harrell asked, "Virginia, do you have anyone in mind for the Board?"

"I don't know exactly what you want in a Board member, but Ashley comes to mind. She has a good head on her shoulders. She has done wonders with the education project, which was her idea to begin with."

"She would be a solid selection. She can certainly handle the work, but I'm not sure she would take it. I think she wants to settle down and raise a family."

Harrell called a Board meeting for the next week. He began the meeting, "I have been thinking that we need to consider enlarging the Board. I asked the lawyers how we might do it and they found a little noticed addendum to our original charter, which was signed by Clark and Grant themselves. They apparently realized the Trust would be much larger some day and complicated enough to need more Board members than called for in the original charter. They prepared an addendum to the agreement, which allows the number of Board members to increase as the operation grows. The Board can vote to expand the number of members, without the descendants voting. In the same document, they modified the stipulation that Board members have to be Cannon descendants—a Sheffield or a Robley descendant is also qualified. Let's first address the size of the Board issue." After a brief discussion, the motion was made and passed to add two members to the Board.

Harrell mentioned the new Board members could initially be selected by the present Board, with the descendants voting for subsequent members. He then brought up the idea of needing at least one woman on the expanded Board. Everyone agreed if they could find a qualified woman, she should be offered the position. They started talking about possible new members. Ashley's name came up more than once, but no agreement was reached.

Harrell finally said, "Let's look through the list of people we send checks to each month. We should be able to identify worthy candidates."

Harrell later decided to talk to Ashley to gauge her interest, "Your name came up several times as a possible new Board member. If it were offered, would you be interested?"

"Sorry, but I'm not the least bit interested. I'm going to finish the school year and find my replacement. Then I'm going to stay home and raise my two children. I really don't want a job."

"The Board only meets every two weeks, so you would not be going in to work every day."

"I understand that, but I also don't know much about business. A Board seat is just not in my wheelhouse. I can tell you who would make a good Board member—Ruth. She has owned her own business, a construction company. Ask Wyatt about what all she had to do to get over her dad's mismanagement to make it successful."

"Hmm. I had not thought of her. But you're right, she might make a fine Board member. I'll talk to Wyatt. She's pretty low profile now but he would know her from before."

Harrell asked Wyatt about Ruth and he responded, "She took over a business her dad had run into the ground. He was an evil man and the firm was in terrible shape. I looked at all the numbers, and she single handedly brought the company back by doing jobs others might have considered too small or whatever. She paid off all the debts and made a good living for her and Ashley. Ashley was strong-willed and Ruth managed to get her into womanhood quite well. I think she would be a fine choice."

"I'll talk to her. Do you have anyone else to recommend, possibly from the Sheffield family?"

"Joe is the only Sheffield I know."

"You got a recommendation for VP of Finance?"

"I think you need someone from the outside. I don't run in

the finance circles so I don't know those people. But don't rule out Jake. John has checked him out as much as anyone can be checked out. He has impeccable character. He may be younger than you want, but I think he could do the job."

"Hmm, you have given me some names to think about. Is Joe well enough to handle the two jobs?"

"I think he is. I would not mind going into any hairy situation with him. I'm seeing no problems with his mental ability. He still has mobility issues, so I don't want to put him out front in situations that might involve a firefight. I think he can hold his own but he can't run if it becomes necessary. But Hilary has him close on those remaining issues."

Harrell had some thinking to do. He was fairly sure the Board would support his choices. He went to talk to Ruth after lunch.

"Ruth, we are expanding the Trust's Board of Directors by adding two positions. You have been recommended to me for one of those positions. Do you have any interest?"

"I'm not a Cannon descendant. Isn't that a requirement for being on the Board?"

"Actually, we recently discovered that a Sheffield or a Robley descendant is also qualified. Wyatt thinks of you and he seems to know a lot about how you ran your construction company. He says you brought it back from some bad management and rough spots."

"He should know. He spent a lot of time investigating the company when he was with the FBI. I'm proud of saving the company and making it profitable. I hated to sell it but I wanted to be close to my grandbabies. Let me talk to Lenny and think on it for a few days. I think I will be interested."

Harrell had his staff pull the names of everyone who received a Trust check, along with a thumbnail sketch of their current positions. More descendants were qualified for the finance position than for the Board position. He and the other Board members narrowed the list to five for each position. The Board implicitly agreed to Ruth for one of the Board positions.

Security was given the names for the other positions. John and Sara did thorough background checks. Several were dropped because they had run afoul of regulatory Boards—one was likely to be indicted any day for fraud. Another was far too sketchy for such a high level position. A few were from back east and could not be counted on to come to the regular Board meetings. Other potential candidates pulled their name from consideration because they already had a full plate.

The Board spent an entire day discussing the people and the jobs. Ruth was voted in quickly. Joe was discussed for a long time, primarily because of his medical condition. He was selected late in the day. Jake's age was a major point of discussion—he was young for a VP. After considering an internal candidate, Jake was the choice. Now Harrell had to convince Ruth, Joe, and Jake to take the jobs.

Ruth said 'yes' quickly since she had been considering the job for several days. Ashley, Margie, and Virginia put a lot of pressure on her to accept, as did Wyatt. Lenny joked that she would officially be his full-time boss, not just at home.

Joe was not at all sure about being a Board member and asked for a couple of weeks to think about it. Jake was shocked by the offer and also asked for a couple of weeks. Joe and Jake were honored to even be considered, much less being offered the jobs.

––––––––––––––––

Joe knew he had to spend a night or two at Freedom Town. Wyatt said he would take him and Carrie down there. Carrie was totally sold on him joining the Board, but he wanted additional input from Miss Lily.

Jake also wanted to get away to think. Wyatt suggested he and Sara go to the restored cabin across the road from the Interpretive Center. Clark and Margo had lived there a while and it was where Martha and the boys had done so much to help Dale. The restored site was closed on Mondays and Tuesdays so they could stay Sunday night and Monday night.

Joe had a vivid dream the first night at Freedom Town. Miss Lily came in the dream and almost scolded him, *"Why are you out here seeking my opinion? You know you are qualified to be the first Sheffield on the Trust's Board—the Trust that controls the money I left for our descendants. Manny and I will be with you all the way. Go take what is yours. You will do a great job!"* Manny was in the background but kept quiet.

A complication arose regarding Jake and Sara staying in the restored cabin—John! When they approached John, Wyatt was there to support them.

Jake said, "Sir, we would like to spend a couple of nights in Clark's restored cabin. If you insist, you can go with us. I need to think about the Trust's offer for the VP of Finance position. Wyatt thinks staying there might help me with the decision."

John just sat quietly for a long moment. He knew why Wyatt wanted them to stay there, but was not happy about the request, "A short few months ago I would have told you that you needed to get out of my sight and never come back. I might have used some pretty bad language to convince you to forget it. I know Wyatt's motivation, but she is my daughter. This is a tough question. I trust both of you but I know what can happen between two people in love. But you have my blessing. Please don't disappoint me. I'm not threatening you now but I am depending on you being a gentleman and Sara being a lady. Of course, I will still hurt you if you're not, but I am trusting the two of you, as hard as that is for me to say. Don't let me down."

Sara gave him a big hug and Jake shook his hand from a distance. He was sweating profusely.

John turned to Margie and said, "Give this young man a glass of water—I think his throat is dry." It was.

They went to stay at the cabin as soon as possible. Neither was sure what to expect. The first night Jake had a vivid dream. A person who looked a lot like the paintings of Clark entered his dream, as did a woman who looked a lot like Margo.

The man said, *"Why are you stalling on accepting the job? You can handle it. We know it and so do others. You have the education and training. We want people of your character protecting the wealth we put aside for our descendants. You have a chance to be directly involved with protecting and growing those assets. We will be behind you and helping with important decisions."*

The dream was so real that Jake woke up and could not go back to sleep. He went into the living room and built a fire to ward off the chill.

He was sitting wrapped in a heavy blanket when Sara came in. She was cold and somewhat baffled at what had happened. She had dreamed about two women and they looked like the paintings of Martha and Margo. They talked to her about being a Cannon woman and bearing Cannon children. It was not frightening, but nothing like that had ever happened to her. She got under the blanket with Jake. They talked for a few minutes about their dreams. The room warmed as the fire worked its magic. Both went to sleep in each other's arms. The sun was peeking over the eastern horizon when Jake awakened.

Sara was still asleep. He looked at her sleeping and knew he wanted to be with her for the rest of his life. He also knew he would accept the job.

When Sara's eyes opened, she saw Jake looking at her and knew he was the one she wanted. He said, "Let me ease out and build the fire up. I'll get the coffee pot going. You just stay here and keep warm."

She was warm from an internal glow. It warmed her body better than anything ever had. She had to remember the promise they had made John. It would have been a lot easier to forget it.

Jake came back with two cups of coffee. His was black. Hers had Italian Sweet Cream, just the way she liked it. He got back under the blanket and warmed up. After a few moments, he said, "I am getting my own blanket to keep more layers between us."

She said, "I think that would be a good idea for a lot of reasons."

They were still in their separate blankets when someone knocked on the door. It was John and Wyatt with breakfast.

Wyatt threw a couple of pieces of wood on the fire and asked, "How did you sleep?"

Jake responded, "Very well. But I had the most vivid dreams I've ever had. It was like Clark himself came to visit me. I know it sounds crazy, but it seemed so real."

Sara added, "My dream had Margo and Martha in it. It was more real than any dream I've ever had. They talked to me and welcomed me to the family. I swear it was like they just came by for a social visit."

They all ate breakfast. It was fast food breakfast. Jake said, "I would like to stay another night. I have never experienced anything like this. Have you?"

"Yes. Grant and Dale, along with others, have visited in my dreams when I go to Dale's cabin. It's a little weird, but I get good guidance from those dreams. They are so real."

John said, "Margie and I have experienced it and Joe also has down at Freedom Town. You don't really want to talk about it to outsiders because someone may put you in an asylum. It's does seem so real when it's happening. That's why I agreed for you two to come out here. Looks like you have been in those blankets for a while."

"We have been. It's hard to go back to sleep after something like that happens, and it was cold about daylight. We watched the fire, caught up in our own thoughts for a couple of hours."

"Okay, one more night. Just be careful. When you are in love, some things happen that are hard to stop once you get started. I remember those days."

"Thanks, John. It seems life has become clearer after the dreams. I know what I'm going to do. I will be working with you guys soon if Harrell's offer is still open. Clark told me I could do it and he wanted me to be looking over his and Grant's investments. He said he would help me through the rough spots."

"Margo was so nice to me in the dream. I wish I could have met her in real life."

"Maybe you did."

John said, "I hope she didn't say you were pregnant!"

"Not yet, but I will be coming here often after we are married. Kind of an early alert system it seems." Everyone laughed at her comment.

Jake said, "Tell Margie we will be home early and probably will be wanting one of her marvelous breakfasts. This one was good, but it wasn't Margie's!"

Jake and Sara puttered around the cabin all day. There was nothing much to do so they just sat and talked all morning. They talked about children and life together. Their house had been started ten days ago. Like all construction, it went on in spurts. The foreman said he thought they would be finished with Carrie's by around June or a little earlier. They were trying to finish before her baby arrived, but it was not likely possible.

Sara wanted to make sure she had a room dedicated to her computers. She could work from home with the right setup. Jake would also have an office. A Vice President would make a lot more than he was now making. He wanted the house to be open and big enough to accommodate two or three children.

Jake knew the Trust checks had the signature of the Vice President of Finance. He wondered if his dad would even notice or care. He also wondered if any of his family would show up for the wedding. Probably not. The thought made him sad, but not for long.

The stables near the cabin contained an array of horses. He called Tommy about riding that afternoon.

Tommy replied, "Let me come look at what's there. Some are stallions we let others breed to, along with a few other horses. I'll run down and pick out a couple for you. There's land behind the Center you can ride on. I'll be there in a few minutes."

Tommy and Cole drove up in less than an hour. Tommy said, "I saw you two riding pretty well the other day. Jake, you can ride this stallion. He's gentle for a stallion—just keep him under control. Sara, the little gelding should be just right for you. We will help you get them saddled and across the road. Don't try to ride them on the road. Some idiot will blow a horn or something and they might blow up on you."

"Great! We just wanted to ride a little. Not much to do in the cabin. We are going to spend the night."

"Does John know?

"Yes. He approves.

"Good! I don't want to get crosswise with that man."

The ride was relatively brief but highly enjoyable. Tommy and Cole were still in the stable and helped care for the horses. It was almost dusk when they left. Jake and Sara went to eat at a nearby restaurant. The food was good and both ate too much.

When they returned to the cabin it was time for bed and to see what this night brought. Both were anxious to find out. Jake built a large fire and they got their blankets. They were dozing in each other's arms before long. As the fire died down, the dreams started.

Chapter Twelve

The dreams started as soon as they fell asleep, or so it seemed. Clark came and talked to Jake about the strategies they used initially, which were fairly rudimentary for the present day. They basically bought land that had a good chance to have gold. Grant preferred to buy land good for cattle or horses. He bred high-quality horses and owned some of the foundation stock that later became the famous Quarter Horse strain. Banks and hotels were also in their wheelhouse.

Clark was interested in knowing about investment strategies used today. Jake explained, or tried to explain, stock markets and various financial instruments. The Trust was very diversified now, but land, horses, and cattle were still part of the Trust's core strategy, along with banks, hotels, and resorts. The Trust's wealth was growing steadily and every descendant was wealthy, unless they wasted their money.

Clark was delighted their descendants were still enjoying the fruits of his and Grant's labors. He was also glad the core of the wealth was still centered on what he and Grant invested in so many years ago.

Margo talked to Sara about her years as a captive of her own family. She did not understand how someone could hurt their own flesh and blood, even if it were by marriage. Margo said, *"John took care of them down in Mexico. You don't have to worry about them anymore. He has also taken care of the Russians who came after you. We also had to fight to survive and prosper. I thought they had killed Clark one time. We had a hard ride to get to a Denver doctor. We rode in the back of a wagon, with me holding his head all night. Medicine was not so good back then, but his strong spirit brought him through. You also have a man with a strong spirit. Stick with him. He will always protect you and those children you want."*

"You are so bright and know those computers so well. Clark was smart, but all he had was a pencil and paper. Your kids will make you proud when they grow up. They will get both your and Jake's intelligence. They will lead the Trust in the next generation. Good night. Get some sleep so John won't be concerned with shadows under your eyes."

The dreams seemingly stopped as soon as they had begun. Both Sara and Jake slept soundly the rest of the night. Jake put a log on the fire a couple of times and they slept on the floor in front of the fireplace. They lay in each other's arms until dawn, when Jake made them a pot of coffee. They drank the coffee and talked more about their dreams. Both were as happy as they had ever been.

They were ready to depart by full sunup. Jake could almost smell Margie's bacon cooking. Sara said, "We will visit this place when we face tough decisions. I feel calmer and more collected than at any other time in my life. For me, it was almost like finding love from a mother who I've never known. I know Margie loves me, but this felt different. Amazing experience!"

Jake said, "I agree. I've never had anyone talk to me like that. My father kicked me out because I wouldn't follow his wishes for my life. He bullied my mother mentally and she could not support me. We are very much alike in not having good parental guidance. John and Margie are the closest we have, but the last two nights made me feel like I have loving ancestors who will help me get through life's rough spots. Leaving us wealthy is not so bad either."

Margie was just taking the biscuits out of the oven when Jake and Sara arrived. Everyone sat down to a big breakfast. John asked, "Well, what happened? Was it a fruitful two nights?"

Jake responded, "More than you can imagine! I expect the experience will change my life. Clark visited in my dreams both nights. An old codger stayed in the background, but Clark was the star both nights. I will be taking Harrell's offer. Clark gave me straightforward advice. The second night, we talked about the changes in the Trust since he and Grant set it up. It was an illuminating talk—my dad never talked with me that way. It changed my thinking so much."

Sara said, "Margo came to me, along with Martha. It was what I think a talk with a mother and grandmother would be like. Margie, you have been a great mother to me, but the talk with them was so life-changing. We did not talk about any specific children but we talked about raising children. We will apparently have several. No, John, they will not be coming soon."

"Good!"

Jake said, "John, I'm so glad you let her go with me. I'm positive you can trust us after these nights. Not because we did not want to go further or your threats, but because we respect each other. You don't have to worry about us. We will not have sex until we are married."

"You know, deep down I knew you wouldn't. It's just that

Sara was hurt so much in her early life, I want no one to ever hurt her again—I couldn't help myself. You are going to make her a fine husband."

Jake said, "We need to talk to the builder. We are going to need space for Sara's computers and an office for me. I think we will need bedrooms for three children and us. I think that adds two rooms. I hope we are in time. I need to go talk with Harrell about the job before he leaves for work. I also need to thank Wyatt for pushing us to stay in the cabin."

John said, "You go talk to Harrell and I will get Wyatt and Ashley to come over here. I'm sure Margie wants to talk to y'all."

Jake walked over to Harrell's and knocked. Harrell came to the door in his robe and said, "Come in. I hope you have good news for me."

"I have news and I hope it is good for both of us. I will accept the job offer. I have spent two days thinking about it and I know I can do it if you will help me. You know I'm jumping a few levels and don't know exactly what you expect."

"You are going to do a great job! I will help you understand the various expectations. You will have a good group to handle the day-to-day activities. You will need to provide guidance and let them do the work. That's likely the biggest adjustment for you, and the hardest thing to do. Come by the office today and I will have the paperwork ready. I assume you will have to give notice to your present company."

"I'm sure. I wasn't thinking about quitting so I'm not sure about the rules. I will go in and get the process started this morning. I will come by your office when I have the information."

"Welcome aboard! I think you will find us a good organization with lots of interesting people and history."

Jake returned to see Sara and found Wyatt and Ashley were also there. TG was with Cassandra. Wyatt shook his hand, "I understand you had more dreams at the cabin."

"We did! They were the most realistic dreams I've ever had. As I told you yesterday, I dreamed the first night. Those were specifically related to joining the Trust. Last night, it was more of a conversation. We talked about finance and how he and Grant put together the holdings and formed the Trust. I told him about modern finance and he understood quickly. He must have been a brilliant man."

"He certainly has that reputation. He had a brilliant mind for business and Grant had one for property. They bought only a few duds, which is remarkable. Knowing the difference between real gold strikes and the hundreds of flash-in-the-pan strikes was a skill the two of them combined seemed to have. It was said Grant could look at a piece of land and know if there were real gold chances. Clark could look over a mine's records and tell if they gave a true picture of the property. Having the intelligence to set up the Trust to protect their descendants from frittering away the fortune was a brilliant stroke. Many fortunes were made in the late 1800s, but few remain today."

"Sara, how was your time at the cabin?"

"Great! Margo and Martha came the second night and we just talked. It will make a great difference in my life, I think. I will never be the same and I know Jake is the one for me."

Ashley gave her a hug. "We're almost sisters now and the bond will be even stronger when you are married. I've never had a sister."

"Nor have I!"

It was time to get ready to go to work. Jake went to his apartment to get dressed. He had less conflict in his mind than he had had in a long time. He had even come to accept his family's rejection. He would send them an invitation to the wedding as a courtesy, but would not get his hopes up. He had a family even if some of them showed up only in his dreams.

He went to his employer to submit his resignation. He was informed he had to work for thirty days from his resignation. He had been hoping for two weeks but expecting thirty days. At least he knew the exact day. Of course, he had more than thirty days of vacation coming. He asked about it and was told he could use his vacation and leave immediately. If he stayed, he would be paid for those days. He elected to leave immediately.

He left and went by Harrell's office with the news. Harrell had the paperwork ready to sign with him starting the next day officially. The new Vice President's salary was three hundred thousand dollars—quite a raise! The salary combined with his descendant's checks put his total annual income a little over half a million dollars, which almost took his breath away. He was tempted to call his dad but passed on the thought. He did go down to the security floor to tell Sara.

She was thrilled they would be working only a short elevator ride from each other. Wyatt and John also came over to welcome him to the work family. After visiting everyone, he went back up to Harrell's office to be introduced to the people who worked in finance. They were a little surprised at his age. His office was almost as big as his apartment—it included a private bath and a desk that could land a small plane. He sat at the desk and realized it was larger than his previous office.

Jake went to the payroll office to be added. It only took a signature and a social security number, plus a few questions about deductions. He went back to see Sara and nothing much was going on. Sara wanted to see his office so they went back up.

She said, "This is the biggest office I've seen, except for Harrell's. You might get lost in here."

He introduced her to the office staff as his fiancé. He had two secretaries and five others in his suite. He planned to carefully analyze each job description and corresponding workload to determine all the positions were needed.

Before they left, he asked the secretary to pull the personnel files on all the employees so he could get to know them. He had once read the book *The Prince* by Machiavelli. It said a Prince should do all the atrocities early when taking over a country. His professor in a management course said this relates to firings and downsizing, so he wanted to get those kinds of things addressed during his first few weeks.

He realized firing someone would be difficult, but he had to have an efficient operation. In his limited experience, one or two people who did not have enough to do caused problems for everyone.

He and Sara went to lunch. She talked about the wedding even though it was still nine months away. He did his best not to show he was not much interested in the planning. She asked a question about his family attending the wedding.

Jake responded, "I want to invite them but I doubt they will attend. Don't plan for any of them to be involved in the wedding for sure. My mother might come and maybe the brothers. I certainly do not expect my dad."

"I'm so sorry. I will have John and Margie. John will give me away. Ashley will be the matron of honor along with Carrie. Who will you be using for your groomsmen and best man?"

"I'm not sure. Probably Wyatt for the best man. Or maybe Harrell. The guys you work with will likely be the other groomsmen. I'm not sure. To tell the truth, I haven't thought much about it."

"Margie and Virginia want to know. They are planning more and more each day. I think it's best to just let them run with it. They're really pushing me for a date. Virginia says a Vice President marrying the stepsister of another Vice President will truly be the social event of the year. I think her being limited on Carrie and Joe's wedding means we are going to be her showcase wedding. Maybe we should just run away and find a judge."

"I would love it! But after John softened me up, he would turn those two women loose on me. You would be married to a simple mud puddle."

"I'm afraid you're right. Let's get back to work. What are you doing this afternoon?"

"Looking over the employment records of people in my bailiwick. It will be very boring, I'm sure."

Jake was correct, it was seriously boring. But he found a few people who seemed to do very little. He put these in one pile for further consideration. He decided he needed a confidant who knew what people really did. He decided to look over the secretaries since they often knew more about what was really going on. Nadine, his personal secretary seemed a likely choice. He planned to study the files for several days and talk with her before he made any decisions. Before he knew it, quitting time arrived.

He and Sara had a meeting with Willie Gray, the Head of Construction, to see if they could alter their plans a little. Willie responded, "We already have the foundation poured, but we can add another floor. You can easily add three bedrooms upstairs and very little will change downstairs. We will have to make sure the bottom floor has substantial walls. Let me take the blueprints to the architect and get them adjusted. This might put us a week or two behind schedule."

"That's okay, if we can get these changes made. We both are going to need an office now."

"I knew she carried a big load in the IT area. Why do you need one now?"

"I have changed jobs. I'm now working for the Trust."

"What will you be doing?"

"I am the new Vice President of Finance."

"Yes, Sir, I will have a copy of the new plans tomorrow morning. We'll get right on it." He was amazed at the motivation generated by the title of Vice President.

He and Sara were going horseback riding. The weather was typical late fall weather for Colorado—cool bordering on cold and clear. A few clouds seemed to be building in the west, which would likely bring the first snow. Their ride was very relaxing. A few snowflakes began to fall just as they finished the ride shortly after dark.

John was having a drink and Jake joined him. Margie had supper ready soon. It was chicken and dumplings, which was one of their favorites. It was also Wyatt's favorite so he and Ashley came over with TG. TG was beginning to eat real food and he also liked the dish. Everyone sat around the table and talked about their day.

_____

No one was experiencing any excitement except Ashley. The first bus trip for the wives was coming up soon. The women on the ranches were excited. They would take the bus to the nearest large town to begin Christmas shopping. It was the first trip to a large city for some of them.

Ashley intended to go on the first couple of trips to make sure everything went smoothly. Cassandra and Wyatt would take care of TG, with Margie serving as backup. Ashley was not overwrought like she sometimes got. Ruth was going on the bus trip to help prepare for her new Board position. It would be good for her to get some experience with the workers on the remote properties.

Jake said he had been reading personnel files to get to know his people. He said, "It seems like I have a lot of deadwood in the finance area. I guess I'm going to irritate some people almost before I get started."

John and Wyatt both said if he was fair, he might be surprised. Wyatt added, "Everyone in the division knows who's not pulling their weight. They may be happy to get them out of the way. Gale was not a very good manager and ran a loose ship. I'm thinking you are likely to find quite a few deadbeats."

Margie said, "Oh, Jake, you're not firing people just before Christmas, are you? That seems so cruel."

"They will be taken care of through the first of the year. Some will retire. We will try to help the others find employment. Some just seem not to be doing much. I am going to use my secretary, Nadine, to give me more insight on who the good and bad performers are. I have seven secretaries. With computers, I'm not sure they are all needed. I see a lot of nail filing going on. I just don't think the division has enough work for all of them."

Margie asked Ashley the next morning, "When do you leave next week?"

"Ruth and I will catch the bus in Williston, North Dakota, and pick up half the women from each of the two ranches south of there. We will take them to Bismarck for two days of shopping. We have a few activities planned beyond shopping. Then, we will take those women back and pick up the other half at each ranch. A few of the women have been to larger cities, but this will be the biggest for most of them. Walmart is going to have an invasion, I fear. But that's why we are going. I think it will be a great experience for them. The cultural events should be even more exciting for them. We probably will need another bus to do this right. Wish I knew someone at the top of the Trust and maybe someone in the finance area." They had a good laugh over her comment.

Margie said, "I know a couple of women who can help get you an appointment with both of them. If I threaten to cut the biscuits off, I bet the finance dude would listen to you. Speaking of biscuits, I better get home and cook a batch. I think Jake is coming out before his big day and take Sara in with him." Sure enough, his car was in the driveway.

Margie finished the breakfast while Sara and John got dressed. Jake nibbled on the biscuits while waiting. Actually, he ate a whole biscuit by pinching off a little bit at a time. The sausage was from a little place north of Denver where Margie bought most of her pork.

John came in and asked, "Were you able to get the house changed to what y'all now want."

"Yes. The strange thing about it, Willie Gray was explaining the difficulties and such and asked me what I did. I told him I was the new Vice President of Finance, and all his problems seemed to disappear. We are going to have the same footprint, but it will now be two stories. The kid's bedrooms will be upstairs."

"Kids! What do you mean, kids?"

"In the future, Gramps. Margo told Sara we would have multiple children. Who am I to disagree with things I don't understand? Ashley and Carrie seem to have received solid information."

"They did, which reminds me. Margie, what are we getting TG for Christmas? He has so much of everything. Is there anything he doesn't have?"

"Not much. He's getting so big and hard to buy for."

"Maybe one of those electric cars or a bike."

"A tricycle might be good. Why don't you start looking around for one."

Sara came in and they ate. It was time to go to work.

John said, "Jake, you get one of the parking places close to the elevator. It will have your name on it, I'm sure. The paint may not be dry, but it will be on the wall next to the doors, bigshot."

————————————

The horses started acting up in the barn late that night. John and Wyatt went out to see what was going on. Wyatt spotted a large cougar running from the barn. He was afraid to shoot for fear they were protected in this part of Colorado.

He called Denver's animal control division and, sure enough, cougars were protected. The Director said they would send a trapper out the next morning to trap the cougar and take it to the mountains.

Wyatt, John, and Joe decided they would take shifts in the barn for the rest of the night. John said, "We should have just used the 'three S' approach—shoot, shovel, and shut up. I would rather sleep in a bed all night. If he comes back, I am going to fear for my life and shoot."

Joe said, "Me too!"

Wyatt actually agreed with them. The trapper showed up early the next morning and found where the cougar was getting in. A large limb was close to the fence and the cat could jump from it into the enclosure. He set up two traps, one near the barn and one near the limb, and baited each with red meat.

He felt sure the cougar would not return until after dark. Wyatt closed the barn as tight as possible and planned to be back before dark. He ate an early supper and fixed a bed in the hay loft.

Just after midnight, the horses started acting up but quieted quickly. Wyatt was not sure what had happened. They found the cat in the cage near the barn at daylight. It had fed and slept, but was not happy. It hit the end of the culvert trap and screamed. It then just sat there and glared at the three men. If looks could kill, they would be dead men.

Everyone came out to look at the cougar. He was not happy with the humans and just sat in the trap hissing and spitting. He looked like he wanted to kill them all. Wyatt called the trapper to tell him of the success.

The trapper responded, "I will be there in an hour and take him way up in the mountains. Do you have someone to go with me, or should I bring an assistant with me?"

"We can send someone with you."

Wyatt then called Lenny and asked him to go with the trapper and to make sure the big cat was a long way off before he was released, "That thing was inside the compound for a day, I think." He also called Javier to get the limb cut down.

Lenny and the trapper left on schedule and drove several hours through the mountains to a remote area in a national park. He took his old .45-70, just in case. The process of letting the cat out was simple enough. The trapper got on top of the culvert cage to open the door while Lenny was positioned well back on the ground to make sure he went the other way. But things did not go according to plan.

As soon as the trap opened, the cat jumped out, turned toward Lenny, and charged! He was on Lenny before he could get off a shot. Lenny was knocked down and scratched badly on his chest and both arms. The trapper started yelling at the cat, which attracted his attention. The cat turned and leaped onto the culvert to attack the trapper and both of them tumbled to the ground.

Lenny crawled to his rifle but could not shoot because the cat and the trapper were now rolling around on the ground. Lenny fired into the air from his knees and the cat turned to charge him again. Lenny had a shot and the cougar tumbled—a second shot finished him off.

The trapper got on the radio and called for assistance and an ambulance. Both men were hurting and bleeding profusely. They managed to stop the heaviest bleeding for each other. Two National Park Rangers arrived quickly and got the bleeding slowed down even more.

An ambulance arrived later and the EMTs got the bleeding under control and rushed them to the nearest hospital. Both men were given a unit of blood and the wounds were carefully cleaned and sutured. A nurse called Ruth and the trapper's wife. Ruth and Wyatt headed to the hospital as fast as they could go on the curvy mountain roads.

Lenny was coming out from under the anesthesia when they arrived. Ruth's heart almost stopped when she saw all the bandages.

Lenny grinned groggily at her and said, "You should see the other guy!"

Ruth leaned in and gave him a kiss, "Did he survive?"

"Nope. The park rangers skinned him while we were waiting for the ambulance. Gonna' have a rug made so I can step on him every day."

The cat's blood had been sent to be tested for rabies. It would take a few days to get the results.

John and Ashley came as soon as they could. The doctor said Lenny would have to stay at least one night and probably two. The trapper was a little worse. The cat bit into the back of his neck and would have killed him if Lenny had not attracted the cat's attention.

The results of the rabies test came the next day. Fortunately, it was not rabid, but potential infection was still an issue.

The doctor came to Ruth and said, "I know you want to get him home, but we have him on four antibiotics intravenously. He needs to stay a few more nights to be completely out of danger."

Ruth responded, "Keep him as long as needed. I need this man to live more than I need to get him home quickly."

Ruth said, "Everyone can go back to work. We'll be fine. If somebody is coming this way, please bring me more clothes. I left too quick to get any."

Wyatt asked if the hospital had a helicopter pad, and it did. He said, "You will have clothes on a chopper tomorrow. Ashley can pick them out. We will also fly you back when they release him. It will take less than an hour."

She gave her son-in-law a peck, "Thank you! That will help a lot."

Chapter Thirteen

When Jake and Sara drove into the parking garage, they found a spot with a freshly painted sign, *Reserved for Jake Carr, Vice President of Finance.* It was a few spaces down from Wyatt's reserved space. Sara showed more emotion than Jake—she was so proud to see her fiancé's name and title on the wall. He took it in stride on the outside but was bubbling with pride on the inside.

The Finance and Accounting division was located one floor above the Security division. Most of the offices were large cubicles, with the Finance group on the right side when Jake walked into his office and the Accounting group on the left. He noted many of the Finance cubicles had large screens scrolling stock market data, a setup he was quite familiar with.

The Associate Vice Presidents in charge of the two groups both had nice offices. Each had a secretary and could access Jake's cadre of secretaries when needed. Jake was still puzzled about why he had a pool of seven secretaries.

The Finance area contained groups of employees devoted to the typical finance responsibilities regarding investments and cash management.   The Accounting group focused on general bookkeeping, accounts payable, accounts receivable, budgeting & forecasting, expense management, tax, and payroll.

Jake set up meetings with the two Associate VPs. He wanted to talk with them about a variety of topics, including structure, personnel, strengths, weaknesses, problems, and opportunities for greater efficiency."

———————————

Ashley and Ruth boarded a Trust plane for Williston early one morning. They were headed south on the bus by ten o'clock. The driver, like many, did not obey the speed limit but the women hardly noticed. Everett was a smooth driver and the bus itself was set up to minimize sways and bumps. Ruth would have been horrified if she had known their speed.

The women at the first ranch were ready to go when the bus arrived. The ones waiting for the second trip laughingly admonished Everett to hurry back. They were keeping all the children while the first group enjoyed their excursion. The bus made it to the second ranch by two p.m. and they also loaded quickly. The women from the two ranches did not know each other, but with Ashley's help they were chatting like long lost friends within a short time. Everyone was excited to be going shopping in bigger stores and for simply being recognized by the Trust executives. It made them feel important.

There was much oohing and aahing when they rolled into Bismarck. The size of the stores and the size of town was like nothing most of them had ever seen. Ashley and Ruth understood many of them had never traveled very far from their homes. Bismarck was the second largest town in North Dakota, behind Fargo.

Their first stop was at a Target. Ashley told them they would visit other even bigger stores so they should not spend all their money at the first stop. Most of the women were overwhelmed with the choices and followed Ashley's advice.

Ashley took them to a Cracker Barrel for lunch. She told them before they left the bus that she was paying so they could order whatever they wanted. Once again the number of choices on the menu surprised the women, as did the prices.

Everett drove them to the Kirkwood Mall after lunch. Most of the women were somewhat dazzled by the large number of stores under one roof. Very few bought anything, but everyone seemed to enjoy walking around and looking.

The bus moved on to a Super Walmart about middle of the afternoon. It was even bigger than Target, but they were becoming more experienced shoppers. They found the items they wanted and made their selections. Most bought clothes for their children and husbands. Ashley encouraged them to also buy something for themselves. They quicky bought clothing and, in some cases, a little jewelry.

They left the Walmart at five o'clock. Ashley used the buddy method to make sure everyone was back on the bus. They were staying at a nice hotel, probably the nicest any had ever seen and certainly the nicest they had stayed in. The hotel offered a huge breakfast buffet the next morning and everyone ate heartily— they were used to big breakfasts on the ranch.

The women were able to finish their shopping with another stop at Target, largely because it opened early. The rest of the day was devoted to sightseeing, with stops at the Bismarck Art Gallery, the State Capitol, and the North Dakota Heritage Center.

Ashley took everyone to dinner at Laughing Sun Brewing. The specialty beers and excellent BBQ were a hit with everyone.

Immediately after dinner, they went to a movie complete with a box of popcorn and drink. Ashley had reserved all the seats for a private showing and everyone had a great time. The rocking chair seats fascinated them. Ashley thought, *"We should send a recently released movie to the Learning Centers for Saturday nights and Sunday afternoons. I think they would appreciate the entertainment."*

They then returned to the motel both exhausted and content. The bus departed early the next morning to head back home. Everett had to exchange the women and return to Bismarck that day with the second group. He made it back with time to spare.

The sequence of events for the second trip was repeated, except one woman was not at the bus when they were ready to leave Walmart the first day. Everett, Ruth, and Ashley found her trying on a dress. She was terribly embarrassed about losing track of the time. Her name was Lucy and she became 'Late Lucy' for the rest of the trip, but she took the ribbing quite well.

The women loved the trip! A few said it was as happy as they had been in a long while. Others added their husbands would continue working at the ranch since the owners obviously cared about their wives and children. That was the reaction Ashley wanted to hear!

During both trips Ashley asked questions about the Learning Centers and received only a few minor suggestions. The women were especially excited they and their husbands were able to take GED classes. Everyone liked the teacher at their Learning Centers.

All the ranch women were able to take the bus trip before Thanksgiving. The outings were well received, even for the properties closer to larger towns. One lady commented, "Yes, we are close enough to Bismarck for me to shop there, but I have children tagging along and usually a husband not wanting to shop or spend money."

Ashley was planning field trips for the school children before Christmas, beginning shortly after Thanksgiving. The field trips would be to places near the properties, with three women going along as chaperones. She tried to make each trip include something significant in history, which as a challenge. She planned two-day/one night trips and had them laid out as Thanksgiving approached.

Jake was settling into his new Vice President position. He completed his analysis of all the personnel and felt several in each section were unnecessary or underperforming. He asked Nadine to come into his office to help with the final decisions. She was not comfortable at first, but got into doing what was needed. She confirmed Jake's analysis. She also pointed out two people who were consistent troublemakers, including one of the secretaries.

They spent all morning at the worktable in Jake's office. They discussed each finance employee and he added the two troublemakers to his list. She also thought seven secretaries were too many and that five could easily get the work done. She named the two who did not hold up their end of the work and one of them was a troublemaker.

She added, "We can hire temps pretty easily when we get overloaded with work, which happens only a few weeks each year."

Jake was extremely satisfied with the decisions. Ten positions were selected as the ones to eliminate. Jake asked, "Who assigns the work to secretaries?"

"Really no one. It just sort of gets done."

"That will be added to your job description. You will be the Executive Secretary and be given a raise. You will work only for me and have the supervision responsibility. You did an excellent job on this difficult discussion and demonstrated great insight."

He went up to visit with Harrell about his decisions. Harrell would have to approve the terminations and Nadine's new title and duties. Harrell looked over the list of position terminations. He approved all of them and asked, "When will they take effect?"

"I don't want to terminate anyone before Christmas. I will let them know around December 1, to take effect on January 1. A few can retire. Others will use vacation time to leave immediately. Some will work the month of December. I expect all of them to appeal to you. I would like for Nadine's promotion to be immediate. She was a great help with these decisions."

"I approve all these moves and will back you. I know how challenging these decisions were, but from what you have said all are deserved. Get HR to help you with the letters. Actually, they will do the letters and you and HR will sign them. I will initial them before they are sent. Good job. Terminating a worker is one of the most challenging decisions you will face, because it affects so many people."

Jake decided he would keep the firings under wrap until after Thanksgiving. He told only Nadine. He went to HR to find out what he needed to do to reclassify her as his Executive Secretary. It was simpler than he expected and was completed with a phone call to Harrell. Nadine received a substantial raise immediately. The only person who complained was the secretary Nadine identified as a troublemaker, who found out from another troublemaker in HR.

It was now time to start planning for the new year. Jake had a few ideas about making the division more streamlined. One of the first items was a new cover sheet required to accompany every request for additional funding. It would give them a place to start while evaluating the proposal and provide a summary to take to the Board.

The Thanksgiving meal at the compound turned into a great feast. Virginia and Carrie helped Margie prepare the meal, with Margie doing most of it. They cooked and celebrated at Harrell's house. The entrees were turkey and ham. Margie made a fantastic pecan-topped sweet potato casserole with sweet potatoes from Vardaman, Mississippi. The other dishes were traditional fare for Thanksgiving. Rolls and pies were bought at a nearby bakery. The coconut chess pie was to die for. The pecan bourbon pie was almost as good. Apple and cherry pies were also served.

Everyone lay around watching football and generally adding pounds after such a meal. Jake and Sara later decided to go for a horseback ride. It was a cold, raw day, but the exercise felt good. The fireplace also felt good when they returned to the house.

The snow began at eight o'clock. It began as a blizzard roaring out of the mountains. By ten o'clock, most roads were closed and the snowplows were out in force. John told Jake it was too dangerous for him to drive home. The electricity failed a little after midnight. But the compound's large generator came on with hardly a flicker of the lights.

Jake was assigned the couch, but he and Sara got pillows and laid on the floor watching movies almost all night while Jake kept the fire going.

John came in at four a.m. to join them. Margie followed John as soon as she ran a brush through her hair. John and Margie sat on the couch under a blanket. When the fireplace needed another log, John just nudged Jake with his toe and said 'wood.'

John made coffee at daylight, if you could call it daylight with the blizzard still howling. Everyone was content to stay inside for the duration. Wolf was curled up near Margie on the floor. John thought to himself, "*This is almost perfect. If Wyatt, Ashley, and TG could make it over, it would definitely be perfect.*" Margie called them and they decided they could make it.

They came in and found more blankets. After everyone was settled, John said, "Here I am, the oldest man in the family, and you two young whippersnappers are already Vice Presidents. It just doesn't seem fair!"

Sara shushed him so she could hear the movie, and he responded, "Geez! I can't even talk in my own house!"

Ashley and Margie joined the shushing. TG crawled into John's lap to console him.

It was almost ten o'clock when Margie put biscuits on and sliced leftover Thanksgiving ham. Everyone loved the simple breakfast.

The snow finally stopped a little before dark, leaving at least two feet on the flat areas and up to six or eight feet in the drifts. It was beautiful, especially since no one had to go to work for two more days.

The next morning, John and Jake worked on the walkways between the houses with the compound's two snowblowers. Wyatt used the tractor and blade to clear the driveways.

The snow began melting around mid-afternoon. The night was cold and clear, and ice formed on the streets. The big snowplows got most of the roads cleared by Sunday afternoon. Joe used the tractor to clear the compound's roads again.

Everyone went to work on Monday. Ashley was anxious because the first field trip for students was scheduled for Tuesday. The North Dakota ranch children were going to Rapid City. They would visit Mount Rushmore and the Badlands. The roads were in good shape. Since several mothers were going as chaperones, Ashley was not going along.

———————————

Harrell received a highly disturbing call at ten o'clock

Wednesday morning. A group of neo-Nazis had kidnapped the entire busload of children!

They were demanding five million dollars to be delivered the next day by noon or they would start shooting children, one per hour. They warned if the police were called, they would blow up the bus.

Harrell told them, "I need more time to get that much money together." It worked and they were given until six the following morning.

The entire security team was alerted and ready to begin searching for the bus. Ashley insisted on going and Wyatt tried to tell her no, but it did no good. Sara also demanded to go since she was part of security. Jake said he needed to go along to take the money, which they had in cash. Wyatt protested but realized he was not going to win the battles. He put together the armaments he thought they might need.

He did not think the kidnappers were a large group, so they mainly took long range rifles and side arms. They boarded two twin-engine planes and a helicopter so they could search the roads. John and Wyatt narrowed down the likely places to hide a bus. There were plenty of forest roads, but many were still snow covered. They searched all along the route the bus was supposed to take. A rest area about two hours from the ranches would have made a good rest stop, so they concentrated the search around on the rest area.

The bus tracks were somewhat distinctive and they found where they thought it had turned onto a road heading into the mountains. The planes flew the road at the highest altitude from which they could see. One of the planes saw a glint in a small camping area. The helicopter came to check it at a lower altitude. It was the bus.

They flew to a small airport not too far from the camping

area. The planes and chopper landed and the group developed a plan. First, they needed ground transportation. Frenchy called a man he knew with Fish and Wildlife. Wyatt called the local FBI office and explained the problem. The FBI sent an SUV and the Fish and Wildlife sent two large pickups. The FBI also provided a ten-person SWAT team.

The Trust's security team and the two agencies agreed they had to try to take the bus without endangering the children. They realized only a lightning fast strike had any chance if a bomb was on board.

Wyatt called Everett to find out about the delivery instructions for the money. He also desperately needed to know how many kidnappers were on the bus.

Everett caught on quickly, and said, "I'm so sorry I let this happen. These six people jumped me when we stopped at the rest area. I'll see how they want to handle delivery. It's going to have to be one person or people will get killed."

Wyatt turned to his group and said, "We have six bogies and we need to take them out all at once. If we can surround the bus, we may be able to eliminate all of them. But all six probably won't leave the bus. If we put snipers in the woods before daylight and pretend to start the ransom delivery, we may be able to get clear shots. I think it's our best chance. Does anyone have a better idea? Each shot must put one down for the count." No one offered a different plan.

Everyone on the SWAT team was a qualified sniper. One hundred yard shots were easy for a sniper, but Wyatt wanted two shooters on each kidnapper. He put one SWAT man in each of the six teams, so four of the teams included two SWAT snipers. Frenchy and Mitch went with the others to fill out the two-man teams. The FBI brought high-quality communication pieces so everyone could know when to shoot.

John and Jake would take the satchel to the bus. Joe and Wyatt would try to slip to the back of the bus in their snow camo. Ashley and Sara would be backup and ride in the backseat of John and Jake's SUV. They would slip out when Jake opened the SUV's back door to get the satchels of money. The plan's success depended on precise timing.

The SWAT team, along with Frenchy, Mitch, Joe, and Wyatt began the long walk to get to the side of the door-side of the bus and were in position by four o'clock. Wyatt and Joe were able to get close to the bus's back door.

The dance began when Jake called Everett to tell him two people were coming in with the ransom money. John insisted he be allowed to board the bus to make sure the children were okay. The kidnappers allowed him to board and look around. When satisfied, John turned and stepped off the bus for the money transfer. The kidnappers made a huge mistake—four of them exited the bus behind John. One stood inside the front of the bus and another one stood at the back. The SWAT team radios were active, with each team being given the color of the coat worn by their target.

On a countdown by the SWAT commander, the firing erupted with six almost simultaneous rifle shots. All rifles were aimed at heads. Five of the six were totally out of the fight, but one mortally wounded kidnapper tried to pull himself up the bus steps. Everett saw him coming and made a diving tackle when the man mounted the first step. Everett was a big man, and the wounded kidnapper was not. Everett landed full force on him and knocked the dying breath out of him. The children were surprisingly quiet.

The FBI bomb squad arrived at the bus almost before the echoes of the shooting died down. The children were taken off the bus as quickly as possible and the squad began a slow examination of the bus. They found no explosives.

While the FBI was combing through the bus, three large fires were built. The children made a game of gathering dry, dead branches from the edge of the woods. Ashley, Sara, and the chaperones tried to comfort the few young children who were upset. The six kidnappers were placed under a tarp away from the children.

The local Sheriff and deputies arrived and the coroner came to examine the scene. They talked to the lead FBI Agent and Wyatt. The shooting was quickly ruled justifiable.

Other than the dead kidnappers, only three others suffered injury—one SWAT officer twisted an ankle walking in, one chaperone had a nasty cut over an eye from one of one of the kidnappers, and Everett either broke or severely sprained his wrist and received facial bruises and scratches from trying to fight off the kidnappers. An ambulance and another bus driver were called for and arrived shortly. The TV networks picked up the story and reporters soon arrived on the scene.

Wyatt, the lead FBI agent, and the local Sheriff were interviewed by reporters. One of the main questions was whether it was necessary to kill the perpetrators. The FBI agent explained that the group threatened to blow up the bus and it was necessary to prevent an explosion.

The bus and the children started back home as soon as they were released by the police. Everett would not leave his bus, so the EMT just put a splint on his wrist and told him to go to a doctor as soon as he had a chance.

Chapter Fourteen

The next day, a team of psychologists was dispatched to each of the ranches to help the children and their parents deal with the kidnapping trauma. They were scheduled to stay on the properties for at least a week. Ashley wanted to go but Wyatt said she needed to stay in Denver to start planning how to prevent kidnappings from happening again.

Everett finally went to the doctor about his wrist. The doctor said he had broken a small bone in the wrist rather than a complete fracture. Everett asked when he would be able to drive the bus again and the doc told him 'whenever you can stand the pain.' But he advised him to wait a month or so. The doctors also checked the bruises and scratches he got from tussling with the kidnappers. He was acknowledged as a hero, having faced down armed men by himself. Someone might have died if not for Everett.

Harrell agreed they needed a planning meeting. He attended along with the entire Board, the security team, Ashley, and Tommy. It was a tense meeting due to the gravity of the situation. Everyone knew the Trust had the money to pay a ransom, and a few thought they should pay it to protect the employee's children. Actually, the payment question was the first question addressed in the meeting.

Wyatt commented, "I do not believe the Trust should pay ransoms. Paying ransoms invites copycat actions by other groups. The fact that we handled the kidnappers with deadly force will make anyone think twice about further kidnappings."

John added, "Kidnappers almost always kill the hostages, whether or not they are paid a ransom. We have a potent security force to handle such cases and we can get professional help from other law enforcement agencies. I think you should develop a policy of not paying to get our people or other assets back from kidnappers. I think the Trust should formalize such a policy, and the policy should be made public in some fashion."

After a short discussion among the Board members, they decided to confirm the 'no payment' policy. Jake was asked to work with Wyatt and John to develop the written policy.

They then discussed how to publicize the policy. Holding a press conference was mentioned and discussed, but some people questioned that direction.

Harrell mentioned, "Everyone knows about Chris Stoneman and his popular Denver talk show. If you have not seen it yet, he likes to interview local community leaders. I have had pleasant experiences with him. Before the interview, he asks what kind of points the interviewee wants to make. Essentially, I could set him up with questions I would like to answer. I think it could work well." The Board encouraged Harrell to pursue that approach.

The group then moved on to discuss how to protect the buses in the future. Frenchy said, "We have to have security on the buses. In addition to preventing bad actors from kidnapping a busload of students, we have to guard against an individual student being targeted. You just can't figure out what teenagers might do. If one is targeted for harm, we won't have time to get Security to the scene. I'm not sure exactly how we should do it, but arming two drivers like Everett is a good start. Maybe two or three chaperones should be trained and armed, including the women. Nothing more dangerous than a mama bear protecting her cubs. We would certainly need to train the chaperones. I'll bet we could easily get volunteers for such training."

Wyatt said, "That's a really good idea. How can we implement it?"

Sara said, "John took me from knowing nothing about self-defense to being able to hold my own in a dicey situation. I'm comfortable with my pistol and my hands and feet. I think those farm and ranch women have a big head start compared to where I began."

Wyatt added, "We have a security person on each ranch and farm. They could go on each trip."

Ashley added, "I have been thinking we need two drivers on the bus for longer trips or those returning late at night. If we train and arm Everett and a relief driver, I think we will be in good shape. How do we get all these people trained?"

John spoke up, "I can help train, but we need to do it before we schedule any more bus trips. Actually, several of us are qualified to do the training. We're not trying to create supermen and superwomen. I can train Everett, the new relief driver, and the security people on each property. One or two of you train the chaperones."

Ashley said, "I think a video of me and the carjacker in D.C. and one of Sara in a practice session with John or Wyatt would show the women they can do the job. The kidnapping probably motivated them to learn how to protect themselves and their children. Maybe we could show training videos at the Learning Centers."

Wyatt responded, "Great idea! It will speed this up by a lot. We can begin immediately and should be done by the new year. You can pick back up on the field trips in January."

The idea was discussed and tweaked a little. Wyatt thought he could also get videos of how the FBI taught people to be observant for possible threats—those were on the way before lunch. They also videoed Sara and John practicing hand-to-hand techniques after lunch.

The training went into high gear before the week's end. Many women were eager participants and some were very good. The pistol training had to be done in person, with Lenny and Mitch leading the training. They were surprised at the number of men who also wanted the training. Maybe it was to protect themselves from a trained wife.

———————

A speed bump popped up three days after the training began. Rosie called Wyatt to say a gold shipment had been stolen, and Lawrence was badly wounded. His survival was in serious question.

Wyatt told her, "Oh no! You stay with him and a security team will get there today to run the thieves down." He started calling in the troops for immediate departure.

Mitch remained in Denver to keep the defensive training going. Frenchy stayed to handle outfitting issues because waterfowl hunting was in high gear. The plane arrived in Alaska after dark. Of course, Alaska's days consisted of a few hours of dim light at this time of year. John and Joe went to the mine's stamping mill to launch the investigation. Wyatt and Lenny went to see Rosie and Lawrence.

Lawrence was severely wounded, but the doctors thought he had a good chance of surviving. He would have a long recovery and rehab due to three chest/abdomen wounds, and each arm was hit. Rosie was very emotional because she sent him to guard the shipment and she was not there to help him.

Rosie did not have much information about the robbery. She speculated the thieves might be the same ones who had stolen Trust diamonds previously, but she had no real evidence.

Wyatt asked incredulously, "Aren't they still in jail?"

She responded, "I don't know for sure, but I doubt it. It's pretty easy to get bail around here and I don't think they have had a trial yet. I wish I could help you, but I think I need to stay with Lawrence. If you need more muscle, call me. I have a couple of guards who I think are trustworthy. I might be able to slip away in a few days if Lawrence perks up. I would like to get my hands on the ones who shot him. Oh, he killed two of them, so you have a place to start. They were sheriff's deputies."

"Really! I think we will have a chat with the Sheriff. I want to know if those diamond thieves are out on bail and what the dead bodies can tell us. John and Joe are at the mine seeing what they can develop. Do you think it could be an inside job?"

"It could be. The people up here are pretty tough and don't like wealthy people. Most people agree that a goodly proportion of the workers around here are wanted somewhere. We do background checks, but I expect some bad actors slip through the cracks."

"If you need anything for Lawrence, call Denver and talk to the Director of Mining Operations or Harrell. We will get him whatever he needs."

"Thanks. Do we have insurance?"

"Yes. Plus, his injury was in the line of duty, so everything will be covered. If he needs to go to the lower 48, a Trust jet will pick him up and deliver him wherever he needs to go. Gotta run by the Sheriff's office to get some answers."

Wyatt went into the Sheriff's office to check on their investigation. The deputy on duty said they had turned up nothing.

Wyatt asked, "Are the men arrested for the diamond thefts still in jail?"

"No. We didn't have enough evidence to hold them. We're now working on the latest thefts. No evidence yet."

Wyatt politely asked, "May I use your phone?"

It was handed to him and he called Harrell. "Harrell, this is Wyatt. The Sheriff here, or at least his deputy, says they have let the diamond thieves go for lack of evidence. Each of them signed a confession and the evidence was overwhelming. They also have done nothing about the gold shipment robbery. If you will call the Governor, I will call the FBI. Maybe we can wake this guy and his deputies up. Let me put you on speaker so the deputy can tell his boss exactly what we are doing."

Harrell responded, "I will call the Governor immediately to see if the state can take over the county's law enforcement. I will wager a malfeasance charge will be made when they arrive. We have warned the Sheriff before, so he has no more chances. Wyatt, you get the Feds involved. Why don't all of you get in a safe place in case the Sheriff decides to try to take you on, hoping they can survive? Mr. Deputy, you call the Sheriff and tell him what's going to happen. Have a nice day."

The first State Trooper arrived in half an hour and another ten pulled up to the Sheriff's office within an hour. The lead State Trooper for the district arrived with papers signed by the Governor—the Sheriff was removed and the state would temporarily operate the Sheriff's office. The Governor also called up a National Guard contingent of Military Police to help out.

The FBI began arriving the next morning. A task force of six Agents was on site before noon. The chief of the Alaskan State

Troopers came to help decide who would be doing what in the next few weeks. It was a delicate job as no group wanted to be underneath another. Eventually, they decided all but two of the State Troopers would return to patrolling the highways. The MPs would act as deputies in the county. The FBI would lead the investigation of the Sheriff and his office. The two State Troopers and two MPs would work with Wyatt's people to investigate the theft of the gold shipment.

John and Joe were already on the trail. They were certain someone on the inside was involved. The Trust's security man at the gold mine and stamping mill named two men. He had no evidence, but the two had been acting suspiciously. They took an unusual interest in exactly when the gold would be shipped and how much would be in it.

He also suspected the Sheriff might have some culpability. Deputies arrived on scene over two hours after they were called. Their delay affected all other first responders. The ambulance did not take Lawrence to the ER until after the Sheriff's deputies arrived, which was one reason he lost so much blood. It was an all-around mangled situation and the Sheriff's office seemed to be the main problem.

Wyatt knew he wanted to get back to Denver before Christmas. The quickest way to see if the suspected inside men were involved was to let John chat with them.

As the targeted men were leaving the mill, Wyatt, Joe, and Lenny asked them to come with them. They led the men toward two small storage buildings. John was waiting in one building. As was his usual approach, he first talked to both men.

John said, "Gentlemen, you two men provided information to the gang who stole our gold. You have two options. First, you can tell me their names and we will hand you over to the police. If not, option two is that I will take whatever measures are necessary to make you give us the names."

"I don't enjoy inflicting pain, but I'm willing to do what I have to do to get those names. Why don't you gentlemen discuss those two options? Just remember this, I have spent the last thirty years getting tough guys to talk all over the world. You decide whether you want to talk now or after my 'enhanced questioning'."

Both men thought they were tough and decided they would just keep quiet. If the Trust had any real evidence, they would be in jail.

John went back into the shack after a moment and asked if they were ready to talk. Neither said anything. Wyatt and Lenny took one man to the other nearby shack.

John asked, "Are you ready to talk?" The culprit just shook his head.

"Too bad. Now I'm going to have to hurt you."

Those outside heard a couple of blood-curdling screams. Wyatt said, "John offered them the chance to leave here intact. Too bad they didn't take it."

John came to the door with the first hoodlum and got the second one. The first man was bleeding and holding his hand and ribs. John took the second man inside.

"You don't have to get hurt. Just tell me the names and where are they."

"I'll tell you all I know. It's three men who used to work at the diamond mine. The Sheriff was also involved, along with a couple of deputies."

"Who shot the guard?"

"We were not at the robbery. We just told them when a large shipment was leaving the mill."

"Where are they?"

"They talked about a cabin off the railroad near Talkeetna.

It's near the last stop before Talkeetna. I've never been there—I just heard them talking."

John walked outside and said, "Let's get these two scoundrels to jail. It was those three guys from the diamond mine and the Sheriff. I know where they are or where they better be."

He looked directly at the second man, "If they are not there, I know where to find you."

They drove to the jail, now operated by the MPs. Wyatt asked if one of them would help them follow the directions provided by the culprit.

State Trooper Clark offered to accompany them to help keep everything legal and John replied, "You are welcome to go with us, but we don't do the Miranda thing before we go in."

"Suits me fine. Let's try not to kill them unless they fight back."

"The Sheriff was in on it. Do we know where he is?"

"He went to his house."

"He needs to be arrested."

The other Trooper said, "I'll pick him up."

Wyatt said, "These two need medical attention. They resisted. I would not hurry to get them assistance—they just have a few broken ribs and one has an injury to his hand. Slipped on ice and broke it, I guess. If you want to, you can wait until you get backup to take them over to the hospital. You never know, they may try to run again."

Trooper Clark said, "We need to go to Fairbanks to catch the train. You fellows better buy good winter gear, the best you can find—heavy parka, gloves, and hat. Avalanches occasionally stop the train for two or three days. The perps may also run, so we better take snowmobiles. I have one and we can rent three more. Those things are a bitterly cold ride. Make sure you take everything you need. We'll be going into wild country and can't call for backup."

The railroad ran from Fairbanks to Anchorage. It supplied the little settlements along the way and individual houses that were off the grid, except for the railroad. They bought the supplies and clothes Trooper Clark thought they needed and boarded the train. The train cars were comfortable when compared to the outside. They had small wooden stoves in them, which by no means really warmed the car.

They got off the train where the insider told them the cabin was supposed to be. The conductor watched them unload and commented, "Interesting. The Sheriff got off at this same spot yesterday."

They were now sure they were in the right place, but the thieves had forewarning from the Sheriff. The Sheriff's snowmobile tracks were easy to follow to the cabin. But the cabin was deserted, with four sets of snowmobile tracks leading away from the it.

Trooper Clark said, "They know they are being chased and are heading into mighty rough country. This is going to be the coldest chase you've ever made."

Trooper Clark radioed for a helicopter to assist with the tracking. The tracks were easy to see, but the chopper could range ahead and reduce the likelihood of an ambush. They soon heard the thumping of chopper blades.

Two hours later the helicopter had to return to base for fuel and could not return because of an approaching snowstorm. It would have to stay on the ground until the storm blew over. The snowmobile ride was brutal. The temperature was nearly forty below and the icy wind could penetrate any opening not secured tightly. The cold hurt. The thought that kept them going was knowing the thieves were in the same weather. The storm grew worse and they had to stop to find shelter and fire. They got under the canopy of a big fir tree, or as big as they grew in the area.

They broke off dead limbs from the trunk and quickly started a fire. Trooper Clark had a fire starting kit on his machine, as well as tarps to sit on. It was not truly comfortable, but it was so much warmer than on the snowmobiles—it actually felt wonderful.

The snowstorm began playing out in a little over three hours. They had made two pots of coffee on a small folding camp stove. Each man also ate an MRE provide by Trooper Clark.

They could not start the chase because the snowstorm had covered the snowmobile's tracks. Fortunately, the helicopter was able to return an hour later. It took the helicopter only thirty minutes to locate the tracks. The helicopter guided them to a shack at an old mining operation. The chopper pilot told Trooper Clark the tracks did not continue on.

They were sure the shed covered an old mine shaft. They surrounded the opening and yelled to the robbers, who were nearly frozen. But they were not ready to give up peacefully. One of the thieves fired a shot and missed badly.

Everyone returned fire. At least one thief was hit and the others had to be scared. The Trooper ordered them to come out without their weapons. The thieves yelled an obscenities and fired again. The posse poured fire into the shack.

After more yelling, a voice rang out, "We are coming out! Don't shoot!"

"If you have a gun in your hand, you will be killed! No exceptions. Come out with your hands up!"

Four men came from the shack. Two had been wounded and the other two appeared to be nearly frozen. The wounds were not too bad—at forty below the blood freezes quickly.

The criminals were cuffed and their guns unloaded and put on the machines. Trooper Clark built a large fire in the mine shaft entrance so everyone could get warm—it took a while.

The four thieves got on their machines. Each driver was handcuffed to the machine.

John said, "If any of you try to run, I will shoot you for attempting to escape. I do not miss."

Trooper Clark knew which direction to head out. They would hit the Talkeetna River, which he thought would take three or four hours if they had no problems. It was a cold ride and took a little over four hours to reach the town. After a perilous river crossing, they warmed up in the general store. The next train heading for Fairbanks was expected in six hours—a sturdy jail awaited the prisoners. The good guys needed a good meal and a serious sleep.

They ate great tasting soup at the general store and took turns watching the criminals. John gave them the same warning again. He did not think they would try to escape—they were beat. The wounded men were now leaking blood, but not an alarming amount. The posse did not much care if they were helped.

Lawrence was lying in a hospital bed, shot up much worse and they were nearly frozen. Each man got a few hours' sleep in the store. When the train finally arrived, they loaded up and handcuffed the prisoners to a seat, but not very close to the heater. The men complained to no avail. The posse caught a few more winks and dreamed of the steak Wyatt promised to buy them.

It did not take long to get the prisoners checked into their accommodations in Fairbanks. The steak was incredible and the bed was presumably comfortable—no one was sure because they were all exhausted. They shook off the last few icicles in a hot shower and were asleep when their heads hit the pillow.

Wyatt called Denver before he drifted off and talked to

Ashley and Harrell. He told them they had caught the robbers. Harrell asked about the gold.

Wyatt said, "We could not bring it on the snowmobiles. They left the gold at the cabin and we had a long chase away from the cabin. I'm going to find people up here to bring it out, probably the Trooper who helped us and a few other tough men. It's now near fifty below and snowing. He says he can find it when the weather gets better."

Ashley said, "Rosie says Lawrence is improving. The doctors are also much more optimistic. TG is looking for you and Santa Claus—not necessarily in that order."

"Tell him I am near the North Pole, but I haven't seen the gentleman. If I do, I'll tell him to be sure he comes to our house. Hope to get home tomorrow. Tell the pilots to pick us up in Fairbanks. I plan to visit Lawrence before we depart."

The plane arrived early and they went to see Lawrence. Trooper Clark assured Wyatt he and a couple of his Trooper buddies would retrieve the gold and take it to Fairbanks, where it was headed originally. After they retrieved it, he would need a few days to get it through the evidence process. He also assured them the Sheriff and the other three thieves would face trial.

The plane arrived in Denver the next day. The men went straight to the office, hoping to never have to chase down criminals in the Alaska winter. TG was with his mother at the office. He was almost two years old and looking forward to Christmas. He was also running and talking—constantly.

The men went up to see Harrell. John said, "I don't know what you pay those people who work up there, but I do know it's not enough. I have been cold twice in my life, and both times were on this trip."

Wyatt said, "You need to decide how much to give the men who go back to recover the gold. They didn't even mention money, but it's a really nasty duty. I think we are all going home and have a gallon or two of hot chocolate and warm up. Call if you need us. I'm as tired as I have ever been."

Everyone, including Ashley, went home. The men slept until the next morning. None, not even John, got up early.

Chapter Fifteen

It was a few days before Christmas. The trees in the compound were decorated and TG was excited. He did not remember much about his first Christmas, but he had watched enough TV to know what was coming. Santa Claus was high on his list of favorite people.

The people living at the compound decided to celebrate at Wyatt and Ashley's house. Everyone wanted to see TG's reaction to all the things Santa was going to bring him. They planned to have a late breakfast of rolls and assorted pastries. Harrell and Virginia would host the mid-afternoon lunch. Rather than spend days cooking, Virginia ordered a turkey and ham from the hotel along with all the fixings. Margie, Ruth, and Ashley planned to make desserts.

The activity around the office was light and winding down. Jake was working more hours than anyone trying to keep things together for the end of year push for statements, tax documents, and such. On the investments side, the account managers were busy discussing and making yearend decisions. Millions of dollars could be made or lost depending on the decisions.

Harrell and Wyatt went in everyday but they did not have any major work to address. Harrell received a call one day notifying him the stolen gold had been retrieved and deposited. The value was over five million dollars. He decided to give the troopers fifty thousand to split for picking up the stash during their off time.

Wyatt said, "That's generous, but I think we should also give them a nice rifle."

Harrell agreed. Wyatt called a Fairbanks gun store and ordered the three troopers Browning .300 Magnum rifles.

Everyone at the compound was wrapping packages and purchasing a few last minute items. The women kept the bodyguards busy with their shopping excursions.

Christmas Eve finally arrived. All the security people ate at Lenny's. It was a relatively plain meal, with an entree of succulent backstraps from Ashley's elk. Frenchy brought sausage from south Louisiana called boudin—spicy rice and meat stuffed in a sausage liner. Everyone tried it. Some loved it, others not so much.

Ruth also served mashed potatoes, gravy, and huge fluffy biscuits, which was a big hit with everyone. She cooked the backstrap medium rare and it was tender enough for TG handle. He ate from the table out of a highchair. He loved the meat and ate two biscuits. He had fun with the potatoes and gravy, but did not get very much into his mouth. Ashley thought, *"I should have put a tarp under his chair!"*

They opened more than one bottle of good wine supplied by Harrell. After dinner, Lenny made eggnog with an excellent bourbon. Frenchy and Mitch's kids were enjoying themselves watching Christmas movies and petting the horses in the barn. Carrots and an apple were provided for each horse.

Ashley, Theresa, and Jana encouraged the children play so, hopefully, they would not get up at the crack of dawn the next morning—John was highly skeptical. Jake bought a large sack of impressive fireworks to enjoy after darkness fell. Everyone clapped and screamed, including TG—he particularly enjoyed the multi-colored starbursts and the booming did not bother him.

The ones who lived in the compound and Frenchy and Mitch's families exchanged gifts that night. Virginia gave each child a nice gift. Harrell gave checks to the adults—sort of their bonuses for a good year. Mitch and Frenchy took their families home about ten o'clock. Both men knew they faced a couple of frustrating hours of reading directions for assembling toys before they could go to bed.

The ones who lived in the compound started for home soon afterwards. Wyatt had nothing to put together that night. He had already spent hours putting TG's gifts from Santa together. A wonderful tricycle of German manufacture took most of the time. He, Joe, and Jake worked on it into the wee hours one night. Wyatt swore they would never buy another unassembled German toy!

Wyatt was instructed to call everyone as soon as TG woke up. Ashley would try to constrain him until the others could come over. The rolls and coffee were ready to go. Wyatt had bought a large coffee pot and planned to start it before doing anything else. The pastries would be warmed as soon as the presents were opened.

TG was tired from playing and went to sleep with only one horse book being read. As soon as he was sound asleep Harrell, Joe, Jake, and Wyatt started bringing his large stash from Harrell's spare room. Some stores had less than the load Santa was bringing TG!

Wyatt woke at daylight the next morning. He got the coffee going—the big pot took a while. As soon as the ready light came on, he poured a cup and sat down. He soon saw John headed his way. They drank a couple of peaceful cups before pandemonium broke loose. With the first sounds from TG, Ashley went to his room and Wyatt alerted everyone. Most people were more awake than asleep when he called.

When the adults arrived, Ashley turned TG loose. Wyatt thought of a rodeo and letting the bucking broncs loose. This year, TG understood all the unwrapped loot was his. He was not yet aware he would be sharing the spotlight with two other youngsters the following Christmas.

He ran from one toy to the next, not really taking time to explore any. Wyatt was crushed when he did not even get on the tricycle. Everyone watched him play for an hour before they decided to open gifts. TG did not have many wrapped gifts. He started over—looking at and playing with the toys. He was in constant motion.

The adults received some interesting gifts. John had a long and slender package from Jake. It was a Whitworth rifle in superb condition. Jake had sent it to a factory in England to be re-barreled and refinished—it was beautiful and fully operational.

John exclaimed, "We will go out on the prairie soon to see how it shoots!"

"Yes, I have bullets for it and the recommended black powder. The listed range is 600 yards, which is almost unbelievable. I think it's just like the one Bad Cat Jones obtained when Cletus Sheffield was killed."

Jake also gave Wyatt a reconditioned Colt Peacemaker, which was the last gun used by both Angelina and Grant. It came with an exquisite fast draw holster, just like the ones in the paintings of them.

John and Wyatt did not spend much time on their other gifts. Jake was not just an accepted member of the family, he had moved to the top of the list in John and Wyatt's eyes. They finally put the guns down and went on to other gifts when they saw their wives give them the 'evil eye.'

Everyone received gifts that fit them well. Jake received a full cowboy outfit with a beautiful Stetson hat—he was going to look like a westerner now. Many of Carrie's gifts were baby related and she loved them. Sara received large painting proclaiming her a champion fighter. The list went on for all.

Ashley slipped to the kitchen to warm the rolls and pastries after the last gift was opened. One pan of rolls came directly from the hunting lodge. Harrell had the pilots pick them up on one of their last trips. A huge platter contained only a dozen of the rolls, but that was all the group could eat. In fact, two rolls were left over. The other rolls were overshadowed by the lodge's massive rolls.

The excitement began to settle down by nine o'clock. Lunch would be delivered at two. All the men except Wyatt went home to get a nap. TG demanded Wyatt play with him and his new toys. He still was more or less going from toy to toy without giving any one toy much attention. He stayed a little longer with an array of toy horses. One was almost the same color as Chief and it was the one toy he carried from place to place.

After a few hours he took more interest in the tricycle. Wyatt showed him how to get it moving. It soon became his favorite, much to Wyatt's relief. TG was not a very good driver and banged into a lot of furniture, but nothing valuable was broken. Ashley cautioned the two guys often, but they more or less ignored her. He rode the trike for nearly an hour and started playing with a game someone gave him. After a few minutes he laid down on the floor and went to sleep. Wyatt took him to his room and straightened up a little bit.

Wyatt and Ashley sat on the couch before the fireplace and dozed a little. They also talked about what it would be like to have two buck-a-roos. It certainly would not be quiet or calm.

Wyatt asked, "Now, how many did you say you wanted.?"

"Maybe three or four.?"

"I guess we can't start making another while one's in the oven."

"I don't think it works that way but we could try."

They went to the bedroom in case visitors intruded. It was a wonderful quiet time for Ashley and Wyatt. Ashley wondered if something similar was happening with Joe and Carrie and maybe even the older adults.

Ashley, Ruth, and Margie began making their desserts about eleven. Ashley made a wonderful bread pudding from the leftover pastries. Ruth made a huckleberry pie. Margie made a beautiful coconut cake, with a little help from Sara and Jake grating the coconut.

The meal arrived at two. Everyone was ready to stuff themselves and then enjoy another nap. Frenchy called about a group of hunters canceling their duck hunting trip and anyone who was interested could go. A huge flight of mallards arrived on Christmas Eve according to the Louisiana property manager.

All the men decided to go duck hunting. Sara wanted to go, as did Ashley and Carrie. But Ashley and Carrie decided they should not make the trip due to their pregnancies. Sara said she would wait until the other women could go. They received a promise for a hunt on opening day the next year when the lodge would be open.

The men spent the rest of Christmas day getting ready for the hunt and flew out the next morning. It was surprisingly cool in Louisiana, so all they needed was a shotgun, shells, and warm clothes. They would hunt from blinds and did not need waders.

The flight down was smooth and uneventful. The pilots were also going to hunt, which made ten hunters. The newly arrived ducks were not 'blind shy' because they did not know where they were located. The guides set out more than fifty decoys in front of three blinds. The guides were excellent callers in the distinctive Louisiana style, which had a little squeal at the end of the series of notes.

Jake's years of shooting skeet came into play and he bagged a limit of four green heads in short order. It took the others longer, but not too much longer. A few gadwall were flying and they filled out the six bird limits with them. A flight of teal came through the decoys, ducking and jiving so fast no one connected, which shook the group's confidence.

While the guides cleaned the ducks, five other guides arrived to take the group fishing. They caught a limit of redfish and most of a limit of speckled trout. Everyone enjoyed the fishing and listening to the Cajun guides talk. The banter between and in the boats was a key part of the fishing experience. The fish were quickly cleaned and iced. Five ducks were cooking in cast iron ovens at the farm's headquarters. They were delicious, as were the starters made from fish, shrimp, and crabs. A good cigar and bourbon finished the meal.

Harrell asked, "Frenchy, how much does this cost the hunters."

"Five hundred a day for both hunting and fishing. Three hundred for just one experience. If the hunter needs to rent equipment, the fee increases. Most people tip the guides a hundred dollars after a good hunt, and they have all been good so far. Rooms at the motel are in the hundred dollar range for two hunters. Next year, when we have a lodge, we will charge closer to a thousand for an all-inclusive hunt, fishing, and lodging. It will be first class."

"Do you think people will pay that much?"

"Yes. It's close to what the competition is charging. I know it's out of the range for many people, but there are many people in Houston and New Orleans who are willing to pay. Many companies book trips for employees or customers. Our rates will be a little less for mid-week hunts. Duck hunting is expensive and requires a lot of equipment. It's also hard work for a DIY hunt. Putting out and taking up decoys in the marshy bottom is tough duty."

"I will be back and I'm sure these other guys will. We could have a meeting at the lodge and fish in the afternoon. Is there anything for the wives to do?"

"Swamp tours are popular, as are tours of plantation houses and other historical venues. A Cajun 'fais do-do' is a highly memorable experience, as are crawfish and shrimp boils. Some of the food is almost beyond description. We will hire local chefs to cook for the lodge."

"I'm sold! When can we start on the lodge? I'll get someone down here to help get it going. I suppose the building will be elevated."

"Yes, but parties and seafood cooking can be done underneath the structure. I think we should use local builders to make it fit the country."

"Absolutely!"

The duck hunt the next morning went much like the first morning. As Harrell and Frenchy sat in the blind, Harrell said, "I like what you are thinking and doing. Let's get lodges built on all the properties you think we can use for hunting. I think this outfitting effort is going to pay off big. Try to think of things we can do on the other properties during the offseason."

The group flew back to Denver after the duck hunt. They all had work waiting on them. But before they got totally back into the grind, they planned to spend a few days at the ranch to celebrate New Year's Day. Ashley also planned to see if she could acquire a dog or two for the bus. Most casual criminals would not dare brace a protective and irritated Comanche War Dog.

After everyone settled in at the ranch, Wyatt rode two good cutting horses, as did Jake—no one else took advantage of the opportunity. The women spent most of their time talking about the babies expected in a few months and the wedding that would soon follow. Virginia was torn between planning for a grandchild and planning a big wedding. The wedding for an adopted Cannon and a natural born Cannon would be big. All the men decided they were more comfortable outside or somewhere away from the planning.

John and Wyatt brought their new guns and John went first. Jake had researched loading and shooting the gun. Loading was similar to any other muzzle loader. First, black powder is poured down the barrel. A bullet is then seated on the barrel and pushed down with a bullet starter. The ramrod then pushes the bullet all the way down to the top of the powder. Since the rifle was a cap lock, a cap is placed over a small nipple. When the trigger is pulled, the hammer strikes the cap, which sets the power off.

Earlier, Jake had placed a bucket about six hundred yards out. John aimed and the bullet went over the bucket. Everyone was surprised when the bullet whistled until it hit the ground.

He said, "I thought I needed to aim a little high. But it went right where I aimed."

John reloaded and aimed dead on the bucket. The whistling stopped when the bullet tore into the bucket. Everyone was amazed the rifle was accurate at such a distance. John moved to eight hundred yards.

He aimed just over the bucket and hit it dead center. He now understood what the books said about the Whitworth being a scary weapon. People could hear the round coming and were afraid it was coming directly for them. He carefully swabbed and cleaned the barrel. It was Wyatt's turn to try his rig.

He put the holster on to get the heft of the gun. It shot the .45 long colt round, which was devastating at close range. The gun felt good in Wyatt's hand.

John walked over and said, "You know, a lot of fast draw people shoot themselves in the foot trying to cock the gun as they draw. I'd draw and cock after the gun was out of the holster."

"Good advice."

Wyatt loaded and set up six cans at thirty feet. He drew and fired rapidly—all six cans toppled. The cowboys gathered around started calling him a 'pistolero.' Many whoops and hollers erupted when he repeated the performance.

One cowboy hollered, "Gotta' be a son of Grant!"

He quickly added, "And Angelina!"

The men came over to admire the weapons. One said, "Someone must really like you to get you one of those. It's a real one—not a reproduction."

TG was awake and wanting to go outside. Ashley came to the porch and said, "When you boys get through playing with your big boy toys, come get TG. I think he wants to ride."

Wyatt went by to pick him up and walked to the barn. "Slim, please find me a gentle horse to give this guy a ride."

Slim walked out with a beautiful bay mare. Wyatt got on and took TG. They rode up toward the Choctaw land. Actually, TG was getting good balance. Wyatt wondered if he might be able to ride by himself in a year or so. Probably not.

Ashley went down to talk to Earline about one or two Comanche dogs for the bus trips. She responded that she had two nearly ready to go.

Ashley said, "I want them to guard the buses when we start back with field trips."

"Okay, I should go on the first couple of bus trips with them. I will train them to escort the children and stay quiet on the bus. We will have to find a good place for them or the children will worry them to death."

"Good idea! I'll be back in a couple of weeks and you can go on the first two or three trips to make sure they know their jobs."

It was soon time to get back to the grind. Actually, everyone was ready to get back to work. All was quiet at the office except in the financial area. This was a peak time for them. Jake was not familiar with the routine so he tried to stay out of the way. He was pleased to see everyone was working hard and looked like they knew what they were doing.

Cassandra also reported to work that day. She came to Wyatt and said, "Mr. Wyatt, I want to talk to you about my grandson. I am afraid he's headed for serious trouble."

"What's the problem?"

"Teenaged gangs in our neighborhood. He's hanging around with some pretty rough guys. He's not a bad boy, but they will turn him into one. My daughter does not know what to do."

"What's his name and what's the gang's name."

"His name is Alejandro. The gang calls themselves the Banditos."

"Let me do some checking. I will work on it as soon as I get in."

When he got to work, Wyatt first went to Joe to ask about the Banditos, "What do you know about a gang operating here called the Banditos? Cassandra says her grandson may be hanging out with them."

"Of course, a widespread motorcycle gang call themselves the Banditos. They are a tough bunch involved in drugs and a lot more. I doubt it's the one she's worried about. Let me make a few calls to see what the DEA knows."

Joe came back a little later and said, "A young local gang calls themselves the Banditos. Mostly small time stuff, but they are on the DEA's radar. Interestingly, DEA expects the real Banditos will likely come down on this group of kids for using their name, which is one reason the group is on their radar. I can get someone to check on them to see what they are up to if you want."

"Yes, please do. I don't need Cassandra quitting or having anything besides TG on her mind. Keeping up with the boy is a full time job. I better talk to Harrell before we get too involved."

Wyatt talked to Harrell, who knew Cassandra well, "Certainly, you can spend time on this. We will likely hire one of her friends to help Carrie with the baby. How old is the boy?"

"I think he's about fifteen or sixteen. Maybe we can do something to help him if he's not too deep into the gang."

It was a week before Joe got any additional information. The gang was mostly teenagers and they were on the edge of trouble in several areas. Mostly pushing a little marijuana in schools, small time thievery, and general intimidation in the neighborhood. But they were likely headed for bigger things. Unfortunately, the bigger things hit quickly.

A store clerk was shot during a robbery. Two shooters were apprehended—a kid named Alejandro was thought to be a lookout and pulled in with the shooters. Wyatt reached out to the police to find out how involved Alejandro was.

An officer told him, "I don't think he had any idea a shooting would go down. He's on the younger side of a young gang. He's in jail. You can talk to him if you wish."

Wyatt went to see him. Although he tried to show the typical gang member toughness, he could not bring it off with Wyatt.

Wyatt said, "How did you get yourself in this position?" Alejandro just hunched his shoulders.

"Do you want to get out of here?" He nodded his head affirmatively.

"I can likely get you released into my custody, which could be worse than sitting in jail. I have checked and you are not going to school. That will change. You have no job and are just hanging out with a bad bunch. That will also change. Are you still interested?"

Alejandro again nodded his head and asked, "Why are you doing this for me?"

"Your grandmother asked me to help you. Let me talk with some people about getting you released. If you are released to me, you will not be going back to the neighborhood. You will be going to a ranch to work and go to school at night. If you screw up, you will face charges that could ruin your life."

Wyatt went to the Police Chief to tell him what he had in mind and ask what it would take to get him out. He responded, "He was more of a bystander and can be released into your custody. I can talk with the judge and that done in an hour or so."

"Great! I am going to take him to a ranch and let him get dirty and sweat a little. We will keep close tabs on him and see if he can become a productive citizen. Getting him out of the 'hood will be the best thing for him."

Wyatt called the ranch and told Clay what he intended to do. He then called John to see if he wanted to help take a recalcitrant teenager to the ranch to learn the error of his ways. John knew vaguely what Wyatt was working on and said he would love to help.

They drove by to pick up Alejandro and take him to his house to get some extra clothes. He did not have many. Soon after John parked the car in front of the house, two young toughs walked up to their car.

One said, "We don't allow old Anglos on our turf. Leave now or we will have to teach you a lesson."

Wyatt and John looked at each other and shrugged. They

stepped out of the car just as Alejandro walked out the front door. The two 'old Anglos" proceeded to whip the thugs to a bloody pulp in less than a minute. The two guys were the toughest in the Banditos and the older men took them apart without breaking a sweat. Alejandro was seriously impressed.

The drive to the ranch was quiet with no mention of the fight. Clay met them and showed Alejandro a place in the bunkhouse.

Wyatt said, "Clay, he has to stay on the ranch at all times. Find him some hard work to do. If he complains about the work, call me. He likely needs gloves and such. He's trying to earn his way out of jail."

Wyatt then turned to Alejandro and said, "Remember, this is your last decent chance to make something of yourself. Work hard and earn yourself some respect. You are starting over, but it will be on my terms."

Alejandro reached out to shake hands and said, "Thanks."

Chapter Sixteen

Cassandra thanked Wyatt profusely when he returned home. Her daughter had seen the dust up between Wyatt and John and the self-proclaimed tough guys.

"My daughter said you and Mr. John taught a couple of thugs a hard lesson. Alejandro also saw it and was impressed with you 'old guys.' I think it opened his eyes to see his heroes put down so easily."

"We got him out of jail, in my custody. We took him to the ranch and he will be working their until it makes or breaks him. He will be paid and can get raises if he can move up. I know you and his mother will want to see him soon, but letting him leave the ranch now is not a good idea. We don't want him tempted by being around the gang. Maybe y'all can go see him after a month or two. I'm thinking he has a good chance to come out of this a better man. We'll worry about school next year. He has missed too much to make up this year."

Ashley was getting ready for the next field trip and she was very worried. Wyatt finally said, "Everett, the second driver, the dogs, and the armed chaperones will be on the bus—the students will be well protected. Tell you what, Dad and I will follow the bus at a distance to make sure nothing happens this time. Everett and I will have two-way radios."

She threw her arms around him and said, "Thank you so much! I will stop worrying about them if you are following."

"You're not lying about worrying, are you?"

"Well, I can't promise. But I will worry enough less so I won't make your life miserable. That's probably as much as I can do."

"Good enough. Can we have at least one meal where your fears are not the only topic?"

"Yes. Earline is likely to come spend a couple of nights here with the new dogs she's taking on the bus. She will go on the first two or three trips to make sure the dogs know their duties. We also decided the teachers should go on the trips. They can then better discuss what the students see on the trip."

"Both are good ideas. I want to check on Alejandro before the first trip. I wonder how much horse dung he's shoveled in the past week. I hope several tons. Shoveling dung is a great way to make you want a higher-level job. I think he's smart and will be trying to break away from dung shoveling as soon as he gets an opportunity."

The bus trip was the following Monday so Wyatt drove to the ranch Friday afternoon. Cole met him when he drove up.

Wyatt asked, "How Alejandro work out?"

"I'm very pleased with him. He works really hard. He also has ridden horses a few times after work—just helping to exercise them. He's already a surprisingly good rider for a person who's had no training. What do you think about me having Slim take him under his wing and see what develops?"

"Great idea! Maybe it will give him something to take pride in. So far, he's just been on the edge of trouble. If we give him something that holds his interest, I think he will turn out to be a good man. The neighborhood he comes from is pretty distressing and has little for teenagers to do."

"I'll talk to Slim. He came to the ranch needing help to get his head on right. Tommy and Lenny helped him. Slim can relate to the boy."

Cole and Wyatt walked into the barn and chatted with Slim. He was very interested in helping Alejandro.

Slim saddled two horses and walked them outside. They were green broke, meaning they had been ridden, but not very much. They might kick up a little dust to begin with.

Slim said, "Al, come over here and help me—these horses need to exercise. They may think they don't want a rider, so get a good seat and hold on. We will need to be careful because they are almost surely going to buck sometimes during the ride, including at the beginning."

They led the horses into a corral and a cowboy held the horse's heads firmly until the riders got mounted. Both horses bucked, but it was a halfhearted effort and it stopped quickly.

They rode around the corral a few times, and then Slim hollered, "Open the gate!"

Al's horse did not want to go through the gate but with a little urging, he pranced through it. A little soothing talk settled him down and the two horses trotted off. The ride went well in that no one hit the ground. The two horses seemed to take turns creating a ruckus every few hundred yards by dancing and hopping. When they returned to the barn after an hour, both horses were riding much better.

Wyatt strolled over to Alejandro and asked, "How's ranch life treating you?"

"I can't say I'm particularly fond of mucking the stalls every day. But I love the horses and riding. I want to learn more about riding and caring for horses. It doesn't take a lot of training to clean the stalls." Wyatt and Cole chuckled.

Cole said, "I'm assigning you to help Slim. You appear to be a natural horseman. If you listen to Slim and learn from him, you will be working more with the horses. You will still work on the stalls some, but if you turn out as a rider, you will spend most of your time with Slim."

Slim said, "Let's go. We need to ride twenty-five horses each today. You will be sore at the end of every day 'til you get used to it." Alejandro grinned and nodded.

Wyatt watched for a while and Al, as the other cowhands called him, was doing well. Only one horse unseated him and most tried. He rode relaxed in the saddle like a real cowhand. Wyatt was pleasantly surprised.

Earline loaded three Comanche dogs early that morning and headed for the ranch in northwest Wyoming, which would take her about eight hours. Wyatt offered to carry them on the plane, but she was not sure whether the dogs were ready for a plane. Wyatt and John flew and borrowed one of the ranch's trucks to trail the bus. The bus would leave the ranch the next morning with a load of students.

When the students and chaperones collected up, Earline talked with them about the dogs. She emphasized they should not pet the dogs until permission was given—the dogs needed to focus on their protection jobs. But when she concluded, she had the dogs stand by the bus's door. Each student and adult filed by the dogs and petted them briefly. Earline wanted the dogs to remember each person.

When the bus rolled out, Wyatt and John pulled out behind it. They maintained a distance about a quarter of a mile behind it.

Everett alerted them when he planned to stop. They then moved closer, knowing the stops were the most vulnerable time. They parked fairly close to the bus and watched the proceedings from forty to fifty yards away.

Everett drove the bus to a part of Yellowstone not open to the public yet, but the Park Rangers agreed to give them a special tour in the northern part of the park where all the calderas, bubbling mud, and hydrothermal sites were located.

They transferred from the bus to four-wheel drive park service vehicles since patches of snow still remained in spots. The bubbling mud pits fascinated the students—the Rangers explained the whole park was over a huge collapsed volcano that might erupt one day. The hot bubbling mud pits were caused the magma was close enough to the surface to warm the water. They saw many elk and bison in the area because the snow was not too deep and they could easily find grass. They saw Old Faithful erupt, which was an interesting and enjoyable experience.

The SUVs then headed east where there were fewer interesting sights. Everett drove the bus around the big loop to pick them up the lodge on the eastern side. They had sack lunches at the lodge. They then boarded the bus and headed for Cody, where they visited the Cody museum. The museum contained an enormous collection of rifles and pistols from the era of the mountain men and the Wild West. They spent the night in Cody.

The dogs performed just as Earline hoped. All three rode calmly on the bus and Earline worked on having them assume positions between the bus and the restrooms when they stopped. Everett stayed on the bus and the backup driver took a position near the restrooms or near the main focus of the stop. Chaperones were positioned between the bus and the backup driver. A person with evil intentions toward the children would be taking a terrible risk. The rumbling noise the dogs made would stop most brave men in their tracks. No one tried to pet the dogs except the children.

Wyatt and John were in their usual positions at one rest stop when a car pulled up and two young women jumped out and rushed toward the restrooms. John intercepted them and said, "Ladies, you probably don't want to get any closer to that little dog guarding the children."

"Oh my! We drank too much coffee this morning and barely made it here!"

"Let me get you an escort."

John called Earline and waved her over, "Earline, would you please escort these ladies into the restroom area. They seem to be feeling the pressure."

Earline smiled at them and told them to follow her. All three dogs were standing and staring at the two young women. The dog closest to the restroom building rumbled, which frightened the women.

Earline said, "Jocko! Sit! Friend!"

Jocko sat and his tail began to wag furiously. Earline said, "You can pet him now."

"Really!"

One woman was too scared to get close to Jocko. But the other one walked to Jocko, kneeled down, and scratched his ears. Jocko was in heaven.

She asked, "What kind of dog is it?"

"Comanche War Dog."

"I would love to have one like him. He's both scary and lovable at the same time."

Earline waved them inside and asked the young girls if the two women could break in line. They readily agreed.

The protections were likely overkill, but the adults were

highly pleased. Everett and the backup driver were relieved and comfortable with the protective procedures. The chaperones were very happy to be part of the procedures. Even the dogs seemed to like their roles. The other field trips could go on with little worry about kidnappings or other violence toward the children.

Everyone, including Ashley, was comfortable with implementing the remaining scheduled bus trips. The standard pattern was the children spent time studying the areas they visited and wrote a paper on the adventure. It was a great learning experience for them.

―――――――――

Ashley and Carrie were growing bigger by the day. Ashley was not having problems like she had during her first pregnancy. The two women often commiserated with each other. TG was not pleased because he did not fit in Ashley's lap as well as before. The others made a little fun of them and their waddle like walking. Neither thought the jokes were at all funny.

Carrie and Joe's house was almost complete in early spring. Sara and Jake's was six weeks behind that. Virginia was in her element. Planning for the birth of her grandchild and moving Carrie into a new house were the kind of things she enjoyed. An interior decorator was already working on helping her select the furniture and other decor. Virginia and Carrie had several arguments about colors and furniture placement. Joe began spending more time in the barn brushing the horses.

The arguments were usually smoothed over in a couple of days and Carrie won her fair share. Planning for the baby often generated heated discussions, enough so that Harrell also developed a liking for brushing horses. Sometimes each horse got brushed twice a day. Carrie stood her ground on almost everything related to the baby. Virginia did not hold any grudges over their disagreements. Joe was just ready for the baby to arrive and for them to move into their house. Living with your in-laws had its good points, but it was time to be separated, even if by only a hundred yards or less.

A few minutes before midnight on a day in early March, Carrie suddenly became wide awake. She pushed Joe and said, "I think it is time."

He rolled over, blinked at her, and went back to sleep. She pushed him harder and repeated, "I think it is time!"

He was partially awake but said, "Time for what? The baby is not due for almost a month."

She countered with, "The baby doesn't know that! I tell you I am having contractions! Go get mother! Now!"

He was now awake but not totally alert. He grabbed his phone and called, "Virginia, Carrie thinks she is having contractions and wants you to come over."

"It's too early for contractions."

"I told her that, but she still wants you here."

"Okay, I'm on the way. You make a pot of coffee—this may be a long night."

When Virginia arrived, she went to Carrie's room. She asked, "Honey, what's wrong?"

"I'm having contractions and Joe don't believe me. I don't care what the due date is. This baby is coming tonight."

Virginia called to Joe and said, "Wake Harrell up and pour some coffee down him when he gets here. I think we should go to the hospital to make sure she's okay. Do you know if she has anything packed?"

"Yes, we have a 'go bag.' But she's not due yet."

Carrie almost yelled, "Don't tell me again I'm not due! I'm telling you the baby is coming!"

Everyone began getting ready to go and Carrie was not happy with the delay. Virginia said, "Oh well, I'll put my make-up on at the hospital."

They sped off with Joe driving and Harrell in the front passenger seat. Virginia sat in the back seat with Carrie. Carrie gave a little squeal every few minutes. Joe pulled up at the ER entrance. None of the ER personnel seemed to be moving with much purpose. Harrell got highly agitated when one said they could not do much if she is not pre-checked.

He said in a tone any Drill Sergeant would admire, "I want to talk to whomever is managing this ER! Immediately!"

The receptionist's eyes widened and she scurried off. She returned with a weary and annoyed ER doctor in tow.

"Do you know who I am?"

"No, and I don't care."

"Well, you are going to know quickly. My name is Harrell Cannon, Chairman of the Cannon Trust. Are you aware of how many things at this hospital have the Cannon name attached to them? Are you aware I serve on the hospital's Board of Directors?"

The ER doctor's face began to change and show recognition of the name. Harrell continued, "My daughter is having labor contractions a month before she's due. It would behoove you to see her immediately. If that does not happen, you and the hospital will suffer dire consequences!"

The full impact of the man standing in front him finally dawned on the doctor. Everything began to move a frantic pace. Carrie was wheeled into a room with no further ado and an OBGYN was called. The ER doctor and a nurse examined Carrie to make sure she was not in a distressed condition.

The OBGYN doctor showed up quickly. He examined Carrie and said she was clearly in labor.

He had a sonogram done and said a little while later, "The baby appears to be developed enough to be born, even though he's only about five pounds. The major potential problem is his lungs might not be fully developed, but we can deal with that. If they are, he will certainly be fine. I think we should give Carrie something to relax her to see if the contractions will stop." Carrie and the family decided to try it.

The contractions stopped, but she was dilated six centimeters and the doctor thought she might start contractions again. She slept comfortably for four hours, but awoke with contractions picking back up. She was dilated to seven when the doctor told everyone the baby arrive today.

The contractions got more intense and her water broke at daylight. She would normally have had the baby in her hospital room. But they took her to a delivery room because of the premature delivery.

Carrie delivered at 8:10. The baby was put directly into an incubator provided with extra oxygen. Joe was allowed to see the baby after everything was hooked up on the incubator. Tests were run to check his oxygen level, which was so good the oxygen was disconnected from incubator.

Joe came out and said to Virginia and Harrell, "He's so small—five pounds. But he's breathing well and everything else seems to be normal. They are running more tests, but the doctor thinks he will be fine. We can see Carrie soon. They're taking her to the suite now."

He called Wyatt to tell him they had a boy and, so far, everything looked good. Ashley, Ruth, Margie, and Sara immediately headed for the hospital rather than to work. They arrived shortly after people were first allowed into Carrie's room.

The nurses gave Joe a little time to be with Carrie before allowing the others into the room. It was not long before the baby was brought in to meet his mom and dad. Carrie held the baby on her chest for what the hospital said was skin to skin contact.

Carrie said, "He's so small! Smaller than any baby I have seen. Is he okay?"

Joe responded, "The doctor says he's fine. They ran a bunch of tests and all are good. I'm sorry I didn't listen to you about coming to the hospital. You knew what you were talking about."

Carrie looked at Joe and said, "You should always listen to me!" Then she laughed and he knew he was not in trouble.

Harrell and Virginia were the next visitors. Harrell, the big executive, was brought to tears when he held the baby. He definitely did not see that coming!

Carrie said, "Mom, he's so small I don't have clothes to take him home. Please find something to fit him. Don't make it frilly—he's going to be a tough man like his dad."

"I'll try. It is going to be hard to not have a lot of frills on it. I will probably get two—one frilly and one plain but pretty."

"Thank you, Mother."

Others visited in pairs, but were allowed to stay only a short time. Carrie was getting tired—she had put in a hard day's work.

The nurse came in and said, "Everyone needs to leave the room. Carrie needs rest. I'm going to give her something to relax her enough to sleep for a while. Carrie, do you want the baby to stay in the nursery or in the room with you?"

"I want him with me. Can Joe stay with me?"

"Yes, the father can stay if he will let you rest."

"I promise, I'll be good."

Joe realized later he was very hungry—he had missed breakfast. He eased out while Carrie slept. Virginia was perfectly willing to sit with Carrie and the baby. She sat near the baby and just admired what she thought was the most beautiful baby ever born. She imagined him growing up near her house. They decided previously that Carrie, Joe, and the baby would spend the first two weeks at Carrie's apartment so Virginia could help. Plus, the baby's room in their new house was not ready. She aimed to get that taken care of as soon as they went home.

Joe was back when Carrie started to awaken. She wanted her mother to help make her presentable before more visitors came by to see them. She called the nurse to ask if she could get in the shower and wash her hair. The nurse relented after a little begging. A nurse and Virginia helped her—she wasn't quite as mobile as she thought and had to have help. After the shower, she rolled her hair or at least Virginia rolled her hair. She was ready to get out of the hospital gown and again the nurse relented. Carrie could be persuasive.

The people who worked at the Trust started coming by not long after five o'clock. Carrie was radiant by then and ready to receive visitors. No one stayed long—they just wanted to admire the baby and Carrie wanted them to.

Around six p.m., the nurse chased everyone out to give Carrie some pointers on breast feeding. The baby only wanted a little but they managed acceptably well. Joe stayed with her and the baby all night, while Harrell and Virginia stayed in the suite's apartment.

Joe and Carrie talked in quiet tones when they were alone. She asked, "What is your thinking on a name."

"Well, you know Manuel has to be part of it, probably the middle name. All the Sheffield's since Miss Lily have Manuel in their name. I'm thinking Harrell Manuel Sheffield. We can call him Manny."

"I love it! I also thought of that one. Daddy will be thrilled! Manny will never want for anything with that name. We will tell them first thing tomorrow. I want to see the look on Daddy's face when he hears it."

Carrie and the baby rested well. The nurses said she needed to feed the baby every two hours because he could not drink much each time. The nurses would wake her when it was time for a feeding.

Carrie was worried about him not taking much milk each time. But the nurse said, "It's just because he is so small. He will probably take only a few ounces each feeding for his first two weeks or a month. It will keep you busy."

The nurse asked, "Do you have a name for him so we can fill out the paperwork for a birth certificate?"

"We do, but I want to tell my parents tomorrow."

"Okay. He just needs to be named before you check out."

"When will that be?"

"Maybe tomorrow, but more likely the next day."

"I will have a lot of help when I get him home."

"I bet you will with the parade of people you had visiting!"

The two hour feeding schedule did not allow for much sleep. Carrie did not complain, nor did Joe. The baby cried very little. Usually, only when he needed to be changed or was hungry.

Virginia came in as early as she thought she could the next morning. Carrie asked, "Where's Daddy?"

"He will be here soon. I think he was looking for coffee for him and Joe."

Harrell walked in a moment later. He was carrying two steaming cups of black coffee.

Carrie said, "We have an announcement. The baby's name will be Harrell Manuel Cannon. We will call him Manny."

Harrell spilled his coffee when he heard the name. He sat them on a table and hugged Carrie and shook Joe's hand.

"I had no idea you would name him after me! I am so honored."

With tongue firmly in her cheek, Carrie said, "It is not really after you, we just found the name in a book of baby names."

"I will tell everyone he's after me, no matter what you say! I am honored. Yippee!"

Virginia said, "Harrell! Don't wake the baby!"

He went to work to brag on the baby and its name. He was on cloud nine and could not quit grinning. He did not get much work done the rest of the day.

Carrie and the baby left the hospital later in the afternoon. He was a good baby and did not cry all the way home. Virginia had put a cradle in Carrie's room. It was an expensive and beautiful wooden model.

TG came over to see his cousin or whatever it was. He was fascinated with the baby and tried to talk to him. He brought one of his favorite horse books for Manny. He soon realized a baby was not much fun to play with and wanted to go home.

The household settled down in a couple of days. Then Wyatt received a call from Juan, the Purgatoire Land and Cattle Company's manager.

Juan said, "One of my cowhands had been murdered. The Sheriff doesn't seem to be doing anything, probably because it was only a Mexican cowboy."

Wyatt responded, "I will be there tomorrow with help. Try to keep animals and people away from the scene."

Joe came in that afternoon and heard about the murder. He insisted on going with Wyatt.

Wyatt said, "You need to stay with Carrie and Manny. Someone else can go with me."

"No. It's my people and I have to go. With the plane I can get back here quickly if I'm needed. I know Carrie will be upset, but Virginia will be happy to see me go."

He was not wrong about Carrie's reaction. She lit into him,

"How can you leave with a new baby at home? What if you get hurt? What if you get killed?"

"It's my job and it's at Freedom Town. I can't stay here. I have to go and help protect my heritage. I will be careful and Wyatt and John will be with me. "

She pouted as he was getting ready to leave. She said nothing else, but she was mad and disappointed.

As he was finishing packing, she said, "Come here and give me a hug. I'll be over being mad when you get back. Please don't take any chances!"

A similar scene was occurring at Wyatt's house. Ashley said, "What will I do if our baby comes early? How can you leave me a month before my due date?"

"You will call Ruth and Lenny if anything happens. You don't need me and your due date is six weeks away. Have I ever been away that long? John and Joe will be with me."

"Joe! You are taking him away from his wife and child this quickly? Neither of you have to go. It's not even Trust property."

"They need us. It is Joe's ancestral land and he refused to stay here. We will keep the plane with us and can be here quickly if we are needed."

"You make me so mad, always running toward the gunfire. I know I can't convince you to not get involved, so try to not leave me with two babies to raise alone. Get back here as soon as you can. Be careful, please!"

The plane left before daylight the next morning. Wyatt wanted to get to the scene before it was compromised. Juan and two cowboys were waiting when the Trust men arrived on scene. They had camped close to the scene kept cows and other animals away.

Wyatt asked what they had found and Juan responded, "He was shot in the back by a large caliber rifle. It looks like someone rode up behind him and just shot him off his horse. His horse did not run until after the shot. The other man's horse did not run as far as I can tell, but I'm not a trained evidence gatherer. All the Sheriff's office did was pick up the body and put it in the coroner's car. They didn't even look around enough to mess up any tracks. The murder of a Mexican cowboy is obviously not a priority in this county."

Wyatt, John, and Joe drank a cup of coffee before they started looking around. They began over a hundred yards from where the body was found. Joe called Wyatt over after thirty minutes. He found where a man had hunkered down, apparently waiting on the dead cowboy to come along. He had smoked half a pack of Chesterfields.

After a little more looking around, they found where the horse had been hidden. Juan walked over and said, "We can locate this horse if it's around here. It has a cast off right front foot and the back shoes are almost worn out."

"Good to know. I'm going to talk to the Sheriff. I'll try to light a fire under him. He obviously did a sorry or no investigation. I can call in some big hitters we I need to. Why don't you try to follow the tracks while I am reading to him from the Good Book? What is the dead cowboy's name?"

"We called him Shorty."

Chapter Seventeen

Wyatt thought about the Sheriff's performance all the way back to La Junta. The more he thought, the madder he got. He got himself under control and strolled into the Sheriff's office.

He asked, "My name is Wyatt Cannon. I am Vice President of Security for the Cannon Trust. We own a share of the Purgatoire Land and Cattle Company and help them occasionally with security issues. What can you tell me about the murder of a cowboy out near the Freedom Town ruins?"

"Not much to tell. Somebody shot a Mexican cowboy. Happens a lot. Probably a drug deal gone wrong."

"Humph. Two of my investigators and I flew in from Denver this morning. We know the shooter waited on Shorty for several hours. The shooter has small feet, smokes Chesterfield cigarettes, rides a horse with a cast off right foot and old back shoes, and shoots a .45-70 rifle. We were on scene less than two hours."

Wyatt continued firmly, "Now, let me tell you what's going to happen. I'm going to make a few phone calls and the Wrath of God is about to fall on your head. By tomorrow, the State Police and the FBI will be here to help with the murder investigation.

They will also be investigating your office for malfeasance. I suggest you get your fat rearend up and all your deputies out there collecting evidence. Someone should be looking for the rider of the horse and anyone with a motive to kill Shorty. You may think he was just a Mexican cowboy, but he had a mother and father and maybe a family and was a resident of your county. Your job may depend on you never making that statement again on this or any other investigation. Do you fully understand what the Cannon Trust can bring down on you?"

Wyatt turned on his heel and walked out leaving the Sheriff sputtering. Nobody talked to him that way! However, he knew the Cannon name and the influence it had in Colorado. He started calling in all the deputies and thinking of excuses.

Wyatt, John, and Joe went to the bunkhouse, which was Shorty's principal residence. They talked to everyone available. Several cowboys indicated Shorty had one vice—he liked to play poker at a sleazy joint near Las Animas. He was not normally a good player, but he apparently had been on a winning streak.

They drove to the joint and talked to the bartender, who said he knew Shorty. He said, "Shorty comes in most weekends and usually loses. But he won big last week. A cowboy from a different ranch, Runt, lost big. Runt usually wins and he was furious about losing to Shorty. He'll likely come by this weekend."

It was Thursday so the three drove back to La Junta. They saw four State Police cars and two SUVs that looked standard FBI vehicles. They got rooms and waited to talk to the Troopers and Agents, who were staying at the same hotel.

They collected in the bar after dinner. Wyatt knew two of the Agents. The Troopers said they would take over the county Sheriff's office as soon as a Captain and other officers arrived. Wyatt shared evidence they found.

The FBI planned to focus on building a federal case against

the Sheriff. Two of the Troopers would go with the Trust men to the Las Animas bar on Friday night. They had been called to the joint many times, usually to break up a fight.

The Troopers did not wear their uniforms, hoping to remain inconspicuous as possible. A Trooper, however, looked like a Trooper in or out of uniform. They wore cowboy hats to help obscure their identities. Only the bartender knew the Trust men.

Juan's group had lost the tracks when the horse mixed in with a herd of cattle. He was headed in the general direction of Las Animas. Juan joined the group to make the arrest.

The group arrived at the bar just after dark. It was quiet, with only a few customers sitting around. The crowd from the surrounding ranches would roll in later. A low stakes poker game broke out about eight p.m. and John joined in. The Troopers sat at a back table and Wyatt and Joe sat at different one.

John asked, "Any higher stakes games played here?"

A cowboy responded, "Yep. When Will, Josh, Baldy, and Runt get here, they'll crank one up, if Runt has enough money. Shorty cleaned him out two weeks ago and Shorty never wins."

Sure enough, a little after ten, a new poker game kicked off and a great deal of cash was on the table. One of the players asked, "Runt, how did you get your billfold recharged?"

"Don't you worry about my billfold, Ace. Just deal the cards. You notice that sorry son-of-a-biscuit-eater Shorty is not here to let me get my money back. He ain't that good and I aim to get my money back."

John moved to the card table and asked to join in. Runt asked, "Who in blazes are you stranger?"

"Just a cattle buyer passing through looking to make a little cash."

"Alright, sit down and put your money on the table."

While the conversation was going on, the Troopers, Wyatt,

and Joe edged closer to the table. This game where hundreds of dollars passed hands attracted many onlookers. The Troopers put their hands on Runt and he exploded. John kicked his chair and he was suddenly on the floor trying to draw a weapon from his boot. The gun went off and Runt screamed. He had literally shot himself in the foot!

Wyatt and Joe grabbed Runt's arms and pinned him on the floor. The Troopers got cuffs on him without further problems. Runt was yelling curses at everyone. Since Las Animas was in a different county, Otero County's Sheriff was called.

The Sheriff arrived quickly and asked, "Well, Runt, what did you do this time?"

"Nothing! I was just playing cards and these yokels jumped me and shot me in the foot."

The Troopers pulled their badges and Runt let loose more name calling.

Wyatt said, "Let's get him to jail. The charge will be murder. I'll explain when we get there."

"You coppers have to get me to a doctor. My foot is shot off."

"You shot it yourself, trying to shoot us. We'll get a doctor to work on it at the jail. Now shut up or the Sheriff will charge you with disturbing the peace."

"This is police brutality!"

They got the complaining Runt into the Sheriff's car and took him to jail. The Sheriff asked, "You want me to hold him on murder charges until the Sheriff in La Junta comes to get him?"

"Yes, it may take a couple of days. The state is taking over the Bent County Sheriff's office."

"What did that lazy, lard butt do now?"

"Literally nothing. He said it was just a Mexican cowboy who got killed."

The Sheriff standing in front of them was obviously of Hispanic heritage, "I hope you hang him.   He's been an embarrassment for years."

"This won't get brushed under the rug."

It took a while the next morning to get all the paperwork done.   The Director of Public Safety arrived to make sure of a smooth transition from the current Sheriff to a state takeover. County officials were notified and elections were set for the summer.

_____

The Trust plane arrived back in Denver at four p.m.. Joe and Wyatt were ready to face the music from the wives, but they were forgiven.

Carrie said, "Joe, I forgive you for deserting me during such a trying time. But you made this baby and you are now going to take care of him so I can get a good night's sleep. The bottles are in the refrigerator. He gets one every two hours. Make sure you change his diaper when he is through with the bottle. Warm the bottle a little before you give it to him. There's a direction sheet by the refrigerator. See you when I wake up!"

Actually, Joe was happy to take a night. He wanted to get to know the little person who he hoped would become his best friend. By daylight, his opinion had evolved a little. Waking every two hours is not the ideal way to rest up. At daylight, Joe thought, *"Maybe we need a nanny like Cassandra."*

Carrie slept for ten hours. The five days Joe had been away had worn both her and Virginia down. Joe quickly understood why. The feedings every two hours were a challenge but other than that, Manny was a wonderful baby. He did not cry much. He just ate, pooped, and went back to sleep.

She gave Joe his welcome home hug once she was sure he

had done nothing to hurt Manny. They talked quietly for an hour—mainly about moving into their new house. She told him Manny's room was painted a beautiful blue shade with a few butterflies and horses on the ceiling and walls. Joe walked over later to take a look. The last little items were done only after Virginia gave the other work a close inspection.

They, meaning Carrie and Virginia, decided not to use any of the apartment's furniture in the new house, which meant the new house would contain all new furniture. Joe could see the dollar signs rolling up. The new furniture was delivered the day after the men returned. The furniture was arranged according to Virginia's directions. Joe decided the horses needed brushing. Virginia did call him a couple of times to get his opinion—he was very circumspect in his responses.

The new furniture was finally in place. The interior was beautiful and the furniture and accents matched perfectly. They began moving their clothes and a few kitchen pieces in that night. All the men showed up to carry things and the women showed up mainly to admire Manny. He was such a good baby and was putting weight on quickly. They learned Manny had gained a pound at his two-week checkup.

Carrie was positioned in the new house to show the men where things went and did not take long. Harrell ordered pizza which they decided to eat outside. The March weather was wonderful, but most expected another big snow before summer. Everyone had a good time, maybe less so for Ashley who was ready for her child to be born. She felt as if she was the size of one of the horses.

She was thankful no more problems arose during the field trips. The children were learning so much and apparently the parents were arguing over who would serve as chaperones. Ashley was proud of the entire program. It had been a bigger challenge than she expected initially, but it was working well. She was looking forward learning if the children's scores on the standardized tests had improved."

Wyatt wanted to check on Alejandro before Ashley delivered because he knew he would be tied down more after the baby arrived. He and Jake decided to visit the ranch the next day. Wyatt hoped Al was learning and making himself useful. It's much easier to keep someone interested in riding than in shoveling the stalls.

They left early since the ranch was a beehive of activity in the cool early mornings. When they arrived, they saw a rider on an obviously stubborn red dun—it was Alejandro. The horse was putting on a show of defiance, but Al stuck on his back like a leach. The cowboys were cheering in at least two languages. Slim and Cole were part of the audience.

Wyatt walked up and said, "That one looks pretty rank."

Slim said without looking around, "He's as rank as any we've ever had. You know we try to gentle break our horses, but this one refuses to cooperate. Actually, you can brush and groom him but when a rider hits the saddle, the sucker goes crazy. We may have to put him in the bronc riding on the rodeo circuit. I don't like to give up on one with the kind of breeding he has."

"How's Alejandro doing?"

"He's turning into real cowboy. He's the only one who can stay on that horse for ten or twenty seconds. The horse will just stop when he's worn out, but is still defiant. It's a mystery us why the horse refused to be broken to the saddle. I think Al could make it on the rodeo circuit. He may be the best natural rider I've ever seen, superb balance in the saddle. We need to get him on some bulls—that's where the real money is."

Wyatt was amazed at Al's ability. Cole said he was the one they put on the worst buckers.

Cole asked, "You boys want to help him with these buckers?"

He quickly received two loud negative answers. Wyatt continued, "I just came out to check on him before our baby is born. This guy just wanted to get away from wedding planning turmoil. Virginia is in full hurricane mode."

"Wow, that don't surprise me. Has our little secret shown up yet?"

"Nope, but it should be soon."

Jake looked around quizzically but asked no questions.

Al came over to see Wyatt, "This is the most fun I've ever had! Thank you for bringing me out here! When do you think my mother can come to see me?"

"Probably in a week or so. Your grandmother also wants to see you. Somebody will bring them out."

Wyatt paid him from his own pocket. He would get him on the payroll as soon as he was convinced Al was going to stay straight and make a good hand."

———————————

Ashley was not feeling well that night. She had a slight fever when she went to bed, but not enough to be concerned about. She was nearing her due date and her doctor told her it could be any day. Wyatt slept in TG's room so she could rest better. All was calm until four p.m. when Ashley sat up and yelled, "Wyatt, get in here!"

He ran down the hall and only stepped on one toy. She said, "Call your mother to come stay with TG. I'm having contractions. We have to get to the hospital soon."

The way she said 'soon' grabbed his attention. He went from slow motion to max speed in a split second.

He called Margie and said, "We're heading to the hospital! Ashley thinks the baby is coming. Ruth is going with us. Let me call her."

He pushed his speed dial for Ruth and said, "Get ready to go to the hospital! Ashley thinks she's ready."

"I'll be there in a minute. How close are her contractions?"

"I don't know, but she says we have to hurry. We will be ready in ten minutes."

Wyatt called the hospital to alert them they were coming in. Ashley was prechecked so there would be no delays.

The doctor saw Ashley as soon as they arrived. He immediately said to the nurses, "Get her prepped. We will have a new Cannon baby soon."

With those words Wyatt started getting nervous. He was going to "help" Ashley with her delivery. He moved to the head of the bed so he could hold Ashley's hand and encourage her. He silently prayed he did not pass out. He did not and she delivered in less than fifteen minutes.

Ashley soon asked if it was a girl, which is what she wanted. Wyatt responded, "TG has a little brother to play with."

She looked at Wyatt with wicked eyes, "You were wanting a boy all along! Men! I guess we will just have to try again."

Wyatt said, "Sounds interesting to me." Everyone in the room giggled.

When the doctor and nurses finished counting toes and fingers and cleaned him up, they laid him on Ashley's chest. She was already over her disappointment about it being a boy. She held the baby for a while, as did Wyatt.

Wyatt said, "The doctor said he weighs almost nine pounds and is almost twenty-three inches long. He's half grown already! Let me go tell Ruth—she will want all the details. When can the grandmother come in?"

"Any time you want. Just make sure they both have time to rest today. That's a big baby."

Wyatt hustled to the waiting area and told Ruth and Lenny it was a big boy. He gave them the statistics on length and weight. John and Margie arrived and he repeated the vital statistics. TG was left with Cassandra. The two sets of grandparents went in to see the baby.

Wyatt went to get a cup of coffee and a little breakfast while they visited. He did not take long. He wanted to get back to see the baby and they had to discuss a name for him. Ashley had looked only at girl names had not thought about boy names.

The grandparents went to the cafeteria to eat breakfast and give the parents some time alone with the baby. Wyatt asked, "Have you been thinking about any boy names?"

"No, and I don't think Margie Ruth or Angelina Ruth will work."

"We need to be thinking about a good name. No real hurry, but the hospital will want one before we leave."

"I'll start thinking, but I don't know where to begin."

The nurse came in and started getting the baby wrapped so he would sleep. She asked Ashley if she was having any pain.

"Yes, but it is not too bad."

"Let's get something to relax you so you can sleep before your friends start showing up."

The nurse attached a small bag to the IV and Ashley was asleep before she left the room. The nurse said to Wyatt, "If the baby wakes up and you want us to take him to the nursery, just call. Her doctor wants the baby to start feeding in six hours."

"Okay. I'm sure his grandmothers did not get their visit finished. They will likely want to come in to see him and think about how he is one of the best babies in the world."

She chuckled and said, "I understand."

Wyatt went out to tell the grandparents that Ashley had been given something to relax here and would sleep for a while. The baby was still in the room and they could go in to watch him if they wanted to. They jumped at the chance.

Ashley slept until the nurse came in to help her with feeding. She was a pro now and the baby quickly learned. He fed voraciously like a big baby should and went back to sleep. Ashley asked for Wyatt to come in to talk for a minute.

She said, "I don't know if I was dreaming or what, but several names for boys floated by. I think I favor Johnathon Dale Cannon. We can call him Johnny or JD. I think I like JD best. We would have TG and JD. What do you think?"

"I love it! You know John is going like it."

"I hope he does! Nothing can ever replace TG as the first son or grandson. Maybe being named after him will even out the love and favoritism."

"Okay, let me get them. You hold the baby and I will make the announcement when they come in."

Wyatt went out to get the grandparents. John and Lenny napping.

Everyone walked in and Wyatt stepped over to Ashley, "We are presenting Johnathon Dale Cannon. We plan to call him JD."

John, the tough ex-CIA man who would take on any person and beat most of them, was caught completely off guard. His knees buckled a little before he caught himself. His eyes glistened, but he acted as though he had something in his eye.

Margie hugged him to give him a chance to gather himself. He walked over to Ashley and picked up JD.

He said, "Young man, I expect you to grow up to be someone we can all be proud of. If anyone in this place mistreats you, let me know. I'll show them how the cow eats the cabbage."

Wyatt thought he would hate to be the person who

mistreated JD. It could become a capital offense. John sat down in the rocker and just held JD. His reaction was greater than anyone expected. He normally steered his clear of babies and children. When Margie asked if he was going to allow her to hold the baby, he gave the elaborate answer of 'No.'

Ashley broke the tension in the room by saying, "We may have created a monster with the name. John, you really should share the baby a little."

"Why? I'll share after we have bonded properly. Y'all don't mind us. We're good." Eventually John relented and let the other grandparents hold JD.

Not long after five o'clock, the parade of other people who wanted to see the baby started coming by. Virginia visited before that and went back home to keep Manny while Carrie and Joe came by.

Carrie said, "My goodness he's already as big as Manny! Not sure I want to have a baby that big!"

Joe said, "He will be riding a horse about the same time as TG."

Many gifts arrived. Most of the extended family waited until they came home for the gift giving. JD really did not care what he received. He did care immensely that he got fed at least every four hours. He was a very aggressive and noisy feeder, which embarrassed Ashley.

The doctor came by the next morning and asked, "How are you feeling? Do you have much help at home with the two babies?"

"I am feeling good. I have more help than I can use sometimes." He laughed at that.

"I will leave it up to you. You can go home today or tomorrow. You would probably get more rest here, but it's your choice."

"Let me walk around and see how I feel upright."

"Certainly. I will leave orders both ways. Take a couple of laps around the floor and see how you feel. Tell the nurse and she will know what to do. Medically, I don't think it matters."

Ashley put on a gown the covered her rear and started walking with Wyatt. She experienced a little pain at first, but it got better after a half lap. She was tired from the walk, but felt okay.

She said to Wyatt, "I think I'm ready to go home. I won't do anything at either place and I can relax better at home. I want TG to see his little brother."

She told the nurse and the papers were ready in an hour. Wyatt and Ruth took Ashley and JD home, with Ruth talking to JD all the way in the grandmotherly language no one except the grandmother and the child understood. JD just slept and ignored what was happening.

Cassandra and TG came to the car to meet them. TG did not have much to say and JD had even less. Cassandra was talking in a language that was both English and Spanish. She went back and forth sometimes in the same sentence.

Chapter Eighteen

Ashley and JD had been home a week and, other than JD, all the talk had been about the upcoming wedding. It was going to be a huge wedding at the Cannon Hotel. The staff was doing most of the work, but Virginia and Margie were having a ball helping select everything. When the invitations went out, she asked Jake what to do about his parents.

He responded, "Invite them but don't expect them to be here. I will call my mother to see if she and my brothers are coming—I'm sure my dad will not attend. But please save one of the suites for them, at least for now." Little else was said about them.

Jake called his mother the next day. He said, "Hi Mom. I'm getting married on August 15 and you will be getting an invitation. It will be a very large wedding put on by the Cannon Trust. You will have a very impressive room at the Cannon Hotel if you come. Of course, Dad and the brothers are also invited. I doubt if Dad is interested, but I hope at least someone from my family can come out."

"I read the Denver paper to try to catch a word on you, so I knew the wedding was coming up soon. I did not know if we would be invited to the wedding of the Trust's bigshot Vice President of Finance. I pointed out your signature on my check a few months ago to your father. He was impressed, but didn't say anything. He may actually surprise you and come with us."

"That would be great! Remember, I've already arranged rooms for you in the Cannon Hotel. You are going to be surprised at the luxury and it will cost you nothing—you will be treated like royalty because you are a Cannon descendant. I think you will like the girl I'm marrying. She had a rough early life, but has a great one now. She was adopted by a Cannon and is now very well-to-do—she gets the same monthly check we get. Our marriage will be a Cannon descendant to an adopted Cannon. The Cannon name is a very big deal out here. My primary job is to protect and grow the investments so people like Terry and Daryl will have good incomes all their lives. It's a pretty big responsibility."

"Yes, even your dad said you have done well, which is quite an admission for him after some of the things he said to you. You know the reason he was so mad at you is you left him and the business he planned for you to take over. His feelings were hurt because you wanted to go off and make it on your own."

"Yes, I know. You guys should come to Denver early. You will be able to find out a great deal about the Cannon family history. It's quite an interesting family and it has had an important impact on the growth of Colorado and some other states—you will enjoy it. We descended from Clark Cannon. Less is written about him than about his brother and parents. I'll send you a couple of books so you can learn more about the importance of being a Cannon and how your check comes every month."

"With your signature on it now!"

"I hope all of you come. You will have a good time."

They hung up and for the first time thought his family might actually come to the wedding. He called Sara, Virginia, and Margie with the news. He made sure they knew there was still a chance they would not come. He also asked his secretary send Angelina and Miss Lily's diaries to his mother.

The next morning a highly excited Javier came to Wyatt's house very early. He said, "The palomino Paso Fino mare has a baby. It's small and it looks like a small pony is the daddy."

Wyatt woke Ashley up with the news. She put on a house coat and they took a sleepy-eyed TG to the barn. They gazed at a small but beautiful and perfectly formed palomino colt. TG instantly came fully awake when he saw it. He was excited as a boy could be.

His first words were, "Horse for JD!"

Wyatt said, "The two of you will each have a special horse to ride when you are bigger. What should we name her?"

"I don't know. Is it a boy or girl"

"It is a girl."

"Mom, it is a girl. What should we call her?"

"Well, we could call her Princess, or Missy, or maybe even Sacagawea after a famous Indian woman."

"I can't say that name. How about Wea?"

"Wea is a great name!."

The others came to the barn to look at the new colt and everyone was excited. Wyatt and Javier had kept the surprise very well. The mother horse was not too sure of all the attention and she and the colt stood at the back of the stall. It was a great day and gave a little respite from the wedding, but not for long.

A wedding celebration party was held at the Trust's offices a few days later. All the Trust employees who knew both the bride and groom attended and everyone brought a present. A big buffet was catered by the hotel's restaurant. Harrell made a few remarks about the wedding of two members of the Cannon clan— one adopted and one born to the family.

Sara and Jake were somewhat embarrassed by the number of gifts when they already had so much. Their new house would certainly be full when it was completed, which should be before the honeymoon ended. An hour into the party a computer alarm went off and Sara hurried to her computer station.

Harrell said, "I know that alarm. If you want to see something impressive, go to the Security floor and watch Sara spar with someone trying to get into our computer system." Almost everyone went crowded around Sara's office.

Sara took a few minutes to determine the exact nature of the threat. The system was fighting the threat, just as it was supposed to. The hackers running the invasion were trying to make an end run around one of the firewalls. They were getting close to success when Sara began the duel.

Only the IT group understood very much of the detailed action. The head of IT started giving a blow by blow account of the heavy weight bout. As usual, Sara played with the perps for a little while. She wanted to know how good they were and if she needed a permanent patch to counter other attacks by this group. She realized they were good and chose to fight back harder.

She hit a few keys and released a devasting counterattack on the raiders. She essentially caused their malware to ricochet directly back to its source and followed it into their system!

She made a few more keystrokes and added two of her special bombs to their own malware. It began eating the hacker's software and then turned toward their hardware. The hacker's hard drive began shutting down, basically committing suicide.

She said, "That ought to hold them off until I can add more security to our system tomorrow. That was fun! Let's go back to the party!"

Everyone cheered, especially those who understood she had saved them much agonizing work repairing the damage and maybe saved the entire system. The excellent party rose to even greater heights.

More parties occurred over the next few weeks. The office party was the biggest, but the others were attended by more movers and shakers.

Jake got a call from his mother three weeks before the wedding. She said, "I have great news! We are all coming to the wedding. Your dad is actually excited to be coming."

"That's really great news! Everything will be set when you get here. When do you think you will arrive? Please come early so I will have time for you."

"We are coming a week early."

"Great! I'll have a car pick you up."

They talked a little more about what should be worn and such. He told her, "This will be one of biggest events you have ever attended. Most men will wear tuxes and women will be dressed to the nines. The reception after the wedding will likely have a thousand people attending."

"Wow! That's a really big reception. What will we need to pay for?"

"Nothing. The Trust is paying for everything, including the wedding itself."

He let Virginia, Margie, and Sara know about his parents. Virginia said, "We will have a barbeque at our house for your family and the residents of the compound the night they arrive. We really want to talk with them. Can you share with me why you thought they would not attend? I don't want anyone to embarrass them or be embarrassed."

"We'll talk more before they arrive. There was a lot of

tension between my dad and me over me not working in the family investment firm. Some hurting words were said in anger. I want to forget the words and I hope he does also."

The barbeque was the last of the pre-wedding parties and it would be small. The day for Jake's family to arrive finally came. He had a meeting and could not meet them at the airport, but he had one of the limos waiting with the driver holding a sign. The family was surprised by the limo. They were majorly surprised when they got to the hotel and were whisked up to the penthouse.

Tom had asked about a key and was told, "You don't need one. Take this elevator and punch the 'up' button. Someone is always on duty to help you."

When the elevator door opened, James was waiting on them. He opened the door to the Margo Suite. They discovered their bags were already in the suite.

They were awed by the luxury and Tom kept saying, "We can't afford this."

James responded, "Mr. Carr, you will pay nothing for your stay here because your wife and sons are Cannon descendants. Mr. Jake will be here as soon as he can break away from the Board Meeting, which should be soon. You will be guests at a barbeque at the Chairman's house this evening. It's casual, but you may want to wear a jacket. Please let me know if you need anything. I will be here all night."

Jake arrived thirty minutes later. He gave his mother a big hug and said, "Hello, Mom. I'm so glad to see you! It's been over five years and I've really missed you."

She returned the hug and said, "You are a grown man! I have missed you too. Here are you brothers Terry and Daryl. Terry has graduated from college and Daryl will be starting his second year. They are getting so grown up. This room or whatever it is certainly is the biggest and most impressive one I've ever stayed in. Are you sure we don't have to pay for it?"

"Mom, you can't even tip anyone here. They are not allowed to take them. There's four suites on this floor. It would blow your mind if I told you how much each one costs per night."

He hugged his brothers and said, "Guys, both of you have changed so much. Terry, what are you doing."

"I work in Dad's investment firm. It's quite a learning experience."

"What about you Daryl?"

"Just getting into my second year of school. Majoring in Agricultural Finance."

"Wow! We need to talk. We own more than a million acres and our Financial VP doesn't know much about ag finance." Everyone laughed.

Jake then walked to his dad and shook his hand. "Dad, I've also missed you. Hope we can get to know each other again. How've you been doing?"

"I have been doing good and so has the business. Looks like you've been doing better than good."

"Just got lucky when I went on a blind date with a beautiful girl. We will meet her tonight, along with many people I work with. After tonight, I will try to tell you something about them. They're an interesting group, especially Sara and the Cannon man who adopted her."

He continued, "Let's drive out to the compound. We can show you our new house, which is almost finished. We can also look at some mighty fine horses. Sara and I enjoy riding."

They went to the car and Jake drove toward the compound. Tom said, "You called it a compound. What's that all about?"

"Certain Trust officials, including Sara, have been kidnapped or attacked for various reasons. We have built a compound we can easily defend. It was attacked by the Russian mafia because of Sara and none of them survived."

Jake's mother gasped, "You were in a gunfight?" Jake grinned and nodded.

"Why were they after Sara?"

"Russian hackers tried to take over the Trust's computer system and she repelled them rather emphatically and then destroyed their entire system. Made them mad."

Jake turned into the road leading into the compound. They got to the first set of gates and Javier's house and the other houses came into view. Jake pulled up to their new house and phoned Sara, who was at John's house. She came bouncing out to meet her future in-laws.

Jake made the introductions and Sara gave everyone a big hug. Tom said, "How in the world did you find a girl this beautiful?"

Jake proudly said, "Blind date. She's not really fixed up yet. Wait 'til you see her all dressed up. She'll knock your socks off!"

Sara grabbed Alice's hand to show her the house. It was large, as were the other houses in the compound, and Tom was seriously impressed. His boy was obviously doing very, very well, unlike what he had predicted all those years ago. He suddenly regretted not being around as his son grew into manhood. Sara was excited to show off the house, particularly her computer room had been set up.

Tom asked Jake, "Are all these computers for you?"

Jake chuckled and replied, "No. They are Sara's. She's the Trust's computer guru and cybersecurity expert. She protects the Trust from large computer attacks, among other things. You should see her duel with the cyber world's bad guys. She taught herself." He was obviously proud of his wife-to-be.

They walked over to Harrell's house and the barbeque was ready. They sat outside and talked for a long time. The conversation was congenial and enlightening. Margie and Alice were off to one side talking about the wedding and who would be attending. John and Tom talked about life in general. Jake got to know his brothers better.

Harrell stood and made a toast welcoming the Carr's to his house and the compound. He talked about Jake and what he had already done for the company.

John stood up next, "Mr. and Mrs. Carr, I did my best to run your son away from Sara. I threatened him with violent action and I meant what I said. Most sane men would have scrammed, but he didn't. He stood his ground and hung around so much that I actually began to like him. When we had trouble with a bunch of Russians trying to hurt Sara, he carried his share of the load. He saved her life and managed to get himself wounded in the process. I am considered by most people to be a dangerous man and I was when I was a CIA operative. The kind of grit Jake demonstrated carries a lot of weight with me. I decided if they wanted to be together all the time, who was I to stand in their way. Jake, welcome to our family! But all those threats are still in effect if you ever hurt my little girl."

Jake got up and hugged John, "I understand you have and will hurt anyone who harms or tries to harm her. I will help you carry out threats you made to me if anyone harms Sara."

Several other toasts were made and the festive mood continued. Tom asked to see the horses Jake had mentioned and a group moved to the barn. The women mostly stayed and played with the babies. TG went with the men to show them his horse.

It was soon time for the evening to end. Everyone had a good time and got to know each other a little better. Jake was still learning about his brothers and what had been happening over the past several years. Jake drove them back to the hotel and said he would be back to have breakfast with them at eight.

They had breakfast brought up and ate in the common area connecting the suites. Alice said, "This is the most luxurious place I've ever spent the night in. I can't get over that it costs us nothing."

"Mom, the Trust makes more money than you can imagine. Did you read either of the books I sent you? They chronicle the early history of our family. The wealth began with two brothers, Clark and Grant Cannon. Their father discovered gold and did not want it. He showed them where he found the gold and it turned into a major gold strike. They bought land and became hugely wealthy for their time. They created the Trust to protect the money from being frittered away by their descendants and the core investments have just kept growing since the 1870s. We hire good people to manage the varied businesses we own. We are a very large conglomerate and no stock is involved. The family owns the Trust and receives all the profits. This hotel is a perk available free of charge to any Cannon descendant. Any family member can have a wedding at the hotel. Ours will be bigger because it is two family members and because we work here."

"It seems both of you hold high level positions, too." Said Tom.

"Yes, mine may sound higher, but her job is just as critical, sometimes more so. She's a true computer guru, but did not graduate from high school because her stepfather and brother held her captive and made her work for them in the drug trade. She was chained in a room and forced to hack the DEA so her family cold stay ahead of them. They beat her often and he's had many cosmetic surgeries to cover the scars, especially on her back. You met Joe Sheffield last night—he rescued her when he was a DEA Agent and John later adopted her."

Alice recoiled when Jake told them Sara's story, including being marked for elimination by the Russian mafia. They talked until about ten o'clock, mainly about Sara. Jake had arranged for a car to take them to the Interpretive Center the next morning.

"I think you will love the Center. It gives the history of the Cannon's in Colorado. Make sure you ask for the curator. Three Cannon's coming in at one time will excite him."

Jake's family spent the week learning about their family heritage. As the wedding date came closer, the other suites began to fill with Cannon descendants and more were on the next floor down. They distant relatives met and generally had a good time socializing. Some of the other family members knew much more about the family history and liked to talk about it. Alice and the boys were more and more amazed by their ancestors.

Terry said, "Jeez! They were tough as nails and savvy. Even the women wore guns and used them. Margo was not a gunslinger like Angelina, but she was tough. She helped pick up gold nuggets even though she was a rich girl. Wouldn't you love to talk with them about their life on the frontier? Clark must have been good at finance to grow the banking and such."

Everyone was intrigued by Dale and Martha. Daryl said, "Can you imagine wandering around in those mountains with no equipment or anything? He really found the first gold. It's unbelievable that I get a large check today based on wealth Dale, Martha, and their sons accumulated. Thank you to them!"

As the wedding day drew near, Jake and Sara became more anxious, as did everyone at the compound. Jake and Sara continued their habit of riding the horses in the afternoon. It was the only time they had together away from the hustle and bustle of the wedding. As many others have discovered, a mega wedding created some mega problems, like seating priorities and keeping political opponents from sitting next to each other. The two were ready to just find a Justice of the Peace and leave town. Of course, knowing Virginia and Margie would die from apoplexy kept them from eloping.

Wedding day came none too soon for most of the participants. It was a beautiful day in Denver and the dignitaries were arriving and trying to get an audience with Harrell. They all wanted to pitch something to him. Many also wanted a chance to make a presentation to Jake. He agreed to talk to some of the highest level people before three o'clock. It was hectic in the office.

Jake wanted to talk to his parents but had little free time. He and his dad reconciled during the week and he really liked his brothers. He was thankful he and his mother had always gotten along well. He made time between three and six to talk to them.

The wedding began at six, but the dressing of Sara began at two with the hair and nails. Everything was perfect. Ashley was the matron of honor. Ruth, Virginia, and Carrie were bridesmaids. Wyatt was the best man with Joe, Harrell, and Lenny serving as groomsmen. Most of the Cannon Trust's leadership was at the wedding. Several governors would have given their eyeteeth to get into a room with that group.

The wedding topped a thousand attendees and included top government officials from many states, top people from large companies, and longtime friends of the Trust. Most had never met Jake or Sara. Many people gasped at Sara's beauty as she started down the aisle. She was radiant and smiling like someone totally in love. All the women in the wedding were also beautiful and the mothers were very graceful. Few could recall a wedding as perfect as this one.

For a wedding that took months of intense planning, it was over soon. Five photographers strolled around to catch every minute of the event. A dozen of the Trust's bodyguards watched the crowd to make sure nothing disrupted the ceremony. Another dozen were stationed at the door to keep interlopers from getting in without an invitation. The news media tried to bully their way inside but were firmly rebuffed.

When the ceremony concluded, the minister directed everyone to a room down the hall for drinks and socializing while the hotel staff set up for the dinner. Jake and Sara had a private suite to relax in before the dinner commenced. Their parents were the only ones allowed in the suite.

The gladhanding began in earnest during the intermission. Almost everyone in the audience was selling or buying something. Terry and Daryl sat to the side watching the action. They laughingly agreed it was like watching a scene from the Godfather movies.

In just over thirty minutes the hotel staff had the room where the wedding was held and the one next door converted into a dining room. The receiving line consisted of Jake and Sara along with their parents. All the officials wanted to shake hands with Jake and their wives wanted to look over the bride and the mothers. The competition for attention was intense.

It only took thirty minutes for the people to pass through the receiving line and on to their assigned seats for dinner. The staff obtained everyone's order as soon as they were seated. The choices were ribeye steak, a lobster and crab dish, and a vegetarian entree. By the time the last person went through the receiving line the dinner was being delivered. All the meals, even the vegetarian, were superb.

An area in front of the head table was reserved for dancing. Jake and Sara had the first dance and they did a great job. John then danced with Sara. They had been practicing and Margie was surprised and impressed some of John's moves. Jake danced with his mother and they did well in light of not practicing a routine. Many guests wanted to dance with Sara.

The dancing was also a time for politicking and trying to sell ideas. So many wanted to talk to Jake and Harrell that they adopted the same response, "Please send me a proposal. This is Sara's night. I promise I will look at your proposal as soon as possible."

Some people asked Harrell if they could come by the next day for a meeting. Harrell directed them to his secretary to sign up for a slot and the slots filled up quickly.

A little before midnight Jake and Sara slipped out to change. Margie and Virginia went to help Sara. Wyatt and Harrell helped Jake. They came back to the reception as soon as possible. Sara was still beautiful and Jake was as handsome as ever.

Jake announced, "Sara and I are leaving, but you can stay and party all night. If you want to see us off, look out the windows for a helicopter flying by. We will be back in our offices in a couple of weeks. Thanks for coming to the happiest night of our lives."

They went to the roof with their families and closest friends and boarded the helicopter. It rose up and headed for the mountain lodge where a honeymoon suite was waiting.

Most of the Trust people soon began to migrate toward their hotel rooms or homes. The proposals could wait until later. A few guests, however, saw the sun come up.

The Trust seemed to be in good hands with Jake looking out for the return on investment and the others just trying to make sure the new generation would be taken care of in an appropriate manner.

~The End ~

ABOUT THE AUTHORS

Garry Smith and his wife Charlotte have lived in Starkville, Mississippi for over forty years. They have been married for over fifty years. They have two sons, two grandsons, and two granddaughters. Garry was raised on a farm and worked many other jobs, including each summer for five years on offshore oil platforms. His adult life was mainly spent teaching management at the university level. He co-authored many textbooks and novels with Danny.

Danny Arnold and his wife of over fifty years, Peggy, live in Winston Salem, NC, near their son, daughter-in-law, and two granddaughters. Danny was raised on a plantation in Louisiana. His career was primarily spent in higher education as a faculty member and administrator. He is the author of numerous management, leadership, and marketing textbooks. His first western fiction, *Bad Cat Jones*, was published in 2021. He has also co-authored many novels with Garry.